The
Birdsong Promise

(The Butterfly Storm Book Two)

by

KATE FROST

LEMON TREE PRESS

Paperback Edition 2018

ISBN 978-0-9954780-6-0

Copyright © Kate Frost 2018

This novel is entirely a work of fiction. The names, characters and incidents portrayed in it are the product of the author's imagination. Any resemblance to actual persons, living or dead, or events or localities is entirely coincidental.

The moral right of Kate Frost to be identified as the author of this work has been asserted by her in accordance with the Copyright, Designs and Patents Act of 1988.

All rights reserved in all media. No part of this publication may be reproduced, stored in a retrieval system, or transmitted, in any form, or by any means, electronic, mechanical, photocopying, recording or otherwise, without the prior written permission of the author and/or publisher.

Cover design by Jessica Bell.

The Birdsong Promise

by

KATE FROST

The Butterfly Storm Series

Mine to Keep
The Butterfly Storm
The Birdsong Promise

For Judith

Chapter One

'No wonder this place was a bargain.'

Mum stands with her back to me, hands on her hips. I stare past her to what will be our new home, except it's little more than a building site. Thea is cuddled into me, dribbling on to the muslin I've draped over my shoulder.

Alekos turns to us, a huge grin spread across his face. 'What do you think?'

I have no idea how we're supposed to live here with a six-week-old. Panic climbs up my chest with the thought that I've made the wrong decision.

Mum takes my sweaty hand. 'The location is stunning,' she says. She turns back to Alekos. 'It's just where the hell are you going to live with a baby while you're doing the damn thing up?'

Relieved I'm not the only one with that concern, I let go of Mum's hand and step through the long dry grass towards Alekos. 'I thought you'd stayed over here to get this place ready for us to live in? I knew it was going to be basic, but this...' I waft my free hand towards the crumbling single-storey stone building.

Alekos catches my hand in his. 'This isn't where we're living – this is what we need to do up for guests.'

Still holding my hand, he leads me through the fronds of grass. Mum follows us round the other side of the building to a similar building which stands alongside a whitewashed house that's grey and ingrained with dirt. The courtyard is full of weeds, but there's a single olive tree in the centre.

'Our house,' Alekos says. 'There's running water, electricity,' he continues, seeing that I'm still frowning. 'It's pretty basic inside still but it's liveable, has a bathroom, a kitchen, bedrooms. And that view.'

He turns me around until I face the land sloping down to a stone wall and the Ionian Sea beyond. We must have sailed past this place when Candy and I joined Alekos and Demetrius on our overnight adventure aboard *Artemis* all those years ago. How strange to think I had no clue at the time that not only would I end up with Alekos and start a family with him, but we'd return to Cephalonia to live.

'That view is to die for,' Mum says, placing her arms around both our shoulders. 'I don't know about you, but after that journey, I need a cup of tea.'

She sets off through the grass and across the courtyard towards the house. I stroke Thea's soft head and take a deep breath. I clasp Alekos' arm. 'Seriously, I love it, it just seems an overwhelming amount to do with a baby.'

'We'll manage.' He takes my hand again and we follow Mum, Thea still fast asleep as I walk.

I have to admire Alekos' optimism. He had the guts to take on this place, to gamble with me saying yes and that I'd move to Greece for the second time to be with him – with a baby. But this was what I've been longing for and what I've talked about since almost the moment I met him.

The entrance hall is gloomy but the thick stone walls at least mean it's cooler out of the sun's glare.

'We've knocked through to make a big kitchen-diner, and to make the most of the view we can put patio doors in like the ones at the back. The buildings to the side of the courtyard can be turned into guest rooms…'

'You mean the buildings that are falling down?' Mum asks. We follow Alekos through an archway into an open, light room that runs from the front to the back of the villa. 'Okay, now this is more like it.'

I hoist Thea a little higher on to my shoulder, resting my hand on her warm back, feeling the rise and fall of her chest with each breath. There's a kitchen, an actual modern fitted kitchen, white and sleek with wooden work surfaces. The patio doors beyond open out on to a jungle of bushes and trees at the back of the house. The floor is tiled, the walls are bare crumbling plaster, and the living area only contains one sofa facing a window that looks towards the courtyard and the sea.

'That's where you mean to put more doors?' I point towards the window.

'Exactly,' Alekos says. 'So we can see the view, open the doors right out on to the courtyard. Seriously, what do you think?'

Mum walks down to the kitchen, opening up the cupboard doors. Thea gurgles and snuggles further into my neck, her hot skin connecting with mine. Right then, holding my daughter in my arms, with Alekos standing in front of me in our new home, there's no better feeling in the world. His tan has deepened since I last saw him, his hair longer, and messy from the heat and dust, his cream T-shirt stained with dirt and sweat. I've never wanted to kiss him more. I walk over and take hold of his hand, pulling him to me and looking into his eyes, Thea cradled between us.

'I can't actually believe you bought this place for us.' I reach up and kiss him. His saltiness tingles my lips. 'It's perfect, I mean it will be perfect. It was a brave thing to do.'

'It was a gamble, I know, but it paid off. I had to do something – I couldn't lose you.'

Tears sting my eyes as I drink him in, his face, his taste, his smell, all so familiar. 'You never really lost me, you know.'

That moment in the airport, seeing him for the first time after months apart and introducing him to our daughter is one I will treasure forever. It reminded me of seeing him for the first time aboard *Artemis*, when my stomach flipped and I knew I wanted to get to know him. Watching him kiss Thea's smooth cheek and hold her for the first time as she gurgled made everything else peel away; the airport noise and people jostling around us. Even Mum faded into the background until it felt as if Alekos, Thea and I were the only people in the whole world. As tears slid down my cheeks I realised it was the relief of finally being back with Alekos and knowing that everything was all right.

Lost in the moment, my head resting against Alekos' chest, I realise Mum's disappeared. I pull away from him and look around. 'Where did she go?'

'Out in the garden. Come take a look.'

Cradling Thea, I follow him through the kitchen doors and back outside. Behind the house, the garden is wild and untamed, with years' worth of growth, a tangle of trees and bushes consumed by tall, brown-tinged grasses.

'You have lemon and orange trees.' Mum's standing in the middle of the wilderness. The sun's straining through, casting patchy light on to the overgrown grass and bushes. 'Those are olive trees over there. And what's that one?' She points to a taller tree by the fence.

'Fig,' Alekos says. 'And there's a cherry tree at the back that you can't really see.'

'Right.' She puts her hands on her hips. 'I know what I'm going to be doing while I'm here.'

'I thought you wanted to relax on the beach with Thea for two weeks?'

'I do, but this – I quite fancy hacking this lot back and seeing what else it reveals.' She blows air over her flushed face. 'It reminds me of Salt Cottage's garden when I first arrived – wild and full of weeds, yet I could see through all that and visualise how beautiful it could be. It's the same here, just with more sunshine.'

Thea sleeping peacefully doesn't last. Alekos shows me

upstairs and helps me settle on to the bed in our room, propped up against three pillows, Thea snuggled against my arm as she feeds. Alekos sits on the bed next to me and strokes the top of her head.

'Does this place have a name?' I ask.

'Apparently it's always been known as *Vila Ptina*, or Bird Villa.'

'Bird Villa.'

'Because of the amount of birds there are in the garden, I think. Not too sure where they got the villa bit from.'

I laugh. 'Well, hopefully we can turn it back into something that will resemble a villa.'

Alekos leans down and kisses Thea. 'She's gorgeous, you know.'

'I know.'

'So are you.' He kisses me and leans his forehead against mine. 'I'd better get on with something. Can't leave your mum doing all the work.'

Alekos goes downstairs to help Mum unpack and sort out dinner for us. For the second time, our bedroom is actually his room, like at *O Kipos* when I moved in with him. Not that he's really left his stamp on our room yet – there's only a double bed and an old wooden wardrobe. The floor's been tiled but the walls are unpainted new plaster. We're at the front of the house and the window faces the sea. There are another three bedrooms and a bathroom upstairs, plus another room downstairs that I've already got my eye on to have as a study-cum-art studio-cum-playroom. Even though most of the place is in a state of disrepair, it's everything I longed for while living at *O Kipos*. Life after the emotional ups and downs of the last few months feels complete. There's no going back now to Despina and Takis at *Estiatorio O Kipos* or even back to Mum and Salt Cottage. So much has changed in that time. I've gone from needing to escape a domineering Greek family and fighting Alekos who was too willing to let his mother walk all over him, to unexpected motherhood and

Alekos stepping out from his mother's shadow.

I adjust my hold on Thea, rest my head back on the pillows and close my eyes. The Alekos I first met on Cephalonia is back. I smile, comforted by the memory of the strong-willed, handsome and exciting man I first fell in love with. It finally feels like we've made it through a troubling and confusing few years and emerged the other side, stronger than ever.

Chapter Two

After a simple dinner of grilled lemon chicken and a Greek salad, followed by an early night with Thea sleeping in her new Moses basket by the side of our bed, the plan is for work to start in earnest the next day. It's strange to have Alekos' company during Thea's night-time feeds, even if he only wakes for a bit, strokes her cheek before tiredness takes over and he falls back to sleep. The rise and fall of his bare chest is familiar and comforting, a sight I've missed during the months we've been apart.

With Thea finally asleep in her Moses basket, I should be sleeping too, but I can't, the emotions of the day keeping me awake. It's been five years since I first laid eyes on Alekos on *Artemis*. Now we're back together, living on the island where it all started, where *we* began. There's a comforting familiarity about him. Time apart has made me appreciate him all the more, and it's not just because of his good looks. A sheet covers his lower half, stopping at his bare stomach. He always had been fit and toned but months of physical work clearing away rubble and cutting down the undergrowth encroaching on the buildings has left his chest more defined.

I blow a kiss at Thea and snuggle closer to Alekos, tucking my head into the warm crook of his shoulder and sliding my hand across his hard stomach. He stirs and I close my eyes. The memory of that first time on the beach when he'd held me in his arms pushes away the memories of the fights and distrust that had taken over when we'd been living with his parents.

Sleep is short-lived. Thea wakes me with her hungry cries only a couple of hours later. I slide my arm from off a still-sleeping Alekos, reach over to the Moses basket and pick Thea up.

'What time is it?' Alekos groans and rolls on his side to face me.

I snuggle back against the pillows, Thea in my arms.

'Nearly five. Get used to it – this is our life now.' I smile at him and rub my eyes with my free hand.

He rests his hand on my leg and I'm comforted by his touch even though he falls asleep again almost immediately. His soft snores join Thea's fluttering suck. With dawn about to break, the only other sound is birdsong through our open bedroom window.

'Did you sleep well?' Mum asks, joining us at the kitchen table. Alekos pulls his favourite cream-filled *bougatsa* from the oven. He slides it on to a wooden board, sprinkles icing sugar over and slices it into pieces.

'Thea woke three or four times but it wasn't too bad,' I say, as Mum takes her from me. 'She went back to sleep easily.'

'It must be all this fresh sea air.' Mum strokes Thea's back. 'I didn't hear a thing and slept like a baby, or not as the case may be.' She looks at me and mouths 'sorry'.

Alekos yawns and places the *bougatsa* in the middle of the table. 'I'm used to uninterrupted sleep, so it's a bit of a shock.'

'You barely woke up,' I say, raising my eyebrows.

Mum smiles and buries her face against Thea's cheek. She pulls away and takes a sip of coffee. 'It's going to be a massive change for both of you. You're used to being apart and now you have to learn to live and work together again. With a new baby.' She sticks a fork in a square of *bougatsa* with her free hand and drops it on to her plate. 'Good luck is all I can say!'

'Thanks for the vote of confidence, Mum.'

She pats my hand and looks across the table. 'You're very quiet this morning, Aleko.'

He finishes his mouthful and wipes away the icing sugar from around his lips.

'I think the enormity of what I've taken on has hit me.' He looks at me. 'I mean, I figured with the two of us and some hired help we'd get this place in a fit state to open in a year, but with Thea…'

'Babies take up a lot of bloody time,' Mum says, stroking Thea's cheek where she's snuggled against her, eyes open, gazing up at Mum. 'That's why I think you're mad taking on all of this, *but* it doesn't have to be impossible. You've got me here for the next two weeks, so when I'm looking after Thea, you two crack on, and when Sophie has her, give me tasks, Aleko. I'm here to help. Also, I'm pretty nifty with a hammer and drill. I know I didn't have a baby to look after at the time, but I did do most of the work on Salt Cottage myself. It is possible.'

Mum's pep talk seems to raise Alekos' spirits. We start as we mean to go on, quickly clearing away the breakfast things, stacking them by the side of the sink to deal with later. We head outside to plan the jobs for the day. With Thea back in my arms, Alekos takes us over to a battered wooden table beneath the olive tree in the middle of the weed-filled courtyard. Spread across it are large pieces of paper filled with architectural plans, many of which I'd seen before when Alekos emailed me the designs for the place. It had been difficult then to picture what he meant, but now I can imagine the tumble-down one-storey buildings as guest rooms. Sort of. At least the potential is there.

I pack a rucksack, filling it with baby wipes, nappies, a couple of muslins, breast milk stored in a flask, snacks and a drink for Mum, plus everything else I think she might need for a morning on her own with a baby. Half of me is excited to have the freedom to tackle the retreat, the other half doesn't want to be apart from Thea, even if she's going to be safe with Mum.

'Bloody hell, Sophie,' Mum says, heaving the rucksack on to her back. 'What on earth did you pack?'

I smile. 'You know you can't travel light with a baby.'

'I won't even make it down the hill with this lot, let alone back up again. At least I'll be fit by the end of these two weeks.'

I hand her the baby carrier and she puts it on, adjusting the straps so they sit comfortably on top of the rucksack ones.

I stand back. 'You look ridiculous,' I laugh. With a rucksack sticking out behind her and a baby carrier at the front, she does look quite a sight.

'Well, at least it's not hot…' Mum shoots me a look, her eyebrows pinched together. 'Oh wait, yes it is, we're in bloody Greece.'

'Get back here by midday and you should be okay with the heat.'

'Says the person who doesn't have a baby attached to her front and everything but the kitchen sink to her back.'

'Sorry.'

'Yeah, yeah, I'm only kidding, we'll be fine.'

Alekos strolls over in his work clothes, a paint-splattered T-shirt and an old pair of shorts, Thea in his arms, looking up at him and gurgling.

'Now there's a lovely sight,' Mum says, taking Thea from him. With one hand supporting Thea and making sure her feet are through the leg holes, she pulls the straps up and tightens them until Thea is close to her chest. 'I'll see if she takes a bottle while we're out and then you can feed her at lunchtime.' She takes hold of my and Alekos' hands. 'I want to see an improvement by the time we get back – hopefully you'll have a good couple of hours. We're going to have fun, aren't we, baby girl?' Mum rocks from side to side and kisses the top of Thea's head. 'I'll take her for a walk down to the beach before it gets too hot and then we'll come back up here and have a rest in the shade. I can read my book, Thea can sleep. I have it all figured out, don't you worry. You two get on with turning this place from a wreck into a little piece of heaven.'

'If you walk thirty minutes that way, down the hill and along the beach,' Alekos says, pointing to the south. 'You get to the village. Lots of nice tavernas by the beach with sofas where you can feed Thea in comfort.'

'Ah, civilisation. Sounds good.'

I place Thea's sunhat on her head and kiss her cheek, drinking in her delicious baby smell. I wave them off with a lump in my throat, and watch Mum head along the track that leads to the sandy path down to the beach.

I turn to Alekos. 'Where the hell do we begin?'

'The builders are starting tomorrow on the outbuildings, so there's not a lot we can do there till all the major work is done. Our house needs finishing – there's painting, tiling, cleaning, the garden to clear…'

The list is endless. I stand in the middle of the courtyard, hands on hips, like Mum when we first arrived. The impossibility of working on the place while looking after Thea is a daunting prospect. Alekos has settled into a way of working on his own and I begin to understand the divide between us. The easy way we used to be with each other has stalled. I've come into Alekos' life, much like when I first moved to *O Kipos*, except this time it is *our* home, not a place we'll be sharing with his parents. Alekos has come alive here, relishing being in charge and not bossed about and talked down to by his mother. Long may that last. Now all I need to work out is where I fit in.

Chapter Three

'I can't believe it's been a week already,' Mum says, sipping a frappé Alekos has just made.

We're sitting in the courtyard beneath the olive tree. The workmen are packing up for the day, loading their tools into the back of their van after working late. Thea is in my arms, staring up at the silvery-grey branches of the tree above us.

'I know,' I say. 'It feels like it should be longer, particularly considering how much progress has been made.'

Alekos laughs. 'I've been working on my own for months, apart from occasional help from friends. You three turn up and look what happens.'

'The dream team.' Mum winks and nods towards the workmen by the gate. 'That and four burly builders might have something to do with it.' She places her frappé on the weathered wood of the table. 'You know what you two should do, go out and celebrate. Have a relaxing meal somewhere while I look after Thea.'

'That's a great idea,' Alekos says. He heads over to where one of the workmen is gesturing to him. 'You sure you don't mind?' he calls back.

Mum waves her hand. 'Of course not.'

'Mum, it's fine,' I say, stroking Thea's soft cheek. 'She's still so little… there's no need for us to be going out…'

'My God, Sophie, take the opportunity while you can.

She'll be fine with me for a couple of hours,' Mum says firmly. 'Once I've gone home you won't be going anywhere.'

'You do realise it's quite normal in Greece for kids to go out with their parents in the evening?'

'Maybe it is, but how about the opportunity for a last evening on your own without a screaming baby with you?'

I gaze down at Thea with her pink rosebud lips and smooth, squashable cheeks. 'As long as you're sure.'

'You know I am.' She leans towards me. 'You have a seven-week-old; I know sex is unlikely to be on the agenda tonight – well, yours at least,' she says, raising her eyebrows and glancing towards Alekos. 'But a bit of romance won't go amiss, now will it? A romantic meal, a couple of glasses of wine…'

'I need to breastfeed her later.'

Mum takes my hand. 'There are enough bottles of expressed milk in the fridge for you to not worry about having a drink tonight. Go out, enjoy yourselves and remember the reasons why you got together in the first place. Here, let me take her.' We gently transfer Thea from my arms to hers. Mum settles back in her chair, Thea still gazing up into the branches. 'Go get ready and out of here while the going is good and Thea is happy.'

I jump in the shower, towel dry my hair, leaving it to dry naturally and wavy in the warmth of the evening. I put on a grey maxi skirt and a thin cotton top, slick on mascara, lip gloss, and I'm done. I hear Alekos in the shower and meet him in the hallway. He has a towel wrapped around his middle and his bare chest is beaded with water. He kisses me, his stubbly cheeks damp against mine.

'I'll meet you outside in a couple of minutes.' He heads towards our bedroom but turns back before closing the door. 'You look beautiful.'

This reminds me of the evening he proposed, and all the hope and expectation we had for our future. A hot and sultry evening that started with a thunderstorm over Olympus and those butterflies dancing in the air. A perfect evening with a picnic on the hill by Platamonas Castle, the romance of it, feeling so completely and utterly in love and happy before Alekos' proposal back at *O Kipos* to end the night. I remember hesitating; not because I wasn't in love or didn't want to marry him, but because of my uncertainty at living at *O Kipos* beneath Despina's shadow. After everything we've been through, to come full circle to this moment where life couldn't be more perfect, I practically skip downstairs and out into the fading light.

Alekos is true to his word and is downstairs and back outside in minutes, in jeans and a dark blue linen shirt.

'You both scrub up rather nicely,' Mum says, smiling. 'Now get the hell out of here and have fun.'

I kiss Mum's cheek and lean down and kiss a sleeping Thea, breathing in her scent and warmth. I walk with Alekos towards the gate, tears pricking my eyes at the thought of this being my first evening away from her.

Alekos takes my arm and with a wave at Mum and Thea we walk towards the car parked on the lane. In the dimming light, it's the first time I notice how dark the place is, just the yellowy-light from the house spilling across the courtyard, the other dilapidated buildings shrouded in darkness.

We drive along the dark lane and join the main road. It would be lovely to revisit Fiskardo where it all began, but it's too far up the coast for a quick meal out, and much too long a drive to be away from Thea all evening. Instead, it's only a short drive to Omorfia where Mum walked to earlier with Thea. We park the car on the outskirts and walk hand in hand through the village. The buzz of the popular resort is appealing and is such a contrast to the peaceful location of our villa.

Alekos takes us to a fish restaurant by the beach. It seems forever since I ate proper Greek food, apart from what I cooked for Mum at Salt Cottage. It tastes different in Greece though, the tomatoes sweeter, the peppers thinner and crunchier, the olive oil richer; maybe it's being back in a place where the air is hot and smells of Greece – salt, lemon, grilling meat, cigarette smoke, an oddly comforting combination. There are English voices but lots of Greeks too, drowning out the foreigners with their loudness and laughter. It's funny how Greeks, even if they're simply chatting about something mundane, can sound like they're having an argument. I relax back into my seat, acknowledging how much I've missed the laid-back Greek life. Even if tensions had reached breaking point at *O Kipos*, there was still lots about the place I loved. It was feeling suffocated by my domineering mother-in-law to be that was the problem. I falter at the thought that Alekos and I should have been married by now. Last month in fact. Having been fully swept up by giving birth and dealing with a newborn, I hadn't given it a thought. I wonder if we should talk about it? I glance across the table at Alekos chatting to the waiter and ordering our dinner. His face is shadowed, the flickering candlelight accentuating his tan and high cheekbones. His hair's a little longer than normal, but I like it. He's as handsome as ever. I sip my white wine. I know exactly what Candy would say, 'you lucky, lucky lady'.

The waiter finishes taking our order and leaves us with a nod. Alekos leans back in his chair, a smile on his face. He looks at me and picks up his bottle of beer.

'This was a good idea.'

I pick up my glass and tap it against his bottle. 'It was indeed.' I take a sip and relish the crisp coldness. 'Besides working, what have you been doing? They seem to know you here.'

'I ate out a lot. Even though the kitchen was the first thing I finished, it was still months without anywhere to cook. And the food here is great. Really great.'

'Don't ever let your mum hear you say that.'

'Mama doesn't specialise in fish or seafood. Now, if I was in a place that served grilled meat and moussaka, then I'd be in trouble.'

'Didn't you get lonely here on your own?'

He looks away from me, out towards the beach, where the dark sea glints from the lights lining the seafront.

'I spent most of the time working on the villa. And when I wasn't doing that, sleeping. I missed you.' He reaches for the cross around his neck and folds it between his fingers. 'Like you wouldn't believe.'

I take his hand in mine. It's rougher than I remember it, from months of hard physical work scraping walls, shifting rubble, painting, clearing – so very different to the life he had before, waiting on tables and playing his guitar when he got the chance.

'I missed you too.'

'I do still have friends here, mostly up near Fiskardo, although some of them are seasonal like me. There are still a few musician friends on the island. But seriously, working was good and I wanted to get the place fit enough for you and Thea to come over.'

'You've worked so hard, thank you.'

We share plates of fried mussels, grilled octopus, Greek salad, grilled cheese and crunchy sardines. I'm transported back to Fiskardo with Candy and our fish dinners by the harbourside where I first saw Alekos.

'Are you thinking back to when we first met?' Alekos asks, stabbing his fork into a piece of the grilled octopus and grinning. He pops it into his mouth.

'How did you know?' I grin.

'Because it's what I'm thinking about. Eating octopus always reminds me of being on that beach…'

My memory of that night is still fresh. He takes my hand in his and rubs his thumb up and down.

'I can't believe how close I came to losing you,' I say, with a lump in my throat, the highs and lows of the last year flashing through my mind.

He strokes my hand. 'Hey, but you didn't.'

'I behaved so selfishly. I don't know what I was thinking

half the time. To think what I would have lost…'

'Don't cry, Soph.' He wipes my tears away with his thumbs.

I laugh. 'Bloody post-pregnancy hormones. I've been emotional about everything ever since I first got pregnant. Probably explains a lot.'

'You might be right about that.'

I playfully slap his wrist and he smiles at me. We fall silent, our minds elsewhere as we tuck into the food. I squeeze lemon over the fried mussels and pop one into my mouth. My taste buds explode with the tang of lemon and the delicious saltiness.

'I hope Thea's okay with Mum.'

'She will be. She seems like a pretty relaxed baby.'

'She has her moments, but I think we've been lucky so far. She'll probably be a nightmare toddler.'

'Or teenager. Like my sister.'

'Lena was a difficult teenager?'

'Knowing what she's like now it's hard to believe, but yes, she gave Mama quite a few sleepless nights: drinking, drugs, unsavoury boyfriends.'

'No way.'

'And then she met Spiros and completely changed. Got married, had babies, was the perfect daughter – that's probably why you didn't realise. Mama wouldn't dream of saying anything to anyone about how Lena used to be. Perfect Greek wife and mother now.'

'And you weren't a nightmare teenager?'

Alekos grins. 'I was just better at hiding it than Lena.'

We leave the car parked outside the gate in an attempt to not wake Thea – if Mum has managed to get her to sleep in the first place. I giggle as we cross the courtyard, my one large glass of wine having gone straight to my alcohol-deprived head.

'I had fun tonight.' Before we reach the light spilling out

on to the courtyard through the villa doors, I tug Alekos into the shadows and kiss him. He cups my face in his hands and kisses me back, then pulls away, grinning.

'The old Sophie is back.'

'What, drunk?'

'Fun-loving and a little bit naughty.'

I playfully whack him with my bag. 'You do realise that kiss is as much action as you're going to get tonight.'

He kisses the side of my head. 'I know.'

We go from the dark night into the warm light of the living room. Mum stands at the sound of us coming in and turns. 'Good night?'

'Yes, thanks, and for looking after Thea,' I say. 'Where is she?'

Mum points behind the sofa to the Moses basket. Thea's lying on her back, her eyes closed, peacefully asleep, the only movement the gentle rise and fall of her chest beneath her Babygro.

'Well done, Mum. I didn't think there was a chance in hell of her going to sleep without a breastfeed.'

'I have the magic touch. Although it might be that she tired herself out after screaming the place down for forty-five minutes straight. Just as well you don't have any neighbours close by.' Mum sits back down on the sofa. 'You two should head up to bed and get some sleep while you have the chance. I'll stay down here with her and kip on the sofa until she wakes, then bring her up to you.'

Of course Thea wakes up crying for milk a couple of hours later, but at least Alekos and I get some quality sleep beforehand, curled in each other's arms. I've missed the closeness and warmth of his body. Mum was right about us needing a night out together, to rekindle our relationship, to remember why we'd got together in the first place and what it had been like to be just the two of us.

Chapter Four

The next day we start with renewed energy and make the most of the last few days of Mum being here. We clear weeds and rubble away by hand from the garden behind the house and outbuildings. The birdsong is drowned out by the workmen knocking down walls and digging out tree roots with a small sit-on digger. More rubbish and rubble is taken away and slowly the charm of the place begins to be revealed as the layers and years of neglect are slowly peeled away. The garden is beginning to reveal its charms too, and beneath the weeds and the rubbish – an old broken toilet, random bits of wood, a grate and rusty pots and pans – is the promise of something quite beautiful.

All too soon, it's Mum's last full day. I'm woken by Thea at dawn to the sound of birdsong. Even though it's peaceful, I have a feeling of dread in the pit of my stomach. I scoop Thea from her Moses basket and walk over to the open window. The scent of blossom in the fresh air filters through. Birds flit between the trees, dark shadows against the brightening sky. I sit in the chair by the window to feed her and wish that Mum didn't have to leave. After wasting so many years being angry with her, not to be able to see and talk to her each day fills me with sadness. But this is the reality of being with Alekos and living thousands of miles away from sleepy Marshton and Mum in Salt Cottage. It's taken years and a child of my own to understand Mum's reaction when I announced I was going to live with a man I barely knew, who I'd only met weeks before. Whether Mum thought it was a holiday romance doomed to fail or not wasn't the point; I understand now that she didn't want to lose me, her only child, to an unknown man and another country.

Thea doesn't settle back to sleep, so with her in a sling I leave Alekos sleeping and head downstairs. I put coffee on and look in the fridge. We need to go shopping. We do have eggs, and bread that's about to go stale, so I whisk the eggs with a little milk and salt, soak the bread in it, heat olive oil in the pan and fry eggy bread until it's golden. The smell brings Alekos and Mum downstairs, yawning, rubbing their eyes and murmuring appreciation.

'The time has flown by,' Mum says, taking a bite of eggy bread and sipping her coffee. 'I'm going to be so sad to leave you all tomorrow.'

'That's why you two are taking the morning off,' Alekos announces. 'I'll look after Thea.'

Mum raises an eyebrow but doesn't say anything.

'Are you sure?' I ask.

'I want to spend time with Thea, and this is Leila's last day. Do something nice. Go have lunch.'

I know Mum won't argue with that. Knowing that tomorrow she'll be off on a plane back to the UK makes me want to make the most of our last bit of time together.

With Alekos on daddy duty, Mum and I, arms linked, take a walk. We leave the garden, the villa, the builders, Alekos and Thea, and close the gate behind us, taking the sandy path that meanders down towards the beach. It's so nice to be outside without a paintbrush in my hand or aching from hefting rubble into a wheelbarrow. We walk along the edge of the beach close to the surf and I can't quite believe this is on our doorstep.

We go to the beachfront bar that Alekos recommended, where comfy seats and sofas spill out on to the sand. We choose a sofa right on the edge of the beach and sit down. I kick off my flip-flops and dig my toes into the warm sand. We order a vanilla milkshake each and they arrive in huge glasses with a plate of bite-sized crumbly biscuits.

'This is the life.' Mum wedges her sunglasses into her hair, tilting her head back and closing her eyes, the sun beating down on her. 'You know, I'm sorry I ever doubted you…'

'Doubted me about what?'

She pulls her sunglasses back down and looks at me. 'Do you remember standing in the kitchen of our old house in Bristol? You'd brought boxes of your stuff over to store and were off to Greece the next day to live with Alekos. I thought you were nuts to give everything up to live with a man you barely knew in a country where you didn't speak the language. I also laughed at your idea of setting up an artists' retreat. I'm sorry I ever doubted you. It may have taken a fair few years and plenty of ups and downs but you're the one laughing now.'

I remember everything about that conversation, every hurtful word we said to each other. I remember wanting to prove her wrong and feeling so frustrated when my life in Greece didn't work out the way I had imagined.

'To be fair, Mum, I felt the same at the thought of you moving from Bristol to Norfolk. You gave up a good job to start your own business; you moved from a city to a tiny village and left behind your friends.'

'You didn't voice it quite as strongly as I did though.' She takes a sip of milkshake. 'Bloody hell, that's good.'

I smile and look out over the honey-coloured sand dotted with sunbathers lounging beneath colourful umbrellas, the sea sparkling in the sunshine. 'There are so many things I love about Greece, but top of my list has to be the guaranteed good weather and all of this.' I wave my hand in front of us. 'Blue sky, a beautiful beach and relaxed pace of life.'

Mum swirls her milkshake around. 'It's why I moved to Marshton – to escape the frantic pace of the city. For the first time ever I yearned for a more peaceful way of life, like the way I grew up, I guess. The Peak District is beautiful but not a place I can ever return to. Norfolk offered me everything I craved: peace and quiet, stunning countryside, beaches and sea. And anonymity.'

'You know, it did surprise me when I found out about you moving there. I didn't think you'd ever give up your lifestyle in Bristol: going out, meeting lots of new people, all the blokes…'

'It all became meaningless and I hated myself for being shallow. You of all people know I needed to grow up.'

'And you have, but in a good way. You've kept your spirit and spunk.'

Mum chokes on her mouthful of milkshake. 'Spunk, eh?' She giggles. 'Moving to Marshton was the best thing I did, next to patching things up with you.'

'Best thing I ever did, besides working things out with you, was telling Alekos about being pregnant and how much I loved him.'

'You'd have moved back to *O Kipos* to be with him?'

'Yeah, I would have. Glad I didn't have to though!'

'Oh yes, this place is just stunning, there are no words really. I can't even begin to imagine how incredible the place is going to be once you've finished it.'

'You've got a good life back in Marshton. I'm going to miss living there. It was really special having that time with you.'

'Oh bloody hell, Sophie, you're going to set me off again.'

'Sorry, I hate having to say goodbye.'

'But it's not like the last time we said goodbye when you went off to Greece to live and we didn't talk to each other for what, the next three or four years. This time it's different. You've got Thea and Alekos and you're living in your own place. And although it means I'm going to miss you even more, we'll talk. All. The. Time.' She laughs.

'And you've got Robert. He's a keeper. You know that,

right?' I hold her gaze. 'He adores you and you seem pretty keen on him too.'

'I am, he's a lovely man and a good friend.'

'He's more than just a friend though, isn't he? Oh my God, Mum, you're blushing.'

'I'm not.' She hides her face by downing the rest of her drink. 'Don't you think it's about time we ordered some food? We've got to walk all the way back and up that hill. I could do with a plate of seafood.'

'Question nicely avoided.' I pick up the menu. I'd love to see Mum finally settle down with a decent man, but whatever happens between Mum and Robert, I'm glad she's got him as a friend.

All too soon it's time for Mum to leave. We're all up early, Mum packing her last few things and me keeping busy with Thea, trying to take my mind off saying goodbye. Alekos drags Mum's suitcase across the courtyard. With Mum's rucksack slung on her back and Thea dribbling on to the muslin across my shoulder, we walk arm in arm to the gate. I pass Thea to Alekos and start crying as I turn to Mum.

She hugs me and I wrap my arms around her, not wanting to let her go.

'I'm going to miss you like crazy,' she says. 'Both of you. All of you.' She releases me and takes Thea from Alekos, cuddling her to her chest and kissing her. 'She's going to be so big the next time I see her. Promise me we'll Skype.'

'Of course.'

'And often. I'm going to miss this little girl. Miss this.' She nuzzles into Thea's thick dark hair, tears dripping down her cheeks. 'I'm a bloody mess.'

With a last kiss on Thea's cheek Mum hands her back to me. I hold her against my shoulder, fighting back my own tears as Mum wipes her damp face with a tissue.

Alekos takes Mum's hands and kisses her on both cheeks.

'Look after them both,' she says.

'I will.'

Mum takes my hand and we walk through the long grass towards the waiting taxi.

We stop by the gate and Mum turns back.

'This place is going to be incredible,' she says, squeezing my hand. She leans into me and whispers. 'Never doubt Alekos again – you bagged yourself a goodun.'

'I won't,' I say, choking on my words. 'And thank you, for everything you've done for me over this last year.'

Mum waves away my words. 'Obviously I didn't think it at the time, but my accident was both the worst and the best thing that happened to me. Who knows where we'd both be now without you having come back to look after me. I hope that you and Alekos would have made it through the tough times, but without time away from each other, who knows. But us, the fact that we have our relationship back together, well I couldn't have asked for more.'

The taxi driver takes the suitcase from Alekos and heaves it into the boot, slamming it shut. He opens the door for Mum and without looking back, she clambers on to the back seat. Thea is warm against me and Alekos slips his arm around my shoulders. I take a deep breath and together we watch the taxi drive up the lane, churning up dust until it reaches the road and is out of sight.

'Right,' I say. With Alekos' arm still across my shoulders and Thea snuggled against my chest, we head back across the courtyard. 'Let's get on with it.'

Chapter Five

Three Years Later

It's early June and the sun is high in the sky, beating down over the gleaming white buildings that surround the courtyard. Purple bougainvillea spills out of clay pots on either side of the patio, vivid against the white. It always reminds me of the hotel Candy and I stayed in on Cephalonia when I met and fell in love with Alekos. I stand in the middle of the courtyard and tilt my head up, enjoying the warmth on my face. It's a rare moment to myself. The stillness of the place is only broken by a squawk of a bird overhead and the sound of the sea. I listen harder, making out the toe-tapping beat of Greek music coming from the only guest room currently occupied.

Thea's at preschool and Alekos has gone into Omorfia to stock up on wine and drinks, and with only one guest, the place is even more peaceful than usual. I open my eyes and look towards the sea, a view I will never tire of. It's different here to *O Kipos*, the majestic mountain replaced by the calming blue of the Ionian Sea. It's the perfect place for a creative retreat and I feel blessed every day that I live here. Over the year we spent renovating and rebuilding *Vila Ptina*, Alekos and I toyed with the idea of turning it into luxurious holiday villas or an exclusive B & B, knowing there would be plenty of tourists eager to visit, but we realised that level of guest turnover and luxury would not only be a huge amount of work but tie me to the kitchen and both of us to running a hotel. In the end, we went with the idea I'd envisaged before I'd moved to Greece – my dream of running a retreat. So Birdsong Villas Creative Retreat was born, still luxurious in its own way, we wanted it to have a homely feel and be a relaxing and creative place for writers and artists.

The peace and quiet is accentuated by the absence of Thea's usual laughter and shrieks as she runs around the place. She charms the guests as only a three-year-old can and we're lucky to have returning guests who remember her when she was a baby, then a boisterous toddler, and now a cheeky pre-schooler.

I make the most of the last couple of hours before Alekos returns with Thea in the early afternoon and the peace is broken. We have a routine. After getting Thea to nap either in her room or on the sofa in the living area, Alekos and I have a siesta to avoid the heat. Afterwards we head to the office to catch up on emails, paperwork and social media. So that's what I do, have a snooze on the sofa in the living room, then check emails and go over the plan for the next few days.

A car crunches over the gravel, followed by the slam of a door. Thea's non-stop chatter signals the end of my peace. I clatter from the study, through the kitchen and out into the courtyard. Thea squeals as she runs towards me.

'Mama, Mama!' She waves a piece of paper in my face with splodges of pink and blue paint smeared across it.

'That's nice,' I say. 'Did you do that today?'

She nods. Alekos smiles at me as he walks past carrying a box of wine.

'It's a dinosaur wedding,' he says, raising an eyebrow before disappearing inside.

'A dinosaur wedding?' I ask.

'*Ne*,' she nods, pointing at one of the pink smears. 'Like the wedding we're going to have here.'

'Oh I see.' I turn the paper to the side and squint, trying to visualise either a wedding or a dinosaur.

'Can I play outside?' she asks, jumping up and down.

'For a bit, yes.'

'With the water?'

'Only if you water the plants over there in the shade.'

'Okay!' she says, skipping off across the courtyard.

'I'm going to help Baba!' I call after her.

She's oblivious, so I head over to the car. I drag a crate of beer from the boot and walk back towards the kitchen, passing Alekos as I go.

'You got everything?'

'For the time being. I'll check through everything before you get back and make sure we don't need anything else.'

'I went through the plan while you were out and I think we're ready. I hope we're ready.'

Leaving the sunshine behind I head into the cool kitchen and set the beer down on the work surface. It feels like we've been stockpiling food and drink for weeks, on top of the usual shop we do to keep guests fed and watered.

Alekos joins me, placing a box filled with fairy lights and bunting next to me. 'You're okay with me finishing decorating?'

'Well,' I say, brushing my hand against his stubbly cheek. 'You can start it off and I'll do the finishing touches when I get back. Is there more in the car?'

'On the back seat.'

I head back outside into the glare of the sun.

I catch sight of Thea tipping the watering can over one of the cats asleep in the shade on the other side of the courtyard.

'*Ti kanis*, Thea?' I shout.

The cat yowls and shoots to its feet, its fur dripping with water as it disappears into the bushes.

'What are you doing?' I slip into English and storm across the courtyard, taking the watering can and crouching in front of her. 'I said you could play with the water as long as it was to water the plants in the border, not the poor cat.'

'Sorry, Mama,' she says, her hazel eyes wide as she looks at me, all innocent and un-sorry as a three-year-old can be.

I ruffle her hair. 'Okay, fine, you're forgiven but don't do anything like that again, plus you're supposed to be helping me – I've got lots to do before I leave tomorrow.'

She curls her arms around my neck until she's practically hanging off me and frowns. 'I don't want you to go.'

'I know, *moro mu*.' I lean one hand on the ground to steady myself before she topples me over. 'But it's only going to be for a few days and then Grandma and Robert are coming back with me. And we're going to have a wedding here and a big celebration. Loads of fun.' I playfully pinch her nose. She giggles and lets go of my neck. 'And that's why I need you to be a good girl and help me today, so we can be ready.'

She swings from side to side pulling at her T-shirt. 'I still don't want you to go.'

I take her hand. 'Ah but you're going to have Baba all to yourself and Yiayia and Papou will be here in a couple of days' time. Seriously, Thea, you're going to have so much fun.'

She follows me up to my bedroom and helps me pack my suitcase by jumping up and down on the bed while I deliberate over what to take. The UK in early June could be hot and sunny or miserable and rainy. I pack plenty of layers, scoop Thea into my arms mid jump and whiz her out of the bedroom and back downstairs.

'All ready?' Alekos glances at me. With Thea still in my arms, we zoom into the kitchen-cum-living area.

I place Thea on the floor. 'You're getting too big to carry you about like that.' I take the oven gloves from Alekos, open the oven and pull out a tray of halved roasted aubergines stuffed with savoury mince. I place them on the work surface. 'All packed I think. It's so strange to think I'll be leaving tomorrow and going back to the UK on my own.' I catch sight of Thea heading for the open doors that lead on to the courtyard. 'Your hands! We're going to eat now.'

'Oh,' Thea says, pouting. 'Can I play outside?'

'Afterwards.'

She stomps back across the room.

'Baba, Baba, Baba.' She yanks the edge of Alekos' T-shirt. 'Can I play outside *first*?'

Alekos picks her up and swings her on to his hip, her arms curling around his neck. 'Did you not hear what Mama said?'

'But...'

'*Ohi.*' He waggles a finger at her. 'Hands, dinner, then you can play.'

After Thea washes her hands, we head outside to the large table beneath the shade of the olive tree at the centre of the courtyard. Our one guest, Arthur, a regular, is already there, sipping a large glass of white wine.

'Ah, lovely Thea, there you are,' he says, putting down his wine. Thea skips up to him and they high five.

I smile. 'Have you had a productive day?'

'Not bad at all, thanks, Sophie, nearly four thousand words written.'

'Amazing. The peace and quiet must help.'

'Oh I'm not so sure about that – they're a rubbish four thousand words but they're down at least. I quite like the buzz of the place when there are lots of other guests here.'

'Trust me, give it a few days and the place will most definitely be buzzing again. You might be wishing for peace and quiet then.'

'Oh, I'm looking forward to a Greek wedding and feel honoured that you're allowing me to be a part of it.'

'As long as we don't distract you from your writing,' I say, dishing the aubergines on to plates.

'Arthur?' Thea says, tugging at his shirt sleeve.

'Yes, Thea?'

'My grandma and my yiayia and papou are going to be here.'

'I know, I'm looking forward to meeting them all.'

'Grandma lives in England.'

'That's where I live too.'

Thea frowns. 'No you don't. You live here.'

Arthur laughs. 'Well, I guess I do live here for a good part of the year. But I have a home in England too.' He leans towards Thea and pinches her nose. She giggles. 'I prefer it here though. Nicer food and weather. The best company too.'

'Thea.' I reach across the table and cut the stuffed aubergine on her plate into bite-sized pieces. 'It's time to sit down and let Arthur eat his dinner.'

Arthur picks up his fork and spears a piece of tomato and feta from the bowl in the middle of the table. 'You really do spoil me, you know.'

'We try our best.' I smile across the table at him. Alekos slips his hand on to my bare leg. I glance at him. The moment is not lost on me; the peacefulness of the place, sitting beneath the shade of the olive tree, the blue sky, the sound of waves, our retreat gleaming white in the sunshine, and Thea, kneeling on her chair taking a sip of water. She takes a spoonful of aubergine and grins when she catches us both looking at her.

After dinner Arthur heads to a bench beneath the cherry tree in the garden to write, and Thea plays outside for a while as promised. I clear away and go through all the decorations, sketching out a plan of where everything will go for the wedding and party afterwards. Alekos potters about, changing a rusty hinge on the gate and repainting the corner of one of the guest rooms where the paint has been chipped. It's gone nine by the time Thea's in bed. Alekos and I cuddle on the sofa, watching part of a film subtitled in Greek before heading upstairs.

'Are you going to be okay on your own?' I wipe the make-up from my face and drop the cotton wool in the bin.

Alekos looks at me. He's lying on the bed on top of the sheet in just his shorts. The heat has intensified over the past couple of days, and our third summer season at Birdsong Villas is about to begin.

'Of course I'll be okay. Remember, I was here for months

on my own before you and Thea arrived.'

'Yes, but it was only you then, you didn't have to look after a temperamental three-year-old.'

'We'll be fine. Anyway, it's only a couple of days and then Mama and Baba will be here. You'll be back soon enough.'

I get into bed next to him, a churning feeling in the pit of my stomach, whether it's from nerves about being away from Thea for the first time, excitement about going back to Norfolk and seeing Mum, or Alekos being here with his mother, I'm not sure. The last time I'd said goodbye to Alekos, leaving him in Greece while I escaped to the UK, we'd come so close to losing each other.

Alekos' lips on mine pull me back into the present. His hand smooths across my stomach, dipping under my vest top until he's cupping my breast. 'I'm going to miss you.'

'I'm going to miss you too.'

He kisses me and pulls the bow on my shorts loose.

'I do have to leave very early in the morning,' I say with little conviction.

'We'd better be quick then.'

Chapter Six

The last time I flew to the UK, I was twenty-eight and desperate to escape Despina's suffocating grip. Now at thirty-two, I'm leaving behind a three-year-old and our successful creative retreat that four years ago I never dreamed would become a reality. It feels very different returning.

I slip into the window seat of the plane and look out at the runway of Cephalonia International Airport. How much has changed. It's not simply because I'm older – I'd had so much anger bubbling inside the last time I made the journey. Anger towards Mum and frustration with Alekos and our life in Greece that it had turned out so differently to what we'd promised each other on Cephalonia.

I click my belt together and rest back in my seat. A trickle of air filters from above. This time I'm torn, my emotions fighting each other. Being away from Thea for the first time fills me with trepidation and sadness, combined with excitement at seeing Mum and revisiting Marshton. The thought of being able to sleep in past six-thirty in the morning without being woken by Thea jumping on me is pretty sweet too.

We taxi to the runway. Soon enough we're roaring into the air, climbing higher and higher leaving behind Cephalonia, my home and family. I wipe away a tear and silently curse the hormones that I swear haven't returned to normal since having Thea.

I close my eyes and rest my head back, focusing on the thought of seeing Mum again and Robert; I never thought I'd miss him, but I do. I feel better about living thousands of miles away knowing that Mum has him in her life. I allow sleep to take over, the worries of the last time I did the journey from Greece to the UK a distant memory. The novelty of not having to entertain a young child makes sleep a priority.

Three years of driving on the opposite side of the road makes me a bundle of nerves navigating leaving the airport in my hire car. The contrast of life on Cephalonia with the traffic clogged motorways outside of London is startling as I leave the M23 and join the M25 heading east.

It takes me a while to relax and loosen my arms where they're gripping the steering wheel. I concentrate on the surrounding traffic and steadily make my way around and up past London until I'm whizzing along A-roads, the suburbs giving way to tree-lined verges and vivid yellow fields filled with rapeseed. Memories flood back of the journey I did from Heathrow to Mum's cottage when I picked up Alekos and had the shock of Despina turning up too. The sight of her in a fur coat and gloves, wearing bright red lipstick will forever haunt me. The journey back to Salt Cottage had been tense, yet once we left behind the motorway, the beauty of the countryside had become apparent even to Despina who only ever considered England to be cold, rainy and built-up.

The weather is a perfect mix of white cloud and sunshine, much fresher than in Greece. I relish the breeze through the open window as I whizz along clear roads once I'm in Norfolk. Thetford Forest envelops me in its lush greenness. The road cuts through the trees, dappled sunlight filtering through, casting patterns on to the tarmac. It's slow-going through the market towns that look so English with red brick buildings alongside houses made from the local flint.

I've missed this place. It feels a lifetime ago since I was living here. The last three years on Cephalonia with Thea and the retreat were both harder and more wonderful than I could ever have imagined. Mum has been our biggest supporter, cheering us on via Skype, week after week, month after month, year after year, as bit by bit the place slowly turned from dilapidated hell-hole into a stunning retreat. Thea changed and grew as quickly as the retreat did, those first few weeks after Mum left a trying time of little sleep, too much work and frequent regret at what we'd taken on. Then between twelve and eighteen weeks old Thea wouldn't sleep for more than two hours at a time; she'd scream for an hour before falling asleep and repeating it all over again two hours later. Alekos and I would end the day exhausted and in tears but we survived.

Now, the sea view at Birdsong Villas is nearly topped by the view as you drive down the lane from the main road to the sight of our gleaming villa set back from the main courtyard, backed by a garden bursting with fruit trees and bushes that explode with colour throughout the year. The once crumbling L-shaped building now houses the guest rooms and is our biggest achievement. On one side is the courtyard, the other side a brand new pool with views towards the Ionian Sea. I often wish I had the time to be a guest myself and take a few days out from running the place to simply draw, sleep, eat, swim and walk down the hillside to the beach.

The bubble of excitement in the pit of my stomach intensifies the closer I get to Marshton. I speed past woods, fields of pigs, an occasional roadside garage and signs to odd-sounding villages like Weasenham and Little Snoring. Being back here reminds me of a time gone by and how confused I was about everything – relationships, family, my future – and how in control of it all I am now. I've settled into motherhood, my relationship with Alekos is back on track, and even the amount of work we do has adjusted from those crazy early days at the retreat to the decent work-life balance we now enjoy. Living in the most beautiful place has its price though. Having repaired my relationship with Mum, we're now thousands of miles away from each other. That's my biggest regret, not being able to see her every day like I used to. She's flown out and stayed with us three times, but in the life of a three-year-old, they were fleeting visits and I regret that she's missed out on so much of Thea growing up. Even Despina and Takis living in the same country haven't seen Thea or their other grandchildren as much as they would like, with *O Kipos* keeping them busy and tied to mainland Greece for the best part of the year. Although I know that's about to change.

Chapter Seven

My arrival, over the brow of a hill to where Marshton is revealed, is oddly familiar with the village green leading up to the church on my right and Robert's pub directly in front. I follow the sharp bend in the road round to the left and back out of the village, passing cottages on both sides. Nothing has changed, except unlike the first time I arrived in Marshton nearly four years ago, I'm on my own in a hire car rather than a passenger with a nervous Robert chatting non-stop. I turn down the bumpy potholed lane that leads to Salt Cottage, pull into the gravelled driveway and turn off the engine.

Like the village, the view in front of me is unchanged, even the blue sky and sunshine is reminiscent of when I first set eyes on Mum's cottage. The grey flint is typical to the area and blends in subtly with the surrounding garden which bursts with colour in the June sunshine.

I step out into the warmth and slam the car door shut. I pull my suitcase from the boot and hear the front door creak open.

'About bloody time, Sophie,' Mum calls. She stands on the doorstep with her hands on her hips and a huge grin. 'It's quite something that I have to be getting married for you to come visit me.'

I drag my suitcase over the gravel, along the path and fling my arms around her.

'It's not like we've not seen each other these past couple of years, and you know you're always welcome to come stay with us. I would have been over before but, well you know, it's been hectic.'

'I know, I'm joking.'

'But hey, I wouldn't miss your hen do for the world.'

I pick up my suitcase and follow her inside, through the cool dark hallway and out into the kitchen at the back of the house.

'Journey okay?' Mum asks, flicking the switch on the kettle.

'Long but not too bad. Much easier without a baby in tow.' I go over to the open back door and drink in the familiar view down Mum's sloping garden to the wooden fence at the end, trees casting their shadows across it. Beyond, open fields lead up towards the church at Blakeney just visible through the trees. I turn back to Mum.

She drops teabags into two cups and leans against the counter, her arms folded. 'Is Alekos going to cope with Thea on his own for a few days?'

'Despina and Takis are arriving tomorrow so he's only got a short time on his own. They're staying until after your wedding.'

Mum raises her eyebrows. 'That should be fun.'

I laugh. 'Don't worry, I've given Alekos strict instructions that his mum can't interfere with your wedding plans in any way.'

'Because his mother is the sort of person who'll listen to that advice.' The kettle boils and Mum fills the mugs. 'Actually, to be honest, maybe it would be better if I let someone like Despina take over – I'm a wedding planner who's loathing planning my own wedding. Go figure.'

'That's because it's different organising your own to someone else's.'

She puts the tea on a tray with a small carton of milk and I follow her outside.

'Mind you,' she says, setting the tray on the table on the patio. 'You've done most of the organising, sorting the paperwork and arranging everything at the retreat. I guess I'm terrified of turning into bridezilla.'

'Hell would freeze over before that happened.' I sit down on one of the chairs overlooking the garden and put my sunglasses on. 'It's probably just nerve-wracking making big decisions because it's your own wedding, rather than someone else's.'

Mum bites her lip and looks away, picking up her cup of tea and blowing on it. She stares down the garden towards the fields.

'What's up?' I ask.

She shakes her head. 'Nothing, I'm being silly.' She puts her tea down on the table and leans forward. 'It's a big decision getting married, and I didn't think I was the marrying type.'

'You love Robert, right?'

'Of course. Apart from having you, he's the best thing that's happened to me.'

'There you go then, if you love him it's not such a big decision after all.'

She breathes deeply and exhales. 'You're right. It's bloody pre-wedding nerves, that's all. I want to keep it low-key and simple – there seems to have been an awful lot of planning going on.'

'Well, the bureaucracy in Greece hasn't helped.'

'Damn paperwork.'

'It was *you* who decided you wanted to get married in Greece. We'd have happily come over here for it.'

She takes my hand. 'I'll let you into a little secret. It was actually Robert who persuaded me to get married in Greece – his reasoning being we wouldn't feel like we had to invite everyone we know, keep it exclusive to our closest friends and family. I liked that idea. Also, you and Alekos live in the most beautiful place.'

'Almost as beautiful as here.' I cast my eyes across the field to where a grey horse is grazing.

Mum snorts. 'Yeah right, it certainly has its charms and today is a glorious day weather-wise, but trust me on a miserable day in the middle of winter with driving rain and gale force winds, I wouldn't mind swapping this for a slice of Cephalonia.'

'Well, I can't wait for you to come back over and see what we've done to the place – photos don't do it justice.'

She takes my hand and squeezes it. 'I can't wait to see it again. I can't believe it's been nearly a year since I was last there. And Thea. Oh my God, I've missed her.'

'She's missed you too, crazy Grandma Keech.'

'Enough of the crazy.' She sips her tea and grins. 'Tell me you've gone easy on who you've invited to the wedding from Alekos' side?'

'Just Alekos' parents and Alekos' best friend, Demetrius and his wife.'

Mum raises an eyebrow.

'That's not many – you can't have a Greek wedding without at least a few Greek guests to create a party atmosphere. Plus, they know how to Greek dance.'

Mum folds her arms and leans back in her chair. 'I guess you're right.'

'You know I am.'

'By the way, I said we'd go down to The Globe and have a meal with Robert and Ben this evening, if you're feeling up to that?'

My heart skips. 'Ben's in Norfolk?'

'Uh huh.' Mum drains the last of her tea and puts the cup on the tray. 'You going to be okay seeing him?'

'Of course, I just thought he was still living in London. I wasn't expecting him to be here.'

'Ben's persuaded Robert to have a stag do. Well, I say stag do, I think they're going to have an evening playing cards and drinking beer round at a friend of Robert's.'

'And what are we doing for your hen do?'

'Oh, I'm going classy, Sophie. You're going to be damn proud of me. Kim and Jocelyn are coming over from Bristol, and with a couple of friends from around here we're going to have a picnic and drinks at my friend's beach hut, followed by drinks, nibbles and games back here.'

'Sounds pretty low-key and sophisticated to me.'

'I know, I surprised myself. Right,' she says, standing up and stretching. 'You go get settled in and then we'll head to the pub. Robert's dying to see you.'

Mum picks up the tray and goes back indoors. I scrape my chair back and follow, puzzled by the uneasy feeling in the pit of my stomach. I close the back door behind me. Mum's leaning against the frame of the kitchen door that leads to the hallway.

'By the way, you and Ben are going to be stepbrother and sister in two weeks' time…' she pauses, her eyes briefly shifting from mine. 'I don't know how to put this delicately, so I'm just going to come out and say it. That "thing" you had with Ben when you were here after my accident – you two didn't actually have sex did you?'

'No! Mum, seriously, no!' Heat spreads through my body and my cheeks burn. My thoughts immediately return to our fumble in the sand dunes by the salt marshes near Stiffkey. 'It was nothing like that, I mean we kissed and stuff, but no, nothing more.'

Mum holds up her hands. 'Okay, okay. I had to ask – I knew something happened between you, I wasn't one hundred per cent sure what and figured it would be a little bit awkward you two going from ex-lovers to step-siblings.'

Chapter Eight

Armed with a torch for walking back in the dark, we stroll down to The Globe a couple of hours later after I've settled myself into Mum's spare room, freshened up and got changed. Life in Cephalonia, even with a three-year-old to look after while running a busy creative retreat, is pretty chilled out, yet the peacefulness of Marshton still strikes me. It's one of those rare perfect English days, when it's warm and sunny with a light breeze, a beautiful temperature and not the least bit humid. Days like these were what made me fall in love with Marshton and north Norfolk as much as I had with Greece.

We round the corner and the cream walls of The Globe come in to view with the village green and the church beyond. Mum pushes open the heavy wooden door and we step inside. My heart thuds faster. I will myself to calm down. The waitress greets Mum with a hug and I glance around looking for Ben. The pub is busy with families and couples occupying most of the tables. Robert catches my eye from behind the bar and waves. He strides over, takes my hand and hugs me.

'It's so good to see you, Sophie.' His deep voice booms as he steps away and smiles.

From being irritated by him when we first met, to warming to him when he was a shoulder to cry on when I found out I was pregnant with Thea, I've grown to like him a lot. His hair is a little greyer, the lines around his eyes a little more pronounced, but he radiates a familiar warmth that eventually won me over during the months I spent living here.

'It's really good to see you too.'

He kisses Mum gently on her lips and then leads us through the bar, out into the light and airy restaurant. 'It's a lovely evening,' he says, pushing open the conservatory door. 'I thought we could eat out in the garden.'

I have so many memories of being here. This garden was where Robert organised a party for my twenty-ninth birthday; where I had a heart-to-heart with Despina and she beat into me the importance of family; and it was where Alekos punched Ben thinking there'd been something going on between us. I shudder; I guess there was something going on but I remember being confused as hell about my feelings towards Ben and frustrated by the situation with Alekos. Not that any of that should have been an excuse for how I behaved.

Ben is sitting at the far side of the garden at a table that's bathed in the last of the evening sunshine. Like Robert, he's a little greyer, his dark hair more salt than pepper than it was three years ago, yet he's achingly familiar. His T-shirt hugs his toned chest and his tattoo pokes out beneath the sleeve. He looks up from his mobile and wedges his sunglasses into his hair as we walk across. My heart quickens the closer we get, my hands clammy. Confusing emotions swirl inside at the memory of us kissing and my ill-fated desire to do more. I know my cheeks are flushed by the time we reach him.

He stands up and kisses Mum, then turns to me.

'Hello, stranger.' His stubble brushes my skin as he kisses my cheek. He stands back and meets my eyes.

'Hey there. It's been a while.'

I wipe my hot palms down my linen trousers as I sit. Robert pulls out a chair for Mum and she sits opposite with Robert next to me.

'Well,' Robert says, not allowing a moment of silence.

'Life certainly sounds like it's treating you well living out in Greece.'

'It is, thank you. It's been hard work but worth it.'

'I for one can't wait to come out and see what you've been up to.' Robert catches the eye of one of the waiters and nods at him, then turns back to me. 'Are you still cooking?'

'We do breakfast and lunch for guests staying at the retreat if they want it, and then group dinners twice a week – usually a barbecue and salads. Then the rest of the time guests either go out to eat or cook in the communal kitchen.'

'That sounds like the perfect balance.'

The waiter comes over with a bottle of champagne in a wine cooler and places it on the table with four glasses.

Robert thanks the waiter, stands up and pops the cork. 'I thought we should start the celebrations early.'

'You know I'll never say no to champagne.' Mum smiles at Robert as he pours foaming champagne into the glasses and hands them to us.

'Congratulations, Dad, Leila,' Ben says tapping his glass against each of ours.

'Congratulations,' I echo.

'Not long to go now.' Robert takes Mum's hand and gives her a look that would melt the most cynical heart.

With sunglasses shading her eyes it's difficult to tell the expression on Mum's face. I think back to my childhood and realise how much she's changed – the strongly independent woman who was passionately against marriage, now engaged and only days away from saying 'I do'. I push the thought that she looks worried to the back of my mind and take a sip of champagne.

Our dinner arrives and I tuck into crab salad, the perfect dish for a warm summer evening after an early start and a long day travelling. Mum and Robert chat and the silence between me and Ben grows. I chew a mouthful of crab and wash it down with a sip of champagne.

'Mum said you're still living in London,' I finally say. 'I

thought you were hoping to move out here?'

'I was.' Ben nods and puts down his knife and fork. 'I still want to but the reality of living far away from Bella and Fraser just doesn't make it viable at the moment. Perhaps once they both finish school and are away at university that will be my chance to escape here. Although the thought of them being old enough to go to university makes me feel ancient.' He takes a bite of his burger and chews it. 'But hey, you've found your perfect place to live – wasn't it what you always wanted? A place by the sea away from your in-laws?'

'Yes, true. It's everything I wanted and more. For a place that I didn't see or know about before Alekos bought it, he got it spot on. Well, you'll see for yourself in a couple of days.'

Ben leans forward and lowers his voice. 'He's okay is he? Your boyfriend. About me coming over for the wedding?'

I swirl my champagne round in my glass. 'Why wouldn't he be?'

'You know exactly why.'

I blush once again at the memory of our fumble. 'You're Robert's son – of course you're welcome.'

'Because you know I have to be there, you mean, not because you really want me there.'

I put my glass down and stick my fork into the creamy brown flesh of the crab. 'You really think that?' Mum and Robert are still deep in conversation. I turn back to Ben. 'It was nearly four years ago; we've all moved on and are adults. Me and Alekos have a child, are living and working together. Do you really think he's worried about you?'

I realise too late how harsh I sound. I grab my glass of champagne and sit back in my chair. 'Sorry, I didn't mean to be so…'

'Don't worry.' He shakes his head and grins. 'I'm glad you've lost none of your feistiness.'

'You know where I get that from.' I nod towards Mum.

'Yeah, Dad's got his work cut out with you Keech ladies.'

'What was that about us "Keech ladies"?' Mum asks,

pulling her sunglasses down her nose and shooting him a look.

'Just saying you're feisty.'

Robert's laugh booms across the pub garden.

'Oh,' Mum says. 'I can live with that.'

Mum and Robert resume their conversation. Ben slides his hand over mine where it rests on the arm of the wicker chair. He leans closer to me. 'So, you have no regrets about staying with him?'

Chapter Nine

I wake to birdsong and sunshine filtering through the spare bedroom window. I glance at the clock and groan. I'm away from home without Thea bouncing in to our bedroom at the crack of dawn, yet I'm still wide awake at seven o'clock. I close my eyes and settle back to sleep but I can't nod off. I lie there, thinking back to the evening before at the pub. Ben's question about whether I have any regrets choosing Alekos has been playing on my mind. Was there ever any chance of me choosing Ben instead? I didn't think so, but those few confusing weeks are still a blur of uncertainty. Being in Marshton and seeing Ben has brought the past flooding back, with the insecurities I had back then about my relationship with Alekos. I roll on to my side and hug the pillow. I have no idea why I should feel like this though. Our life couldn't be more different now than it was when I was last here. We escaped *O Kipos* and Despina's domineering personality, and Alekos gets to run our retreat the way we want to. Life has never been better. I rub my eyes and push the niggling thoughts to the back of my head. Reaching across the bed, I pick up my mobile from the bedside table and ring Alekos.

'Mama!' Thea screeches down the phone.

'Hello, baby,' I say, wishing I was there to cuddle her, missing her flinging her arms around me and smothering me with kisses. 'Are you having fun with Baba?'

'Yiayia and Papou are here. They gave me a new scooter. It's red and has lights in the wheels and I've been going round and round outside on it…'

'That sounds amazing.'

'Baba's going away today and Yiayia said we can have meatballs for dinner.'

'Baba's going away?'

'Thea,' Alekos says in the background. 'Let me talk to Mama.'

'You're going away?' I ask.

'The band arrived on Cephalonia a few days early and have lined up a couple of extra gigs. They want me to play with them this evening. They're playing at your mum's wedding, it's the least I can do.'

'Yeah of course, that's great, but who's looking after Arthur?'

'Mama's happy to, there's not much to do and I'll be back late tonight.'

We say goodbye and it feels odd being separated from Alekos once again. I resign myself to not being able to go back to sleep. By the time I've had a shower and got dressed, I can hear Mum pottering about downstairs.

The kitchen is flooded with light, the back door wide open and the morning air filtering in. The fresh sea air may not be as intoxicating as on Cephalonia, but I love the way the heat doesn't suffocate.

'Morning,' I say.

Mum's buttering toast with her back to me. 'Morning,' she replies without turning. 'Grab the Marmite, could you.'

Even after three years I remember where everything is. I take the Marmite from the cupboard next to the fridge and pass it to Mum. I pour freshly brewed coffee into two mugs, top them up with milk and place them on the kitchen table.

'You must have brought the spirit of the Greek gods with you.' Mum leans on the counter, a piece of toast in one hand. 'With this weather, they're most definitely shining down on us.'

I poke my head out of the kitchen door and gaze up at the blue sky with barely a cloud in sight. The warmth on my face from the early morning sun promises a hot day.

I turn back. 'Maybe so, because they're not shining down on Despina and Takis and they practically live in the shadow of Olympus.'

'Oh?' Mum says with a mouthful of toast. 'What are they up to now?'

'Trying to sell the restaurant and retire.'

Mum raises an eyebrow. 'And if they do manage to sell it, what then? Where will they go?'

I pop a piece of bread in the toaster and push the button down. 'That I don't know.'

'They've given up on you and Alekos taking over then? Or his sister?'

I lean back against the worktop next to Mum. 'Lena was never interested in running the restaurant. Anyway, they live in Athens now. Her husband has a decent job, the kids are settled in schools.'

'I doubt Despina will let it go so easily with Alekos without a fight.'

'We have Birdsong Villas and she knows we're doing well. We've built something from scratch and are making a success of it. It's our dream, like *O Kipos* was theirs.'

'You wouldn't want Thea to take over Birdsong Villas when you and Alekos decide to retire?'

I frown.

Mum points her half-eaten piece of toast at me. 'Think of it from their point of view. Most parents work hard for their kids and want to pass on what they've achieved. It's only natural.'

'I can't believe you're siding with Despina.'

Mum smiles, the creases around the sides of her eyes deepening. She crosses over to the table and picks up one of the mugs of coffee. 'I'm playing devil's advocate. Cephalonia is where you belong.'

I never imagined Mum would have a hen do, but then I never thought she'd ever get married. What she has always liked, though, is a good party, and getting married is the perfect excuse for a knees up. While Robert is having a quiet day pottering around the pub and then having a chilled evening playing cards, Mum has friends from Bristol arriving and a whole day and evening of festivities planned. The drinks cupboard is heaving with bottles of wine, gin and vodka, and there's enough bacon, eggs and bread in the house to help fix even the worst hangover.

By lunchtime Mum's already started drinking. We sit in the garden, a jug of Pimm's bursting with strawberries and cucumber slices on the table between us, and munch on egg mayonnaise sandwiches. Watching Mum top up her glass of Pimm's gives me a flashback to my teens with Mum dancing on stage at a club in Bristol, a bottle of cider in one hand and a bloke twenty years her junior grinding behind her. Robert's mellowed her, in a good way.

A crunch of tyres on gravel makes Mum squeal. We clatter through the house and out of the front door. An engine turns off and car doors slam shut. I was expecting Kim and Jocelyn, Mum's old friends from Bristol, but not a third person. Sparkly sandals and tanned legs appear from the back of the car, the sun reflecting off sunglasses and blonde hair.

'Candy?'

'Surprise.' Mum touches my arm as she goes past me to greet Kim and Jocelyn.

Candy grins as she crunches across the driveway towards me. She flings her arms around me and holds on tightly.

'I didn't think you were able to make it?'

She releases me and wipes away a tear. 'I told Lee he had to have the kids. I put my foot down. Seriously, I need some normality in my life and a bit of me time.'

'Good for you.' I hook my arm in hers and we walk to the

cottage. 'Oh my God, I'm so happy to see you.'

'I can't tell you how good it is to be here. I'm going to miss the kids like crazy though. I've only been away from them for like one or two nights at a time at most, but I figured he's perfectly capable of looking after them for two weeks. The fact he's having to use annual leave to pick them up from school, get them their tea and to bed is better than him taking time off to spend with *her*. About time he stepped up and behaved like a father, seeing as though he's failed miserably at being a husband.'

We head straight through the house and out into the garden. Apart from Mum, Kim and Jocelyn's muffled chatter coming from the house, the only sound is the breeze in the trees.

'Wow.' Candy stands with her hands on her hips, gazing down the garden towards the field of horses. 'It's stunning.'

'You really could just sit all day and look at that view, couldn't you,' Jocelyn says, joining us. She kisses my cheek. 'Hello, Sophie. It's good to see you.'

'Have you not been here before?' I ask.

'When your mum first moved up here, I came and helped out for a few days, didn't I?' She glances behind as Mum and Kim emerge from the house. Mum nods and Kim hugs me. Jocelyn sits down at the table and waves her hand in front of her. 'Looked nothing like this though – you couldn't really see the view through the trees, what with brambles and overgrown bushes.'

'You haven't been back since?' Candy asks, sitting down on one of the garden chairs and crossing her tanned legs.

'No, that's awful isn't it? Time seems to have flown by, and it's not like I can just drop by.'

'It is a bloody long way from Bristol.' Mum picks up the jug of Pimm's.

'So you've not yet met Robert?' I ask.

'No,' Jocelyn replies. 'The infamous Robert, the man who finally managed to win Leila's heart.'

Mum laughs. 'You make me sound like I was some cold-blooded ice-queen, unable to love a man.' She waves the jug of Pimm's in front of us, the copper-coloured liquid glinting in the sunshine. 'Who wants Pimm's and lemonade?'

Kim sighs and winks. 'Go on then, we might as well start as we mean to go on.'

'Tea for me, please,' Jocelyn says.

'Jocelyn, really.' Mum frowns.

'Don't we need someone to be sober to drive to the beach this afternoon?' she asks.

'Sophie's already offered to be the designated driver, haven't you Soph?'

I nod and pop a strawberry into my mouth.

'Have a drink, Sophie.' Jocelyn smiles at me. 'Tea will be fine for me, thanks.'

'If you insist.' Mum pours the Pimm's and I nip inside to switch the kettle on.

'I've met Robert,' Kim says as I re-emerge into the garden. 'He's as lovely and handsome as I imagined he'd be. I think he's been a wonderfully calming influence on you,' she puts her hand on Mum's knee, 'and I mean that in the nicest possible way. You seem happy and content.'

'I am,' Mum says. 'He's the longest relationship I've ever had. Not quite sure how he's managed to stick with me for so long.'

'Are you kidding, Leila?' Candy says. 'You've always had men falling for you – it was you who used to push them away, not the other way round. You're a catch.'

'At fifty-two bloody years old.'

'Better than being sixty-four years old,' Jocelyn says, raising an eyebrow.

'Ah, but, Jocelyn, you've been happily married ever since I've known you. Trust me when I say I've envied you with that kind of stability, certainly as I've got older.'

'But then you've loved being a party girl too,' Jocelyn replies.

Mum shrugs. 'True. Okay, so maybe I was jealous of the stability of a decent man but hell, I did have a lot of fun when I was younger.'

Laughter echoes around the group. I head back inside to make Jocelyn a cup of tea. Snippets of the continuing conversation drift in through the open door. I squeeze out the teabag, splash in milk and return to the sunshine, placing the tea in front of Jocelyn.

'Do you know,' Kim says, smiling at me as I sit next to her. 'I think you were about nineteen or twenty the last time I saw you.'

'Yeah probably, at the end of a messy night out with me looking after Mum.'

'That sounds about right.'

'I hope you're all going to behave yourselves this evening?' I ask, glancing between Mum and Kim.

'Sophie, it's my hen do, which I didn't want, but as I was bullied into it I'm now going to make the most of it. Partying used to be my thing; I may be a little out of practice but I'm in the mood to let my hair down tonight. It used to be Kim's thing too.'

Kim waves her hand. 'Back in the day before I had kids.'

'That never stopped Mum…'

'It never stopped Kim either if I remember rightly.' Mum grins and sips her Pimm's.

'Ah, but that was after my divorce and before I settled down with John – I was a good girl once I did.'

'That's true, then I lost my pulling partner.'

'Those were the days.' Kim sighs. She reaches forward and taps her glass against everyone else's and Jocelyn's cup of tea. 'But now my kids have left home and gone to university I have my freedom back again – at least in term time.'

'Your husband doesn't mind you going out?' Candy asks.

'He likes the freedom too. When I'm away he can play golf or spend the day in the pub. So no, he loves it when I'm not home.'

Jocelyn raises her cup of tea. 'To Leila and her last chance to be wild and single.'

It sounds funny coming from someone who's never been wild or indeed single. One of Mum's few sensible, older and grounded friends who actually stuck by her through everything. Married for goodness knows how many years she's a grandma at the age Mum considers a sensible age to become a grandparent.

I sip my drink and rest back into my chair, smiling at Candy, any earlier unease having lifted. This is the life, no cares in the world, my first few days on my own without Thea, relaxing and enjoying the company of my best friend and my mum.

Chapter Ten

I'm torn between wearing my bikini or the swimming suit I bought after having Thea when I'd been worried about exposing my mummy tummy. Alekos had told me I was being silly and he loved my new curves. After three years of hard work, physically building the retreat and then running it, I'm back to the same weight I was before having Thea, my skin's tanned and even my stomach is relatively toned, but I can see the silvery stretch marks on the lower part of my tummy when I look in the mirror. I know what Candy and Mum would say, that I'm being silly and worrying too much about nothing. I chuck the swimming costume on the bed and wiggle into the bikini instead, throwing a colourful short summer dress on over the top.

We head along the coast in two cars. Jocelyn drives with Mum in the front, and me, Candy and Kim, squashed together on the back seat. Mum's local friends, Philippa and Pamela follow in the car behind us. We drive through Blakeney and past the road leading to the Spar where I bought the pregnancy test. My cheeks flush as we wind our way through Stiffkey, past the pub I'd had lunch with Ben in before our interrupted fumble in the sand dunes. I gaze out of the window, trees, hedges and fields zipping by in a blur.

'You're quiet,' Candy says when we reach Wells and turn to the right, heading towards the centre of the town.

'It's strange being back here.'

'Without Thea and Alekos?'

'Yes, but being here reminds me of such a different and unsettled time in my life... So much changed in the few months I was last here, it's an odd feeling, that's all.'

The road along the seafront is packed with cars and people. There's a crab hut and the buildings that face the seafront are filled with fish and chip shops, cafes, and shops selling crabbing nets, flip-flops, buckets and spades. It's the British seaside at its best and a world away from the shimmering heat of Fiskardo and Omorfia with their beachside fish restaurants and open air bars serving creamy frappés with little biscuits, and cold beer alongside bowls of crisps.

We pull up next to each other in the car park and get out, dragging bags, cool boxes and umbrellas after us. Mum introduces everyone to each other, friends from both Bristol and Norfolk, and we take the path beneath trees that runs alongside the car park. Pamela is the incredibly wealthy, posh and vibrant woman I met when I helped with her daughter's wedding day when Mum was injured. Mum's newest friend, Philippa, is the only one I haven't met before. We follow her up steep wooden steps and back down again between two beach huts, on to a large expanse of honey-coloured sand. Beach huts spread out in both directions, their backs to the trees lining the sand, like a row of upright sugared almonds all purples, pinks, yellows and off-whites. Philippa turns to the left, and we follow, our feet sinking into the sand as we haul bags and cool boxes with us. The sky has clouded over a little from the morning but there are pockets of blue.

It's early in the season, schools haven't broken up yet and it's a weekday. The beach is quiet with mostly retired couples sitting reading their books, plenty of dog walkers and a handful parents with pre-school children enjoying a day out.

Philippa's beach hut is almost at the end of the row, with steps up to a small decked area with views of beach and sea.

'Bloody hell, how much did this cost?' Mum dumps her bag in the sand and stands with her hands on her hips, looking up at the pale-purple hut.

'Don't even ask.' Philippa jogs up the steps and unlocks it, throwing open the door. 'But it was worth every penny.'

Inside, the wooden walls and floor are painted white and there's a tiny kitchenette area to one side with a sink, space to prepare food and a cupboard below. On three white shelves on the back wall are candles, an old gas lamp, tin signs and driftwood frames containing beach scenes. A white coffee table with a vase of dried lavender and a padded bench with blue and white striped cushions against the wall on the right fill the rest of the space.

'My little piece of heaven.' Philippa turns back to us.

'I'm insanely jealous right now,' Candy says, kicking off her flip-flops and padding across the sand to the beach house steps. 'It makes me want to leave Bristol and go live by the sea.'

'Which is exactly what Sophie has done.' Mum puts her arm across my shoulders.

Candy turns round. 'Well, I'm insanely jealous of Sophie too.'

We set up deckchairs in the sand at the bottom of the beach hut steps and put out food and drink on a table up on the decked area. I'd spent the morning in the kitchen before everyone arrived preparing salads and *spanakopita*, plus tomatoes and peppers stuffed with savoury mince and rice. Since running our retreat, I don't cook anywhere near as much as I did when I was working at *O Kipos*, but I realise how much I enjoy creating dishes away from the pressures of a busy restaurant kitchen.

'Goodness,' Jocelyn says, putting the last bottle on the beach hut deck. 'That's an awful lot of wine for just seven people, two of whom aren't even drinking.'

'Better to have too much than too little.' Kim opens a

bottle of white, pours it into five glasses and passes them around. She tops up another two with fizzy elderflower and hands them to Jocelyn and Pamela.

'Cheers!' Kim raises her glass. 'To Leila!'

'To Leila!' we all say, taking a sip of our drinks and sitting down on the deckchairs that have been arranged in a circle.

I dig my toes into the sand and rest back, feeling utterly relaxed on a beach, in the sunshine, drinking wine with good company, and not having to keep an eye on a cheeky three-year-old.

'The last time I saw you, Sophie,' Pamela says, pulling her Dior sunglasses down her nose. 'Which of course was the first time I met you at my daughter's wedding – you were single and had no children and now you're married to a Greek god, if Leila's description is anything to go by, and have a gorgeous little girl.'

'Ha yes, still not married but we do have our little girl.'

'And Alekos is hot,' Candy says, looking at me. She holds her hands up. 'Just saying.'

'Did you meet him in Greece?' Philippa asks.

I nod. 'On a holiday to Cephalonia that Candy and I went on, what, eight years ago now?'

'She was romanced on a sailing boat and spent a night getting up to God knows what on a desolate beach with him. Who wouldn't fall in love?'

'Mum!'

'Candy, am I right?' Mum folds her arms and turns to Candy. 'Come on, I'm in my fifties and about to settle down. This is the stuff of dreams – humour me.'

'Yep, you're right.' Candy grins. 'It was love at first sight followed by sex on the beach…'

'Candy!'

I whack her arm and everyone laughs.

'And I wasn't the only one who got up to no good that night.' I jab a finger at Candy.

'Oh really,' Kim says, grinning at Candy over the top of

her glass of wine.

'Yeah, but my night of passion was ill-fated unlike your romance with Alekos.'

'Ooh, but who was he?' Kim leans forward.

'Alekos' best friend.' I reach out and place my hand on Candy's arm. It's difficult to see her expression behind her over-sized sunglasses. 'He behaved like a twat and had a girlfriend back home at the time.'

'I certainly know how to choose them,' Candy says, her tone not quite matching her bubbly personality.

'So you didn't end up with your holiday romance then?'

'Nope, not a chance there. He had a girlfriend back on the mainland and I was a one-night fling – although to be fair that was all I intended him to be, it's just he could have had the decency to actually talk to me the next day instead of ignoring me completely. I mean I understand regret, but if he was able to shag me he should at least have been civil.'

'I'm feeling rather old and married right now,' Jocelyn laughs.

'Me and you both.' Pamela waves her wine glass. 'I married young and have only ever slept with my husband.'

'That,' Mum says, reaching across the sand and clinking her glass against Pamela's, 'is something to be proud of.'

'I know.' Pamela nods. 'We practically conceived our eldest daughter on our wedding night, so we never really had any time to be a couple if you know what I mean.'

'How about you, Candy?' Philippa asks. 'Do you have kids?'

Candy coughs and rubs her finger where her wedding ring had been. 'Yes, two. A boy and a girl, five and four. I had them close together for my sins.'

'You've managed to get away for a few days then?' Philippa asks, taking a forkful of stuffed green pepper.

Candy takes a swig of wine. 'Uh huh, their dad has them; we're separated.'

'Oh I'm sorry,' Philippa says.

Candy waves her hand. 'Don't be, I'm well shot of him.'

There's a pause, and I get the sense that no one wants to ask the obvious question of why they're no longer together and take the edge off the happy relaxed mood.

'Well, Candy,' Mum says, before anyone has the chance to say the wrong thing. 'I've had my fair share of crap men over the years, so trust me when I say if, at the age of fifty-two I can find a decent, loving man, then you've got plenty of time to find one too.' She raises her glass and we all do the same. 'To finding love, and having sex on the beach with a hot man – if we're damn lucky enough!'

Chapter Eleven

It's the one thing I've missed living and working on Cephalonia, having girlfriends around. Even if everyone here, apart from Candy, are Mum's friends, it's comfortable talking to them, regardless of the differing ages and personalities. Mum unites us and she's loving every minute of being the centre of attention and having a blissful, carefree few hours drinking on the beach and gossiping. When I lived at *O Kipos* I became good friends with Katrina, Demetrius' wife but then they moved away to Thessaloniki and I retreated to Marshton for those few months before returning to Cephalonia. Since having Thea I've made friends with other mums in Greece, but it's different getting together for playdates or birthday parties rather than hanging out with a friend you've known for a long time and can talk to about anything.

Full of food and wine, and having basked on the beach in the sunshine all afternoon, we pack up. Philippa locks the beach hut and we retrace our steps back along the sand, past the multicoloured beach huts, a couple of them occupied with families camped out on the deck, and I glimpse their snug seaside interiors. We split ourselves between the two cars again and set off, back along the coast road, through the villages until we turn off the main road at Blakeney and down the hill to Marshton. From the back seat I glimpse Salt Cottage across the field of horses, partially hidden from view by the trees. The pang of longing for the time I spent here before having Thea takes me by surprise. It was a period of contrasting emotions, but I will always think fondly of the time Mum and I had together rebuilding our fractured relationship. That must be what the longing is for – quality time with Mum.

The cars pull up alongside each other on the gravel drive and we pile out, most of us tipsy, all of us drunk on sunshine and food.

'Make yourselves at home,' Mum says, pushing open the door to the living room. 'I'm going to sort out drinks.'

'Put the kettle on too!' Jocelyn calls out.

'There's absolutely no excuse not to have a drink now we're back.'

'A cup of tea first, then I'll start on the wine.'

Mum rolls her eyes and I follow her into the kitchen.

'I've never been a sensible cup of tea kind of person,' she says, putting the kettle on and taking glasses out of the cupboard.

'More like a shot of tequila type of person.' I reach into one of the cupboards and grab a couple of packets of crisps and nuts.

Mum turns and leans on the edge of the work surface. 'Was I a nightmare to live with when you were growing up?'

There's a screech from the living room followed by laughter. I open a bag of nachos and tip them into a bowl. 'Not a nightmare, no. But you weren't a "normal" mum.'

'No shit.'

'But I wasn't really aware of that until I was well into my teens and by then you were normal for me.'

'Sometimes I think back on my behaviour…' She shakes her head. 'How you turned out so normal I have no idea.'

I open the cashew nuts and find another bowl. Normal is such a strange term – what is normal? Does Mum mean I didn't turn out like her? Having an affair with a much older married man and getting knocked up young? I wasn't a particularly rebellious teen, and I didn't sleep around like Mum used to. I pour boiling water on to the teabag and glance at her. Is this regret coming from the fact that now, in her early fifties, she's settling down with a man so different to the men she used to go for? I wonder how much of her past Robert actually knows.

We return to the living room, each carrying a tray laden with drinks and nibbles.

'Why are you all sat in the dark?' Mum asks, setting her tray down on one end of the coffee table.

The sun's beginning to dip outside, the trees lining the driveway silhouetted against the yellow, reds and deep purple spreading across the sky. Mum switches on the lamps and a warm glow floods the room.

'That's better,' Pamela says.

'You're nutters,' Mum laughs. 'Too much bloody alcohol.' She turns to Jocelyn and winks. 'You have no excuse.' She passes her a cup of tea and a glass of red wine.

'I wonder what Robert's up to?' Philippa asks, reaching for the cashew nuts.

'Whatever he's doing, he's probably not as pissed as I am.'

With Ben there, I guess it might be an alcohol-free evening. I have no idea how he's dealing with all of that, but Robert's always been one to protect him from his drinking spiralling out of control again. It's odd to think that Ben and I will officially be tied together forever by Mum and Robert getting married. I push the thought to the back of my head and tune back into what Mum's saying.

'Not working, having a night in with friends and his son is just what he needs, even if it's not going to be as much fun as our night in!' Mum holds up her glass. 'Cheers, everyone, and thank you, Jocelyn, Kim and Candy for coming all the way over here to help me celebrate, and for those of you who are flying out to Greece for our wedding, I appreciate it.' A grin creeps across her face. 'Bloody hell, I'm getting married!'

The realisation that Mum's getting married but it's only

now sunk in, doesn't surprise me. I don't think I've processed the enormity of it, not just that Mum is going to become Mrs Thurston, but that I'm going to have a stepfather when I haven't ever had a father in my life before. Elliot doesn't count. I don't know him, he's never been a part of my life and our brief, ill-fated and fleeting meeting means very little. Ten minutes out of the thirty-two years I've been alive is a joke.

Alcohol continues to flow and we end up playing a suitably hen party-ish game that Candy and Kim had come up with on the journey between Bristol and Marshton. It involves Mum being grilled with some quite personal questions which she can either choose to answer or decline and down a drink. Mum loves it until Jocelyn asks her a question that hits a little too close to home.

'So, you'll be marrying Robert, but when are you actually going to move in with him?'

'Yes, Leila,' Kim says, a slur coating her words. 'I mean you're going to be husband and wife in less than two weeks.'

Even though she's drunk, I can see that Mum's uncomfortable with the question. Her shoulders tense as she puts her drink down on the table and folds her arms.

'I'm not selling Salt Cottage and he's obviously not going to be selling The Globe. We both live and work in our homes. Makes sense to me to keep both running and a shame to see either of them empty. Not that The Globe would be empty, it's just easier for Robert to live there particularly when he works long hours and late nights.'

Candy reaches for a handful of crisps and Kim downs the remainder of her wine. Jocelyn fiddles with her bracelet and I watch Mum, as she carefully avoids eye contact with anyone, particularly Philippa sitting next to her.

'But you sleep together, right?' Pamela asks, her face flushing with the boldness of her question.

'Yeah, Leila.' Kim places her empty wine glass on the coffee table. 'You must end up staying at each other's when you want to, you know…' she attempts a whistle and falls about giggling.

'Yes, we sleep together. Of course we do. Although he was the first man I ever waited a while to have sex with.' Mum picks up her drink and takes a sip. 'I've never lived with anyone – well, not in a romantic sense. I used to have lots of boyfriends who stayed over,' she glances at me, 'Sophie can testify to that, and we had lodgers for a long time when we lived in Bristol. But I've never shared my house with a man I was in a proper relationship with.'

'That's the problem,' Jocelyn says, nodding. 'You're still thinking along the lines of "my house" instead of "our house". Getting married and committing yourself to someone means it's not just you any longer. You've got to think of you and Robert as "us" from now on.'

One by one we drift off to bed, Jocelyn first, up to Mum's spare room, which I've given up for the night, while Pamela drives home and Philippa walks the short distance to her house in the village. We stay chatting and drinking in the living room until Kim can barely keep her eyes open, and Mum and I leave her and Candy to get to sleep on the sofa and a camp bed. We creep upstairs to Mum's room and tumble into bed without cleaning our teeth, getting a wash or even changing into night clothes.

Mum remained subdued for the last half hour or so of the evening after the conversation downstairs had turned to her and Robert living together. I think I was the only one who noticed. Lying next to her on the bed, I know better than to question her further, figuring if she wants to talk to me, she will. Instead I blurt out the first thing that pops into my head, realising too late that the subject matter is as volatile as questioning Mum's motives for not shacking up with Robert.

'Have you invited Grandma and Grandad?'

It's gone three in the morning, and my head is fuzzy from too much sun, alcohol and partying – at least that's my excuse for asking such an insensitive and difficult question in the early hours of the morning. The sun and heat I'm used to, the late night partying and getting drunk I haven't done for quite some time.

'Do you think I should?' Mum takes so long to reply I thought she'd fallen asleep.

I stare up at the dark ceiling, Mum doing the same next to me. It's so quiet, as peaceful as it is at Birdsong Villas at night when only an occasional car passes by on the main road at the top of the lane. I remember being thrown by the silence the first night I stayed at Salt Cottage before Mum came home from hospital.

'It's not about what I think. It would be a way to make amends, that's all.'

Mum shifts on the bed to look at me. 'It was their fifty-fifth wedding anniversary last month and they had a big party – do you think they invited me? Did they invite you?'

'No. I just thought the gesture of an invite might bridge the gap between you… Between us all.'

'My wedding to Robert is for close family and friends. On my side that's you, Alekos and Thea and what, the three friends of mine who are coming over to Cephalonia with us. I'll have everyone there I want and who I care about.' Mum tucks her hands behind her head. 'Anyway, I have nothing to make amends for. I'm done with my parents punishing me for screwing around when I was a teenager. I'm fifty-two bloody years old, not a naive eighteen-year-old desperate to gain back their respect. I lost respect for *them* a long time ago when they sided with the man who was old enough to know better, rather than supporting their own daughter. I'm done with being a disappointment.'

'You really think they're still disappointed in you?'

'I wouldn't put it past them. But you know what, I don't care.'

'Do they even know you're getting married?'

Silence. Mum pulls the sheet up to her chin, covering up the clothes she wore to go out in. 'I phoned Mum on their wedding anniversary to congratulate them. She told me about the party they were having that weekend. She didn't have to tell me *he* was going to be there, but I knew that was the reason I wasn't invited. So I told her I was getting hitched. She sounded shocked, but I guess when your daughter is in her fifties by the time she gets married, shock is the natural reaction.'

I sigh and close my eyes, feeling nauseous from watching shadows on the ceiling swirling around and around. 'I haven't spoken to Grandma since we went up to confront Elliot. They've never met Thea. I emailed them a photo but they never replied. I even said they could come out and stay with us. I sent them all the details and left it up to them, but nothing. It's sad that Thea doesn't know her English great-grandparents.'

'There are a lot of things about our family that make me sad.' Mum reaches above the sheet and takes my hand. 'I hate how they're punishing you and Thea for my mistakes. But you, well I'm damn proud of you and how you turned out, particularly having me as a mother.'

Even with my eyes closed, the swirling feeling continues and intensifies until it feels like the bed itself is spinning. 'You shouldn't put yourself down,' I say slowly, opening my eyes and fighting back another wave of nausea. 'I may have had an unconventional childhood and you may not have been a traditional mother, but I wouldn't change it for the world. Except maybe that lodger who lived with us when I was seven. You know, the one who used to smoke pot in his attic bedroom. Oh and that other one – the two of you used to make the headboard of your bed bang against the wall a lot…'

Mum buries her head in her hands. 'I was a nightmare – what the hell was I thinking? Seriously, how you turned out the way you have is a bloody miracle.'

'I think I rebelled against what I knew, so ended up being good rather than going off the rails. If you'd been a teetotal, happily married, calming influence I may well have ended up rebelling against that and been a nightmare teenager. I was always more worried about you and what twat of a bloke you were seeing.'

'And it's taken me more than fifty years to grow up.'

'And here you are, days away from your wedding to Robert. Definitely not a pot-smoking, horny twenty-something lodger.'

'He's about as far from that as you can get.' Mum takes her hands away from her face and laughs. 'I'm not sure he even smoked anything when he was young.' She turns to me. 'What the hell does he even see in me?'

'You seriously have to ask that? You're a matured version of who you've always been – the best of both worlds. The same wicked sense of humour, feistiness, beauty. Crazy and lovable.'

'You've drunk too much.'

'Couldn't agree with you more. I need to sleep. This whole room is moving.'

'See, even on my hen do I'm a bad influence. We'll regret tonight with the hangovers we're going to have in the morning.'

'Just as well you stocked up on all that bacon and eggs.'

Mum gags. 'Sophie, please, shut up about food.'

I laugh and close my eyes again. Lying still, I wait for the spinning to ease so I can drift off to sleep.

Chapter Twelve

I groan and open my eyes. The band of pain across my forehead intensifies. Grey light filters in through the gap in the curtains where we hadn't closed them fully the night before, but it might as well be blazing sunshine for how it makes my head throb. Mum snores next to me, her mouth wide open, dribbling on to her pillow. I take my mobile off the bedside table. 08.40. A lie-in for me. But with a thumping headache and needing to wee, there's no point in lying in bed any longer. I swing my legs out from under the covers, sit up and groan again, cursing how much I overdid it on wine and Pimm's.

I text Alekos.

Kalimera. Hope you're all okay. Give Thea a big kiss from me. Will call you later. Filakia xx

I stumble across the landing and into the bathroom. I splash cold water on my face and tie my tangled red hair into a ponytail. I tiptoe back into Mum's bedroom, put on clean underwear, jeans and a loose-fitting short-sleeved top. I leave Mum snoring and head downstairs.

I'm the first one up. I guess that's what becomes of being conditioned to waking up early every morning for the last three plus years. I poke my head around the living room door; Candy is fast asleep on the sofa; Kim gives me a weak smile from the camp bed. I wave and shut the door quietly behind me.

In the kitchen I get the coffee machine brewing and fling open the back door on to a grey morning with light rain pattering down on the garden. I breathe deeply, enjoying the fresh cool air on my face, kicking my senses awake. I pour myself a large mug of coffee with a generous amount of milk and pretty much down the lot.

Kim appears in the kitchen doorway, hands on hips. 'I've not felt this hungover for a very long time.' Her face is pale and make-up free, her dyed blonde hair messily tied up. 'I could cope with hangovers in my twenties and even my thirties, but my fifties? Ugh.'

I hand her a mug of coffee and she sits down at the kitchen table.

'How are you managing to be so perky this morning?' she asks, tucking her hands around the mug.

'I don't feel perky. But I slept pretty well and getting up past eight feels like a lie-in. Since having Thea and running our retreat, six o'clock starts are the norm for me now. Oh, and the coffee is helping.'

'That's what I like about having teenagers – no more early mornings. I just can't handle my drink any longer.' She laughs, then groans, rubs her forehead and blows on her steaming coffee. She takes a sip. 'We were lucky with the weather yesterday.'

'I know; it was a beautiful day. This is what I don't miss about this country; the unpredictability of the weather.' I open the fridge and take out packs of smoked bacon and half a dozen eggs.

'What's the weather like in Greece at the moment?'

'Dry and hot. June's a lovely time on Cephalonia. July and August can often get way too hot.'

'I can't wait.'

'Have you been to Greece before?'

'Once, years ago, to Crete when the kids were little.'

I cut open the pack of bacon and start laying the rashers

out on the grill.

'Oh God,' Kim says, putting her head in her hands. 'You're seriously going to cook that?'

'Yep, a good breakfast will make everyone feel better.'

'If you say so. Glad you're doing the cooking.'

I switch the grill on and put the bacon under.

'I'm so jealous of you living in Greece. It's the stuff of dreams.'

I pour myself a second mug of coffee and stir milk and sugar into it. 'It is, but it's not always been that way. When I met Alekos on Cephalonia I'd fallen so hard for him I hadn't actually considered what the reality of living with him would be when I said yes to moving to Greece.'

'It'd been different if you'd actually gone and lived with him on Cephalonia,' Candy says, wandering into the kitchen in an oversized T-shirt and bare legs, her face make-up free, eyes covered by sunglasses, and her short blonde hair sticking up in all directions. 'I could smell coffee.'

She sits at the kitchen table and looks at Kim. 'She moved in with Alekos and his parents, that was the problem. Of course the reality of a few loved up carefree days on Cephalonia was different to living and working twenty-four-seven in someone else's house.' She glances over at me. 'To be fair I'm surprised you lasted as long as you did before falling out with Despina.'

'The tension built up over time.' I pull out the sizzling bacon and turn the rashers over. 'And Alekos behaved differently at home to how he was on Cephalonia. It was all down to his mother.'

'She sounds quite a character,' Kim says, sipping her coffee. 'I look forward to meeting her.'

I laugh. 'She most definitely is a character and okay in small doses. Her and Mum, well, together they're quite a pair, both as opinionated and passionate about things as each other. Sparks may fly.'

Candy rubs her hands together. 'A week in Greece should

be fun!'

'What's it like now?' Kim asks. 'Your relationship?'

I lean against the work surface next to the oven. 'It's like when we first met – obviously not exactly the same because we have Thea, work, responsibilities – but the spark is back. The difference in Alekos is insane. His parents – no actually that's not fair – his mother suffocated him, trying to push on him everything that she wanted for their restaurant and business, his life and future instead of allowing him to discover who he was and what he wanted to do. It's like he's a different person now – the one I knew and fell in love with.'

Candy slides her sunglasses down her nose and looks at Kim. 'What she means is she's getting plenty of sex again.'

'That's so not what I mean, Candy.' I grin.

'Yeah right.' She glances at Kim and pushes her sunglasses back over her eyes. 'She is.'

I save the bacon from burning to a crisp, and crack eggs into a pan. Jocelyn is next to appear in the kitchen, showered and dressed and looking a lot fresher than the rest of us, but then she'd taken it easy with the drinking the night before. I cut thick slices of bread and pop them in the toaster and shove a few halved tomatoes beneath the grill. Jocelyn helps me set the kitchen table with plates and cutlery and just as I'm about to start dishing out breakfast, Mum pads in, bleary eyed and still wearing her clothes from the night before.

'Ah, you're a star, Sophie,' she says, yawning. 'Coffee, eggs and bacon – the best hangover cure I know.'

We take it easy for the rest of the day, everyone either too tired or hungover to want to do much. The murky day continues with fine drizzle that doesn't really get you wet, but it's not weather any of us want to go out in. After our eggs and bacon, no one fancies lunch, so we settle down in the living room to watch *My Big Fat Greek Wedding* which Kim had brought with her.

'This should get us in the mood for what's to come,' she

says, pressing play.

It may be a Hollywood film and larger than life in places, but it's not actually that far from the truth of Greek family life. If anything, Despina is a caricature of some of the Greek women portrayed. And the bit about 'you must eat', well, I nearly choke on a mouthful of crisps. I've lost count of how many times I've heard Despina say that to me, and it isn't just because she runs her own restaurant. Greeks seem to actively encourage friends and family to eat at every opportunity.

'Well, that's it,' Kim says, as the credits roll. 'I'm so looking forward to the next couple of weeks and your Greek version of this, Leila.'

Mum smiles and nods but doesn't say anything. The trouble is, a 'big fat Greek wedding' is actually the last thing she wants. Intimate and understated is how she plans on marrying Robert. I hope to God having her wedding at Birdsong Villas can deliver on that promise.

Chapter Thirteen

The rest of the afternoon is spent watching mindless TV, playing cards and nibbling on crisps and nuts. I'm in the kitchen downing a glass of water when my mobile pings. A message from Ben. My heart skips.

We need to talk.

I frown and write:

About what?

He replies almost immediately.

I think you know what it's about. Meet me in Blakeney car park.

My fingers hover over the keypad on my phone, uncertain how to reply. I bite my lip and type:

Okay fine. Be there in 10 mins.

I set my empty glass down next to the sink and walk into the hallway. I stuff my phone in my bag and poke my head around the living room door. Candy and Jocelyn are both dozing and Mum and Kim are watching some crappy weekday afternoon telly. Mum glances at me.

'Just popping out to get some milk as we've nearly run out. Want anything else?'

'Oh that's great, and no thanks,' she replies.

I close the door behind me and pick up the car keys from off the sideboard. I catch sight of my red hair in the hallway mirror, tousled where I couldn't be bothered to spend time straightening it this morning. Without much make-up and clear tanned skin, I don't actually look too bad after a late night. I slick lipstick on and crunch across the gravel to the hire car.

I drive the short distance out of the lane and up the hill towards Blakeney. I don't quite know what to make of Ben wanting to meet. I know we have more to talk about than we were able to at the pub the other day, and I'm well aware that it's a wise idea to clear the air before we become stepbrother and stepsister. I shudder and pull into the narrow road that leads down to the harbourside.

I find a space in the car park in front of the raised path that leads to the sea. The day has brightened since this morning and it's stopped raining. There's still no hint of the sunshine we enjoyed yesterday, but that hasn't put people off coming out for an afternoon stroll or crabbing on the harbourside. The ice cream van even has a queue. I walk past it, back towards the road. I spot Ben standing on the bank that leads to the coastal path, a bottle of Coke in one hand, his other hand shoved into his jean pocket. His sweatshirt fits snugly. He catches sight of me and waves.

'Hey there,' he says, as I walk up the steps and reach him.

'Hey.' I follow him along a path off the main one to an empty bench overlooking a large pond filled with ducks, swans and other seabirds I don't know the names of. The hustle and bustle of Blakeney is behind us with cars parking and tourists wandering along the quay. In the direction we're facing, there's only wildlife, marshes and a grey moody sky.

'You've been taking it easy today after last night?' he asks as we sit down on the bench, enough space for another person between us.

'Yeah, it's been a long time since I've been this hungover. Not just me; everyone's suffering today.'

He looks at me with the same intensity he did when I first met him in the hospital restaurant in Norwich, his blue eyes watching me intently. I find it as off-putting and as intriguing as I did all those years ago.

'How about your stag do?'

'I was good and didn't drink. Dad might have had a bit too much. It was a civilised evening of cards.'

'Ours wasn't so civilised, but then it never is with Mum. It was good seeing her let her hair down with her friends though. I know she won't ever admit to it but I think she misses her Bristol friends. I know she felt like she was living a totally different life to them before she left Bristol but lots has changed since then.'

We fall silent, our small talk dried up. Birds continuously flap across the pond, landing in the water or wading through the rushes on to the grassy banks. The subject I assume he's invited me here to talk about lies heavy in the air. He was easy to talk to at the pub when Robert and Mum were there to diffuse any awkwardness. But now…

'Want a drink?' He offers me his bottle of Coke.

'Thanks.' He passes it to me and our fingers brush. I take a swig. 'So, you wanted to talk. Let's talk.'

'You never properly answered my question the other day.' Ben leans back on the wooden bench, staring out at the pond, his right foot resting on his left knee.

'About what?'

'Choosing Alekos over me.'

I nearly choke on a mouthful of Coke.

'There wasn't a choice to make.' I look at him, although he doesn't turn to look at me. 'We were never together.'

'You're still playing that card?' Ben laughs. 'You have a funny idea of what "not being together" is. There was a mutual attraction between us – you can't deny that. And we acted on it, even if we didn't go all the way. I didn't make you do anything you didn't want to.'

'Okay fine, you got me there.' I place the bottle on the wood between us. 'I wasn't in a particularly great place at the time; I was confused about a lot of things, angry and frustrated. I liked you, the same way as I still like you, as a friend.'

'It feels like we have unfinished business...'

'What do you mean?' The question is out before I have time to digest his words. 'Are you seriously talking about what I think you're talking about?'

He shrugs his broad shoulders. 'We'd have been good together and it was a shame we never found out how good.'

'You're just talking about sex, not a proper relationship. So, a one-night stand with me would have satisfied you?' I swivel on the bench until I'm facing him. 'I'm the one that got away and you're pissed about it? Grow up, Ben, we're both far too old to be messing around in that way, not worrying about the consequences and who would get hurt.'

'You really think sex was all I wanted? Is all I want?'

'Are you for real?'

'You think I'm joking?'

'I think you're crazy. There is nothing between us, not any longer. There wasn't really anything back then either. Us messing around and me getting so close to losing Alekos, ultimately proved to me that Alekos was and is the right choice.'

'Ouch. Don't go sugar coating the rejection, Sophie.'

'I'm telling you like it is. You don't seem to get it.'

'I'm only asking you to think about it, that's all. We'd be good together.'

'What, like my mum and your dad are good together? Get real, Ben, think this through and you'll realise how crazy you sound.'

I'm beginning to realise this was a mistake. What I thought was going to be a conversation to clear the air and any past misunderstanding, has turned into something else entirely. Something I wasn't expecting.

'We need to put whatever this is behind us and move on. I'm with Alekos. We have a daughter, for God's sake. Things are good. No actually, things are great between us. We worked through the problems we were having when we were living with his parents and have moved on in all senses of the word

– emotionally and physically.'

'You still cheated on him with me.'

'And he knows about that. He knows everything.'

'And do you know everything about him?'

'What do you mean?'

'You're sure Alekos didn't cheat on you all the time he was on his own back in Greece?'

'You really like to stir things up, don't you?'

'Just saying.'

'I was the one who was stupid and selfish and put myself before our relationship. All Alekos did, despite me behaving awfully towards him, was step up, take a chance and offer me a real life in Greece where we could be together. You understand, that me and you are going to be related in ten days' time?'

'Only through marriage.'

'Oh my God, Ben. We're going to be stepbrother and sister. Let's start acting like that, shall we?'

Before I have time to react, he moves across the bench towards me, knocking over the bottle of Coke. It falls on to the ground with a thump and rolls down the grassy hill to the path in front of the pond. He puts his lips to mine and kisses me. Our eyes meet and he runs his hand up my side and across my back. I should slap him, or tell him to fuck off. He kisses me again, his arms wrapping around me, holding me close. He tastes of mints, his touch not exactly familiar, yet a reminder of a time gone by, and I realise I'm kissing him back.

I pull away.

He holds his hands up. 'Fine, if you honestly don't think there's anything between us, why kiss me back? Or are you always going to let yourself wonder, what if…'

I frown and shake my head, not quite understanding what just happened.

'You're so full of yourself. Unbelievable.' I stand up. 'If you've had your fun, I'm going back.'

He runs his hand through his hair. 'Seemed like you had

fun too.'

I take the car keys from my pocket and walk off, but pause before reaching the steps. I turn back. Ben's watching me, his arms resting along the back of the bench. I stop a few paces away from him and cross my arms.

'We're going to be travelling and spending nearly two weeks together in Greece, please let's not make this…' I motion between us, 'awkwardness become a problem.'

'There's no awkwardness,' he says with a look that sends a shiver through me. 'At least not from my point of view. And if you truly have no interest in me romantically, then there's no reason you should feel awkward either.'

'You were a long time.' Mum sidles into the kitchen as I'm putting the milk in the fridge.

'It was nice to get some fresh air and clear my head after drinking way too much last night.' I close the fridge door and turn to her.

'Everything okay?'

'Yeah, everything's fine. Just hungover. Haven't drunk that much since, well, before Thea was born.' I brush past her towards the living room in the hope she won't question further. For the second time after arriving in Marshton, Ben has got under my skin. Even worse, I can still smell him on me, taste him.

I sit down on a cushion on the floor and Mum frowns as she returns to the armchair facing the TV. I hadn't expected Ben to still be hung up on me. He's not in love with me, he never was, and we were never that serious. What worries me is this lingering feeling that he's still fixated on being with me because I was never a conquest. That makes what we once had sound cheap and awful. And yet, he's still single, still suggesting there's something between us, still making me feel uncomfortable. Confusing me with that kiss. Right now, that's the last thing I want.

Chapter Fourteen

There's palpable excitement early the next morning as we gather downstairs, suitcases and bags packed and lining up in the hallway, ready to be loaded into cars. It feels strange saying goodbye to Salt Cottage and Marshton so soon, but I can't wait to be back home with Thea and Alekos and to show Candy, Robert and everyone else Birdsong Villas and the life we've built for ourselves. I think of Alekos and guilt floods through me about Ben. What the hell was I thinking?

I escape the commotion and wander out into the garden, down to the weathered fence at the end. I lean on the rough wood and look out across the field to the farm hidden in a dip and then the hill beyond, lush green fields lined by trees and overgrown hedgerows. Dew still coats the grass, the sun low on the horizon. The sky is pale blue, streaked with white clouds and beneath the shade of the willow it feels cool. Goosebumps pinprick my bare arms. I'm dressed for and ready to return to the sultry heat of Cephalonia, but there's a part of me that still longs for the quiet beauty of north Norfolk and the English countryside.

'You're hiding away out here.' Candy joins me, leaning on the fence.

I glance at her and then back to the field where a grey mare is grazing. 'I craved a bit of peace and quiet. That's a rarity in my life these days.'

'Tell me about it; the kids follow me everywhere. I can't tell you how nice it's been to use the bathroom in peace these past couple of days, and that's with four other women in the house.'

I laugh. 'It's been alright though hasn't it, all of us together. We've got on really well.'

'Yeah, it's been lovely. I'm so pleased I was able to make it.' Candy turns around to face the house, half-sitting half-leaning against the fence. 'Your mum seemed a bit stressed the other night when Jocelyn asked her about moving in with Robert. You don't think she's rushing into getting married?'

I frown and shake my head. 'Are you kidding? They've known each other ever since Mum moved to Norfolk. They were close friends before anything romantic happened. And they love each other. After the disastrous relationships Mum's had in the past, I think she knows her own mind.'

'I guess you're right.' Candy pushes herself away from the fence and starts walking towards the house. 'I rushed into marriage, that's all. And look how that turned out.'

That's one thing Mum's not done – rushed into things with Robert. After her hen night revelation that Robert was the first man she waited to have sex with, I know she's not rushing things. Her relationship with him is different to the relationships she's had in the past and that can only be a good thing.

This spot by the fence reminds me of my favourite place in the garden at *O Kipos*, looking out across apricot fields to the soaring blue-hued, shadowy Mount Olympus. The view is less majestic here, but still beautiful, understated and peaceful.

I walk back up the garden and go inside, grateful for the warmth of the kitchen and the chatter from everyone sitting round the kitchen table.

'Bloody hell am I looking forward to lots of sunshine,' Mum says, smiling at me.

I sit down on the empty chair next to Candy and listen to Mum's friends discussing the last time each of them had a holiday abroad.

Candy leans towards me. 'I'm so looking forward to being back on Cephalonia. Our holiday there feels like a lifetime ago, doesn't it?'

'Just a bit. So much has changed.'

'Tell me about it. The last time I was there I was single, now I'm a soon to be divorced single mother of two.'

'You weren't single though. You were with what's his name, Paul?'

'And about to finish with him.'

'Cemented by the fact you slept with Demetrius.'

'I was as much an emotional mess then as I am now.' She shakes her head. 'What the hell am I like?'

'You had a few good years in-between.'

Candy grunts. 'I guess that's something.'

'By the way, I don't know if this will bother you or not, but Demetrius is coming to the wedding.'

'Oh shit. He is?'

'With his wife.'

Candy rubs her fingers across her forehead. 'Great.'

'She's not the one he was with when you two hooked up.'

'Thank God for that.'

I rub my thumb along my bare ring finger and lean closer to Candy. 'I should have told you when we were on our own in the garden, about me and…'

Beep. Beep. Beep. A car horn blasts from the front of the house.

'That's Robert,' Mum says, scraping her chair back and grinning. 'Right, let's go get married!'

Shrieks and laughter fill the kitchen as Mum and her friends clatter into the hallway.

'About you and who?' Candy stands up.

'Nothing. It doesn't matter.'

We follow everyone in to the hallway and take our suitcases. Candy heads out of the front door. I'm the last to leave with Mum after she locks the back door and checks the house one final time.

'You sure you've got everything?' I ask her. She closes the front door of Salt Cottage behind us. 'Your dress? Shoes? Jewellery? Your passport?'

'Yes, yes, yes and yes.'

I hug her, and arm in arm we walk to the driveway.

'The next time you're here, you're going to be Mrs Leila Thurston.'

Her arm tenses in mine. 'About that, I think I might keep my maiden name. I've been Keech my whole life – more than half a bloody century. It doesn't feel right somehow to give it up.'

'What does Robert think about that?'

'I'm not sure we've actually talked about it.'

We reach the driveway and there's no time to question her further. Robert takes Mum's hand and envelops her in his arms. 'Ready, everyone?'

Ben catches my eye from the front seat of Robert's car and I look away. Mum climbs on to the back seat along with Pamela. I get into my hire car, Candy next to me in the passenger seat, and Jocelyn and Kim in Jocelyn's car. I follow Robert and Jocelyn, crunching across the gravel and out of the driveway on to the lane. I get out and close the wooden five-barred gate behind us, a final glance at the flint cottage that once was home. It feels strange and a little sad to be leaving after such a short time, but I'm longing to see Thea again, give her a cuddle and listen to her non-stop chatter.

Mum insists on having a glass of champagne on the plane even though we're on a midday flight. It feels like we're heading off on a hen weekend away. Mum's in her element, the centre of attention, off to Greece, going to see her granddaughter and getting married to the man she finally fell in love with and wants to spend the rest of her life with. It's good to see her so happy. In fact, I don't think I've ever seen her this happy.

I worried about her when she left us three years ago, heading back to the UK on her own. Even though I knew she liked Robert a lot, I wasn't convinced that she'd manage to hold on to a romantic relationship with him. But she proved me wrong. They became close during the few months I lived at Salt Cottage but I was never one hundred per cent sure if they were simply good friends or if they were together. She didn't encourage Robert to stay over and apart from catching them snatch a kiss at the end of an evening at The Globe, I wasn't even sure if they'd slept together. For once in her life Mum's relationship with a man was about more than just sex. They spend nights together now, either at The Globe or Robert staying over at Salt Cottage, but I do worry how Mum's ever going to give up her independence and finally live with him. Wherever that may be. It's like our roles have reversed again – the same as when I was a teenager, I'm the one worrying about her, about the decisions she's making and how much of her independence she's clinging on to. I have no idea how Robert feels about their situation, living in two separate places. He's been married before to a woman who, by all accounts, was the perfect wife and mother. Those are quite some shoes for Mum to fill. I need to talk to Robert. I'm worried about them both, that they're not on the same page about how they envisage their marriage to be.

Arriving on Cephalonia to the sight of the deep blue Ionian Sea through the plane window as we dip lower before landing, is the best feeling. It's even better knowing that this time, Alekos and Thea will be waiting for me, our creative retreat thriving. Being with Mum and Candy, seeing Robert and Ben again, and catching up with Mum's friends who remind me of growing up in Bristol, has left me in a reflective mood. A change of place has always allowed me time to think and it's no different now, bringing friends and family from my past to the place where I fell in love.

The eight of us make our way off the plane, wait to collect

our luggage and head out into the sunshine. The warmth is familiar and welcome. The late afternoon sun beats down on our shoulders as we wait to get in the eight-seater taxi Alekos has booked for us. It's funny how the air even smells different – maybe it's the heat, permeating into everything, mixed with the heady scent of flowers and the sea air.

We're an odd group. Robert and Ben are not officially a part of our family yet – a family that's only consisted of me and Mum for nearly thirty-three years. I can't think of Ben as my soon-to-be stepbrother. I've kissed him. Passionately. We did a bit more than kiss. That's really not a great start for a relationship that should only ever have been platonic. Our conversation and his kiss yesterday has left me feeling even more uncertain about how we manage our relationship from now on. I want to forget it even happened, but I know I can't. Mum's friends are an eclectic mix of party-animals like Mum, and grounded types, all mid-fifties upwards. And then there's Candy. I'm so pleased she's here and we found our way back to Cephalonia together where my life with Alekos started.

The party atmosphere continues in the taxi, Robert and Ben forced into the hen party silliness. Robert remains his usual calm and reserved presence, while Ben's dragged into the conversation by Kim and Pamela. I get the feeling he's enjoying all the female attention.

'Remember our first taxi journey across the island?' Candy looks at me through the gap between the seats in front. 'Who'd have thought that by the end of those few days your life would have changed so dramatically.'

'Is this the holiday where you fell in love with Alekos?' Ben booms behind me.

He knows it was and I don't particularly want to discuss falling in love with Alekos with Ben in front of everyone else. Mum catches my eye from the seat across from me. I'm still not convinced that she doesn't think that things went further between me and Ben. Maybe because from Mum's perspective, if it had been her in that situation, I'm pretty certain she'd have thrown all caution to the wind and shagged him in those sand dunes.

'Yes,' I calmly reply. 'This is where we fell in love.'

'Ah, love at first sight,' Kim says, sighing.

'More like lust at first sight.' Candy laughs. 'I found Sophie drooling over a tanned and shirtless Alekos on the dock in Fiskardo.'

Kim giggles. 'Beats the first sight of my husband – picking up dog poo in the local park. It was chucking it down, I was on my way to work and he was walking his dog. We sheltered together beneath this big old tree and got chatting. Definitely not love at first sight though – no bulging tanned pecs for me I'm afraid, but he grew on me and we got together a year later.'

I don't want my first sight of Alekos to be cheapened. Without a doubt his handsome good looks caught my eye, yet it wasn't lust I felt, but a desire to get to know him. And I did fall in love with him on holiday here, but not at first sight. It was on the beach after we'd spent time together talking about ourselves and our lives. I rest my head back and close my eyes, letting the conversation and laughter wash over me. I have a deep longing to be back home, with Thea and Alekos in my arms, and let the unsettled feelings that have cropped up over the past few days be banished for good.

Chapter Fifteen

Like my welcome from Mum when I arrived at Salt Cottage, arriving back at Birdsong Villas feels like a proper homecoming. The taxi stops outside the closed gate and by the time I've paid the driver, everyone's got out and Robert, Ben and Candy have unloaded our luggage. Mum pushes open the gate and a high-pitched squeal rings out. I turn to see Thea in her favourite dress with slices of watermelon printed across it. She runs as fast as her legs can carry her across the courtyard and into Mum's open arms.

I've not even stepped foot inside the gate and I can already feel tears building. Thea clings to Mum, while Mum laughs and plants multiple kisses on her.

Candy puts her arm across my shoulders. 'Photos don't do this place justice. You have so landed on your feet. And Thea, my God, she's gorgeous.'

My eyes are damp by the time I walk through the gate with Candy. I catch murmurs of 'wow' and 'it's absolutely stunning', from Kim and Jocelyn.

Thea releases herself from Mum, turns, clocks me and shrieks, 'Mama!', running at me full pelt, knocking into my legs. I kneel down and envelop her in my arms.

Thea looks up at Candy and smiles.

'*Yasou*,' she says, before continuing in English. 'I'm Thea, what's your name?'

'You are just too cute. I'm Candy, your mummy's best friend.'

'My Yiayia and Papou are here and I've been helping making *pagoto*.'

'*Pagoto*?' Candy asks with a frown.

'Ice cream,' I say. 'She might muddle Greek words amongst the English ones.'

'You're a clever girl speaking two languages.'

'I know. I am clever.' Her eyebrows bunch together to make a serious face.

Candy laughs.

Mum takes hold of Thea's hand. 'I've missed this little girl like crazy.' She catches my eye and I can tell that she's barely able to hold back tears. She bends down to Thea. 'Where's your Baba?'

'*Ekei*.' Thea points across the courtyard to where Alekos has just appeared from around the corner of the villa.

I catch my breath at the sight of him. I know I've only been away for a few days but maybe the physical and emotional break allows me to see him like I did the first time I caught sight of him on the boat: bare-chested, handsome, sexy, dark haired and mysterious. Okay, so he's wearing a short-sleeved cream linen shirt and shorts, and after eight years together the mystery has almost gone, but everything else remains. I wave as he strolls towards us, a grin plastered across his face.

'The last time I saw you,' I hear Robert saying as he bends down until he's at Thea's height, 'you were only a few weeks old. Now look at you.' He ruffles her hair.

'Welcome, everyone.' Alekos reaches us and kisses Mum on both cheeks.

Thea giggles. 'Baba, why are you talking English?'

Everyone laughs and Alekos frowns.

'It's not that bad, is it?'

'You sound silly.'

Laughing, I cuddle Thea to me and kiss the top of her

head. In the hope of Thea ending up being fluent in both languages I usually talk to her in English and Alekos talks in Greek, yet after four years immersed in Greek life at *O Kipos* and now with another three on Cephalonia, it feels natural for me to speak Greek.

Mum is introducing her friends to Alekos and he charms them effortlessly with kisses to both cheeks. He kisses Robert too but shakes Ben's hand and a shiver runs down my spine. He hugs Candy and I can't quite believe the first and last time they saw each other was our life-changing holiday here.

Alekos slips his arm around my waist and kisses me.

I survey the scene, my family all together, extended family too with Robert and Ben. My heart falters as I catch Ben's eye, remembering back to us on the bench in Blakeney, and then the last time Alekos and Ben were in each other's presence. I often wonder if Alekos hitting Ben was the catalyst for the change Alekos made to our lives. If he hadn't thought that he'd lost me to another man, would he ever have stepped up and removed himself from beneath Despina's shadow?

Thea drags Mum across the courtyard and slowly we all follow, the sound of suitcase wheels clattering against the uneven paving as we make our way towards the villa.

'Where are your parents?' I ask Alekos.

'Having a siesta. They'll be up soon.'

Bunting strung up over the courtyard flutters in the light breeze, the colours vivid against the gleaming white walls of the villa and one-storey building that houses the guest rooms. There's a party atmosphere already and we still have more guests arriving later in the week before the wedding party.

Led by an overexcited Thea, we show everyone around, first our home in the main villa, which is now bright and spacious with a lovely communal living, dining and cooking space that looks out towards the courtyard and sea at the front and the garden at the back. Despina and Takis are staying in one of the spare rooms and with all ten of us clattering up the stairs to see the bathroom and to show Candy to the second spare room, we manage to wake them up.

'*Yasas*!' Despina appears in the doorway of their bedroom with Takis standing quietly behind her. She's her usual immaculate self, a vision in a smart cream trouser suit with a red blouse beneath, her black-hair neat, her face fully made-up with striking red lipstick. As always, she leaves me feeling underdressed in my knee-length mint-green skirt and capped-sleeved cotton blouse. Although I've become less tomboyish over the years, I never feel as well-dressed or polished as Greek women.

Introductions take forever, first in English, then in Greek for Despina and Takis. Still led by a constantly chattering Thea, we clatter downstairs and back out into the courtyard and sunshine. Leaving Despina and Takis in the kitchen to make frappés for everyone, I show Kim, Jocelyn, Pamela and Ben their guest rooms that either open out on to the courtyard or the pool on the other side, set away from the main villa. I leave them 'oohing' and 'aahing' and, taking Thea's and Mum's hands, we go to the villa that adjoins ours and upstairs to a spacious guest apartment that's designed for a couple.

'Oh this is lovely,' Mum says, running her hand over the saffron yellow bedspread.

'This is for you and Robert.' I squeeze Mum's arm.

Patterned pillows and cushions are piled on the bed, the walls are a pale honey-colour, there's an en suite bathroom, a wardrobe, dressing table and a two-seater sofa in front of bi-fold doors that open out on to a small veranda. Steps lead down to the courtyard and the view of the olive tree and sea.

'The best room in the place reserved for the soon-to-be newly-weds.'

Mum puts her arm around my waist. 'Thank you, Sophie.'

Thea jumps on to the sofa and kneels, her arms folded across the back of it, looking up at us.

'I picked the flowers from the garden,' she says, pointing to the small glass vase on the dressing table filled with dark pink bougainvillea.

'Beautifully chosen.' Mum smiles. 'I can't believe I'm back here, and for my wedding too.'

She sounds like she's choking back tears.

'It's going to be amazing.'

She nods. 'So there's only this room up here?'

'Yep, complete privacy.' I lean closer so Thea can't hear. 'No need to worry about the headboard banging against the wall.'

Mum slaps my hand. 'Bloody hell, Sophie Keech, as if.'

I raise an eyebrow. 'Anyway, the communal living and kitchen area for the other guest rooms is directly below, but this is separate.'

'Was this not done when I visited a year ago?'

'The bit downstairs was, and the other guest rooms, but not up here.'

'Well, it's beautiful, thank you.' She ruffles Thea's curly chestnut-coloured hair. 'And thank you for the gorgeous flowers.'

'*Pame exo*,' I say, automatically slipping back into Greek.

'Mama.' Thea catches hold of my hand. 'You need to speak English to Grandma.'

Laughing, we head back outside and down the stairs into the sunshine. The large table beneath the olive tree in the centre of the courtyard has been laid out with frappés, jugs of water and a selection of mezze dishes: olives, *spanakopita*, dips, bread and crisps. Encouraged by Despina, everyone slowly makes their way from their rooms and back outside to grab a frappé, eat, chat and soak up the last bit of sunshine.

'It's good to have you home.' Alekos slips his arm around my waist and we stand together, our backs to the villa, our families and friends in front of us.

'It's good to be back. I missed you and Thea like crazy.'

'We missed you too. It was strange being away from Thea knowing you weren't here either. Although she had fun with Yiayia and Papou.'

'Oh yes, how did the gig go?'

'Yeah, it was fine.'

'Just fine? I hope you're going to be bloody fantastic playing at Mum and Robert's wedding.'

'We will be. It's just been a long time since I played with them.'

'After all the time we've been together, I still can't believe I've never seen you play in the band.'

'A few days' time and you will.' He squeezes my waist. 'Your mum looks happy.'

'She does, doesn't she?'

Alekos kisses the top of my head, his words, 'I love you,' get muffled by my hair. The tension I've felt over the past few days fades away being back home with him. Thea is in her element, weaving in out of people, chatting to everyone.

'Baba, Baba, Baba!' she screeches, careering towards us and grabbing Alekos' hand. 'Mama, I need to show Baba this trick Robert can do.'

'Okay,' I say, laughing as Thea drags Alekos to where everyone is gathered around the table.

Mum catches my eye and smiles. I smile back, content to watch for a moment: Candy chatting with Ben and Kim, Mum gossiping with Jocelyn and Pamela, Robert entrancing Thea and Alekos, while Despina and Takis make sure everyone has a drink and something to eat in their hands. Laughter floats into the early evening. This place is made for lots of people.

'I did wonder if everyone would have arrived by the time I got back,' Arthur says, appearing beside me. 'I'd gone for a walk; needed to figure out a gaping plot hole.'

'I'm afraid your peace and quiet has been shattered for the next couple of weeks or so.'

'Oh I don't mind. I like it lively once in a while. Lots of interesting new people can be a source of inspiration, although I promise I won't directly put anyone in my next novel. But I do love a lively character or two.'

'Well, I can promise you there are plenty of those, not

least of all my mother.' I hook my arm in his. 'Come on, let me introduce you to everyone.'

Chapter Sixteen

Candy sits next to me on the courtyard wall, our backs to the dark sky and glimmering Ionian Sea. It's still warm but comfortably so. Yellow light spills from the windows of the villa and a couple of the guest rooms on the courtyard side. Despina and Takis have gone up to bed and Arthur, Pamela and Jocelyn have called it a night too. After a lively meal around the courtyard table, Thea was in bed before anyone else, exhausted by all the excitement and new faces. There will be more people here by the end of the week. Ben's sister, Vicky, is flying over a couple of days before the wedding with her son and Ben's children, plus Demetrius and Katrina will be here for the celebrations. Every room in this place will be occupied for the very first time.

Robert and Mum walk hand in hand across the courtyard and up the steps to their room. Mum's laughter carries on the night air before Robert closes the door to their room behind them.

'I left Ben and Kim by the pool having a sneaky smoke,' Candy says. 'I was wondering where you'd got to.'

'I was clearing away from dinner with Alekos, came out to find everyone but got distracted.'

'By what?'

'All of this.' I wave my hand in front of us. 'With everyone here it makes me realise just how much we've managed to do over the past couple of years. Having a creative retreat was my dream, but having friends and family here to stay for Mum's wedding, well, that's pretty special.'

Candy rests her head against my shoulder. 'You've done amazingly well.' She sighs. 'I'm so happy to be here and have time away from everything.'

'You've had a really difficult year.'

'It's been pretty shitty.'

'Time to yourself will do you a world of good.'

'I've been feeling down all the time. I know my mood was bringing Jake and Holly down with me. I hated that.'

'It's a shame they couldn't come with you. I know, I know, Jake has school…'

'At least they're getting to spend some quality time with their dad. Whatever I think about him I don't want the kids missing out on a proper relationship with him. Plus with me out of his life he has to take responsibility when he has the kids, unlike when we were together.'

'It might make him grow up.'

Candy snorts. 'I won't hold my breath. He likes all the fun bits of having kids but the parenting part, not so much.'

'He doesn't have a choice now.'

'Shame it had to get as serious as him messing about behind my back and us splitting up to take on some responsibility with Jake and Holly.'

The stone wall is rough against my bare legs. Candy's head is warm where she's resting against my shoulder. Alekos emerges from the villa and heads towards the gate, a bag of rubbish clutched in his hand. He leans over, opens the lid of the bin and swings the bag in. He starts walking back, catches sight of us and waves. We wave back.

'Sexy and domesticated. You bagged yourself one hell of a man.'

'It's crazy to think if you hadn't gone back for that necklace in Fiskardo, then I might never have spotted him. We might never have met.'

'And that night on the beach would never have happened.'

'I wonder where I'd be and who I'd be with if you hadn't gone back. It's such a strange thought.'

'I guess it was meant to be.' She lifts her head from my shoulder. 'I've had fun tonight. In fact, I can't remember the last time I had this much fun apart from with the kids. Do you know what, it was probably our holiday here, that's the last time I felt truly free and happy with no worries. Even with Demetrius acting like a dick. I had good times with Lee until he cheated, but me time, oh my goodness, I've craved that. And everyone here's so lovely. It's amazing to see Alekos again and the two of you together… and your mum. Kim's fab, Pamela's a hoot and I can't wait to see Jocelyn let her hair down.'

'That I'd like to see too. Maybe we can get her Greek dancing at the wedding.'

'Ben's nice.' She gives me a sideways glance. 'Good-looking and divorced.'

'And has been for three or four years now. You only split up with Lee earlier this year.'

'Ben's single as far as you know?'

'Candy.' I shoot her a look. I know what she's like when it comes to men she has her eye on, but I also know how much she's hurting right now from Lee and his affair.

She sighs. 'Don't worry, I'm not going to do anything. I just didn't think I'd be in this position again – single, and now two weeks without the kids… I always did like to flirt.'

'You've not changed.'

'Gets me into all sorts of trouble. I either choose the wrong men or get knocked up and married far too quickly. But, you do realise, forget about it being fate – if it wasn't for me being so forward, we'd never have spoken to Alekos, we wouldn't have gone on the boat with them, and that night at the beach wouldn't have happened…' She nudges me. 'Was that the best night of your life?'

'You know it was.'

'Oh indulge me; I'm not getting any action.'

'Everything about that night was magical.'

'Yeah, well, that's where your night ended up being different to mine. It was great with Demetrius until we actually had sex and then there was like no emotional connection between us.'

'That's because he was feeling guilty about his girlfriend back home.'

'I wonder if I have a chance in hell of ever meeting a decent man like Alekos? Most men are cheating bastards.' She runs her hand down the material of her skirt. 'Why did Ben and his wife split up?'

'Not because of cheating; at least Ben didn't cheat. His ex seemed to move on with a new man pretty quickly. They went through a difficult period and I guess their relationship wasn't strong enough to withstand the bad times.'

'Has he been with anyone since?'

'I don't know.'

Guilt-ridden and confused over Alekos, I've never told Candy about my brief relationship with Ben, and despite wanting to say something to her this morning, I don't want to go into it now. I have no idea about his love life since I came here to Cephalonia. I don't like thinking about him at all. He reminds me too much of the old me, always wishing for something else. It's a time in my life, until two days ago, I thought I'd moved on from. All that doubt and confusion about who I loved and where I wanted to be was in the past.

'I can't believe it's only our first night here,' Candy says.

'I know, it's going to be so much fun.'

'We have to go out, do something together, just the two of us. We never see each other any longer. I miss you.'

'I miss you too. And yes, we'll do something, there's plenty of time.'

'Right.' Candy slides off the wall. 'I'm heading to bed. You should too – you must be exhausted after all the planning you've done to get this place ready. Get some kip before that gorgeous little girl of yours gets up.'

Alekos takes Thea to her swimming lesson before everyone else is up, but she'll be back later, her laughter ringing out across the courtyard, and Mum will be pleased to have her back.

After getting a quick shower and throwing on shorts and a vest top, I join Kim and Jocelyn at the table beneath the olive tree. I intend for breakfast to happen as and when anyone can be bothered to get up. I've taken two *tcherecis* out of the freezer and the coffee machine is on. I want the next few days to be as relaxed as possible.

'Did you sleep well?' I place a tray on the table and pour three mugs of coffee.

'I had an amazing night's sleep.' Kim takes the coffee and pours in milk. 'And I usually struggle to get to sleep anywhere unfamiliar.'

'I slept well too, but then I don't usually have any problem.' Jocelyn takes a slice of *tchereki* and I pass her the butter and strawberry jam.

'I think it was the peacefulness,' Kim says. 'There's always traffic noise where I live in Bristol, even at three in the morning. Here there's nothing.'

'Until the dawn chorus,' I say.

'Now that I can live with.' Kim places her coffee down on the table. 'And how dark it is at night. Being able to see all those stars is magical. Like where your mum lives.'

'I think she likes it,' Jocelyn says, smiling.

'I'm jealous of Leila living in Marshton and here… well, I can't even put in to words what I feel about this place. I'd love to live in the countryside or even better by the sea.'

'You'd miss the nightlife in Bristol.' Jocelyn grins and sips her coffee.

'What nightlife? I don't go out any more, not like I used to a few years ago with your mum.' She glances at me. 'A good pub within walking distance would suit me just fine. Or a place like this in Greece.' She winks. 'How many rooms do you have here?'

'Are you considering not going home?' I laugh.

'Oh, don't tempt me!'

'We have ten, not including the two spare rooms in our villa. All doubles, although we usually have a single person staying to write or paint or whatever else creative they want to do.'

'If I was the least bit creative I'd be out here like a shot writing the next bestseller or painting a masterpiece. I can dream.' Jocelyn spreads butter on a slice of *tchereki*. She looks across the table at me. 'Do you still paint?'

I shake my head. 'Not really, not any more. I sometimes sketch. I think my passion for art got sucked out of me when I worked at that advertising agency in Bristol. I'm happy running this place. Everything about it feels creative. It's the same way I felt about being a chef in Alekos' parents' restaurant. We'd create dishes that people kept coming back for. It's kind of worked out perfectly running a business we both love. Having time to spend with Thea and enjoy our passions too. Alekos is writing music again. He played a gig with his old band the other night. First time in years.'

'Your mum's so looking forward to them playing at the wedding.'

'Yeah, I know, it's the only thing she requested – even though she's a wedding planner, everything else she left up to us. She wants live Greek music and what better than the band Alekos has written music for. He wasn't keen to begin with – I think he felt like he was asking the band a huge favour to play at a wedding when they're used to larger paid gigs throughout Greece.'

'They've said yes though?'

'The trade-off has been that Alekos is playing a couple of gigs with them while they're on the island. And the best bit is I'll finally get to see Alekos play in this infamous band.'

'Seriously, you've never seen them play?'

'Never. Crazy, huh?'

'*Kalimera*!' Despina's voice rings out across the courtyard, halting our conversation.

'*Kalimera*!' I call back.

'*Thelete kalo cafe*?' she asks.

'*Ne. Efharisto*!'

'I'm feeling rather underdressed,' Jocelyn says, her eyes fixed on Despina who is wearing white linen trousers and a perfectly ironed pale blue blouse. Her black hair is styled within an inch of its life and she has a full face of make-up. Despina retreats back inside the villa.

'This is normal for her. Anyway, you have nothing to worry about; you look gorgeous.' She does. She's older than Mum and has always had a more mature dress-sense than my fashion-loving mother, but she's elegant in a long flowing skirt and loose cotton top, her short grey hair framing an almost make-up free face, far more suitable for a hot Greek day and lounging around in the sunshine.

'Thank you, Sophie.'

Kim cuts a slice of *tchereki.* She looks across at me and wedges her sunglasses into her hair. 'Jocelyn has always been classy – puts me and your mum to shame.'

'Well, I am a fair bit older than you both.'

'There's not that much difference.' Kim bites into the *tchereki* and wipes the crumbs from her mouth. 'And anyway, we're way past the age you were when we first met, and me and Leila still aren't classy. I still shop in Topshop for God's sake.'

I laugh. Mum and Kim were always a bad influence on each other. Even with the embarrassment they often caused me – particularly Mum's antics – I did like Mum having a friend like Kim, someone she could be herself with, as well as the more stable and sensible Jocelyn.

Once everyone's up, the peacefulness of the early morning

evaporates. I love it though, the familiar voices and laughter ringing out across the courtyard. Mum is in her element, surrounded by people she knows, and Despina is too, relishing organising everyone. She takes over from me when it comes to clearing away the breakfast things.

'You are the host,' she says, a look on her face that suggests she isn't willing to be argued with. 'This is what I do… what I did at *O Kipos* and I like it. You're busy sorting everyone out, making sure they have a good time; keeping the place tidy is the least I can do.'

I don't argue. There's no point when she's in this mood and I'm actually incredibly grateful to be freed up to ensure everyone is okay, while Despina ensures the kitchen is clean and tidy, the washing-up done and everyone has enough to eat and drink.

The first full day flies by with everyone either lounging around the pool or walking the hillside path down to the beach to sunbathe or splash about in the sea. Along with Alekos, I stay at the retreat, chatting to everyone and making sure they have food and drinks to take with them if they're heading to the beach or suggesting where to go for lunch if they fancy walking to the village.

Candy and Ben spend most of the day together round the pool. Candy's a natural flirt which has got her in trouble before when she hasn't actually been interested in a man, but it's obvious she likes Ben and the flirting is intentional. Ben laps up the attention and it makes me feel weird, uncomfortable I guess – the way Candy touches him and the way he leans in towards her to talk. Both of them are emotionally unstable; Candy with good reason and Ben, despite his marriage breaking down years ago. He's single, still taunting me with the 'what could have been' and yet here he is flirting up a storm with my best friend. He's my soon to be stepbrother and the whole situation between us remains filled with tension and confusion.

By the time the sun sets on our second evening, we've

already managed to ease into some kind of routine. Despina takes charge in the kitchen and we cook a feast of stuffed peppers with loads of salads and her famous chips. It's like being back in the kitchen at *O Kipos*, working together effortlessly – the only time and place we really did get along. By eight, with hot brows and Alekos and Takis' help, we carry dishes of Greek salad, the stuffed peppers, baked feta and *melitzanasalata* out into the courtyard where everyone is sitting around the table drinking wine. Thea has red grape juice that she's pretending is red wine. Everyone seems a little tipsy already, with beaming faces having enjoyed a day of sunshine and relaxation.

Once the table is filled with food, Mum stands and raises her glass first in Despina's direction and then mine. 'Thank you both so much for looking after us all so well and for another delicious feast!'

Chairs scrape against the courtyard paving as everyone stands and raise their glasses.

'To Sophie, Alekos and Despina,' Mum says, taking a sip of her wine.

'And don't forget Takis.' I nod at Takis quietly sitting at the end of the table next to Arthur, smoke curling into the night air from his cigarette. 'Without him your wine wouldn't be topped up.'

'In that case,' Mum says, turning towards Takis. 'An extra special toast to Takis for helping to keep us all merry!'

I know Takis doesn't understand a word Mum has said but he smiles and nods anyway as everyone drinks.

'Before we tuck in,' I say, catching everyone before they sit back down, 'I'd like us all to raise our glasses again to Mum and Robert who are the reason we're all out here together having a wonderful time.' I tip my glass towards them where they stand opposite me, wine in one hand, their free hands entwined. 'To Leila and Robert.'

'To Leila and Robert!' echoes across the courtyard.

Chapter Seventeen

I'm not sure what's woken me up. The villa is silent. Alekos is still asleep sprawled next to me, one hand resting on his bare chest. I slip out of bed and pad across our bedroom, throwing a cardigan on over the vest top and shorts I'd worn to bed. I open the bedroom door and creep out, not wanting to wake anyone else, least of all Thea. Candy's door creaks open and I turn. Ben closes the door behind him. We stare at each other for a bit too long. He's in the same shorts and T-shirt that he was wearing the evening before.

'I… um…'

I put my finger to my lips and gesture towards Thea's room. I walk along the landing. Apart from her noisy breathing, it's quiet in her room. By some miracle she's still asleep, probably exhausted by the excitement of the past couple of days. I follow Ben down the stairs and into the kitchen. I feel underdressed and awkward alone with him first thing in the morning.

'Well, this is awkward,' he says, echoing my thoughts.

I don't know what to say. I've continued to feel confused about Ben, the attraction I had to him when I stayed with Mum in Norfolk was short-lived, but him standing in my kitchen with bed hair and last night's clothes on reminds me of the desire I once had for him.

'Why are you up so early and creeping out of her room?'

'Why do you think?' He leans against the kitchen work surface. 'Come on, Sophie, you can't be that naive.'

'I'm not naive. I know the two of you had sex – I know Candy too well, and you were all over each other yesterday.'

'You noticed, huh?'

I ignore his dig. 'What I don't understand is why you're creeping out. How's Candy going to feel when she wakes up?'

'I didn't want the awkwardness of everyone else knowing what we got up to. I figured no one else would be up yet.'

'I have a three-year-old and am conditioned to waking up at the crack of dawn.'

'Well, let's keep this to ourselves,' he says, tapping his finger against his nose. 'No need to broadcast it to everyone.'

I step towards him before he has the chance to move away. 'What the hell are you playing at? You kissed me the other day. She's my best friend and only recently split up from her bastard of a husband. Don't you dare mess her around.'

'I'm not messing her around, unless of course you count sleeping together when not in a relationship as messing about.'

'You know what I mean. Don't break her heart.'

'We were flirting, that's all. She was the one who made a move and asked me back to her room. But I guess you figured that out already. She's not shy.'

'No she's not, but she's also vulnerable right now.'

'She's old enough to look after herself.'

'Maybe so, but you've been divorced for a few years, it's only been a few months for her since she separated from her husband.'

'You're not jealous, are you?'

'No.' I meet his eyes and he grins at me. 'No, Ben, I'm not jealous.'

'But you wish we'd done it while we had the chance. If you'd been as assertive as Candy we would have done, you know.'

I clench my fists. 'Seriously. Can you not hear yourself? Your dad and my mum are about to get married. Us never actually sleeping together is a good thing. Trust me, I have no regrets, and I hope to God Candy doesn't either. I'm worried because two days ago you made a move on me suggesting that we still had "unfinished business" and now you're creeping out of my best friend's bedroom.'

There's a creak and footsteps pad along the hallway upstairs.

'Mama?' Thea's little voice calls out.

'I'm going to my room to grab another couple of hours' sleep.' He pushes himself away from the work surface and heads out of the door into the courtyard.

I take the stairs two at a time and find Thea standing on the landing rubbing her eyes. I envelop her in my arms and take her into our room where Alekos is still spread out, snoring.

Thea snuggles up to me and nods off again, but I lie awake listening to her breathing and Alekos' gentle snores. I'm hot and annoyed. Ben has always managed to get under my skin. Four years ago it was an attraction that wouldn't shift; now it's annoyance at him thinking I regret not sleeping with him when I had the chance. I manage to slide out from beneath Thea. I hold my breath and only relax when I realise she's still asleep. I leave her and Alekos curled up on the white sheets of our bed and slip out of our room.

I creep along the landing towards the bathroom but the door to Candy's room opens and she pokes her head out.

'Thank God it's you.' She takes hold of my arm and pulls me into her room, closing the door behind us. 'I need to talk to you.'

The blind is closed and the room dim without the sun blazing through. The sheet on Candy's bed is crumpled, a dent remaining in the pillow where Ben had been. There's an empty condom packet on Candy's bedside table.

Candy, in a vest and pyjama shorts, sits on the end of the bed and looks up at me. 'I went and did something silly last night and slept with Ben.'

I sigh and sit down next to her, immediately wishing I hadn't. I want to rid my head of the image of Ben with bed hair, wearing only a pair of shorts lying on this bed minutes earlier. 'I know you did.'

'You do?'

'I woke up a little while ago and bumped into Ben leaving your room.' I glance at Candy. Her short blonde hair is sticking up in all directions, her cheeks are flushed. 'He said he was heading back to his room early to avoid seeing anyone and starting gossip.'

Candy waves her hand. 'I'm not worried about him sneaking out of here. I've had enough one-night stands to know the drill.' She stops and places her hands together on her tanned knees. 'I'm thirty-two, a mother of two and divorcing a cheating husband. Ben cheered me up a lot, made me feel attractive again… why the hell do I always have to go sleep with a man who shows the tiniest bit of interest in me?'

This is exactly what I was warning Ben about, not playing on Candy's vulnerability. She's always been confident and forward with men and it's got her hurt in the past. I don't want to warn her off him – she's already taken things too far for that – but at the same time I'm not happy to encourage her either.

'I shouldn't have taken it further than us flirting and having a drink.' Candy rubs her forehead with her hand. 'Is it weird for you, me and Ben?'

'No, of course not, why would it be?' I bite my lip, thinking it feels anything but fine.

'Well, he is about to become your stepbrother.' She takes my hand. 'It's weird isn't it? Robert's son, your stepbrother-to-be.'

'When you put it like that, it's a bit weird…' The memory of kissing Ben and his hands on me in the sand dunes once more invades my thoughts, swiftly followed by the thought of Ben with Candy. 'But it's not weird for the reasons you're thinking.'

'Oh my God, Sophie, you've not slept with him, have you?'

'No, I haven't.' I take a deep breath. 'But there was a time when I wanted to.'

'How come you never said?'

'I was embarrassed and confused. My feelings were all over the place. Ben seemed less complicated at the time than Alekos. I was stupid and selfish and angry at Alekos. So frustrated with how our life had turned out in Greece and me and Ben, well, connected…' I stop, not knowing what else to say, not wanting to explain how much I'd wanted Ben while being in love with Alekos. It's in the past; I've moved on, we've moved on. That discontentment with my life at *O Kipos* has been erased. It feels so right with Alekos. Yet I still feel uneasy.

'You should have told me.'

'Would that have made any difference? Would you not have slept with him?'

'Soph, it's not about that, it's just we've always told each other things. It seems a big thing to not have said anything about, that's all.'

It's true, we always have been brutally honest with each other, about everything. She was the first person I told when I found out I was pregnant with Thea. I guess the enormity of being pregnant with a baby that wasn't planned, meant everything else going on in my life paled into insignificance. By the time I spoke to Candy and could have told her about my feelings for Ben, I had more pressing things on my mind.

'He didn't say anything either, you know, about the two of you.'

'His dad's marrying my mum, I'm not really surprised he didn't say anything about messing about with me.' I sound bitter, but I don't mean to be, and have no way of taking back my words. 'Sorry, it's been a weird morning so far.'

'Tell me about it. I've woken up with a hangover and a one-night stand missing from my bed, only to find out my best friend had a fling with him years ago and didn't tell me.'

'He doesn't have to be a one-night stand you know. Sleeping with someone when you haven't known them for very long doesn't mean you can't turn it into a relationship. Look at me and Alekos. That's how we started.'

'You were never a one-night stand to Alekos.' Candy stands up, stretches, walks over to the window and opens the blinds.

'Maybe not, but we'd only known each other for a couple of days.'

Warm light floods into the room and silhouettes Candy. I stand and go over to her, putting my arm around her shoulders.

'Don't shut Ben out before there's a chance to find out if either of you want it to be more than one night.'

'Okay,' Candy says, leaning into me. 'As long as you're fine about us being together.'

'Yeah, I'm fine with it.'

I leave her looking out of the window over the courtyard with its olive tree and border filled with colourful flowers. I lock myself in the bathroom. I have no reason to be upset and yet there's this weird discomfort in the pit of my stomach. Despite saying the opposite, I am troubled by the thought of her and Ben together. It's not what I want; *he's* not what I want, and yet…

I lean on the sink and stare at myself in the mirror, willing myself to get a grip. I hadn't bothered to take my make-up off last night and mascara is smudged beneath my eyes. My skin is tanned though, my freckles accentuated, my green eyes bright and my skin glowing from sunshine and the Mediterranean lifestyle and diet.

Alekos and I rarely have any time to ourselves any more. Maybe that's what I feel is missing, that quality alone time that we used to have to talk and be together, instead of rushing from place to place and constantly being busy with Thea, work, running the retreat and looking after it and our home.

There are so many people here – people from my past, from a time in my life when I felt out of control, unsettled and unsure of which direction my future should take. There's no reason for me to feel like that any longer.

Chapter Eighteen

I wash away the unsettled feeling with a shower, and as soon as everyone begins to emerge from their rooms for coffee and breakfast there's no time to dwell on the past or the morning's events. By late morning with the breakfast things cleared away, the place is quiet.

I take the wet clothes from the washing machine and heave the basket outside. The garden is peaceful and sunny. Butterflies dance over the deep purple brush-like flowers of the bush on the far side. The air buzzes with insects, softening the silence. I stretch my arms upwards and relish the warmth on my bare skin. I love this time of year before the real heat of the summer takes over. I spot Mum and Kim lounging on a picnic blanket on the grass, half hidden by the fruit trees that dot the lawn. Everyone else is either out or doing something. Alekos has taken Thea to a friend's birthday party with Despina and Takis, Jocelyn and Pamela have gone shopping in Omorfia, Robert's gone for a walk, Candy and Ben are in the pool, and Arthur is tucked away in his room writing. I nip back into the villa, grab three glasses, a carton of *visino* from the fridge and head back outside.

'Can I join you?'

Mum pats the rug next to her. 'Of course.'

'Fancy a drink?' I sit cross-legged between Mum and Kim and spread out the glasses.

'What is it?' Kim asks.

'Sour cherry juice.' I pour three generous glasses full of the deep red liquid. '*Yamas*.' I knock my glass against Mum's then Kim's. 'You two didn't fancy going shopping with Jocelyn and Pamela?'

Mum shakes her head. 'I must be getting old. The thought of a few peaceful hours doing bugger all was far more enticing than traipsing around shops in the heat.'

'And quite frankly,' Kim says, taking a sip of her juice. 'I don't feel there's any need to leave this place. It's truly stunning, Sophie. Your mum was telling me what it looked like when you first arrived. Hard to believe really.'

'It's taken more than three years of hard work to get it looking like this, but yeah, it's a dream come true.' I glance at Mum. 'Remember thinking I was crazy leaving the UK for Greece to move in with a man I'd only known for a few weeks *and* scoffing at my idea of setting up a creative retreat.'

'I did and said a lot of things I wish I hadn't.'

'Me too.'

'I also had a rather negative view about falling in love so quickly and giving up everything for what I perceived to be a holiday romance.'

'It was brave moving out to Greece to be with Alekos,' Kim says, holding her glass towards me before taking a sip. 'I'd never have had the guts to do something like that.'

'Sophie was properly in love,' Mum says with a wistful tone. 'To be honest at the time I didn't believe you were really in love. I figured you'd had some great sex and had fallen in lust with a good-looking Greek. I thought you were going to get your heart broken, that's where my negativity came from. I guess my experience of men and meaningless flings led me to believe that. I was very happy to be proven wrong.'

'Even with all my ups and downs with Alekos.' I pluck a blade of dry grass and fold it between my fingers.

'That's life. If everything was straightforward and easy it'd be boring.'

'True,' Kim says. 'I could do with some excitement in my life. Married for flipping donkey's years, kids at uni now and hubby would rather spend the night in watching football. I miss you living in Bristol, Leila. I can't tell you how much I've been looking forward to this time away with you all.'

'Your husband didn't mind you coming out here on your own?'

Kim snorts. 'Are you kidding? He couldn't wait for a bit of peace and quiet for a couple of weeks. We're quite happy doing our own thing most of the time – works fine for us.' She looks at me. 'Do you and Alekos get to spend much time together?'

'Well, we work together so pretty much spend most of the time with each other.'

'I mean together when you're not working?'

'Not really.'

'You two should go out, make the most of everyone being here to look after Thea. Spend some quality alone time with Alekos.'

'Mum, this is your time before you get married to do what you want to do.'

'And I want to spend time with my granddaughter. You and Alekos too, and my friends of course, but mostly time with Thea.'

'Take the opportunity while you can,' Kim says. 'When was the last time you and Alekos had a night out together?'

'Without Thea or anyone else?' I frown. 'I honestly can't remember.'

'Seriously, Sophie, take as much time out as you want this week – there are plenty of people here to look after Thea, not least of all me and Robert and Alekos' parents.' Mum places her hand on my arm. 'Also, you've got Candy here and you two never get to spend time with each other any longer. I'm sure she needs the time and company after the year she's had.'

I push my sunglasses down my nose and look at Mum over the top of them. 'Lack of company is not a problem for

Candy at the moment.'

'What do you mean?'

'Seriously, Mum, you of all people haven't noticed what's going on?'

Mum frowns and shakes her head.

'There's gossip we're missing out on?' Kim asks, sitting upright.

'Candy and Ben,' I say.

'Oh I can tell they like each other.' Mum shrugs. 'But then Candy has always been a flirt, it doesn't tend to mean anything.'

'It does this time.'

'They've slept together, haven't they?' Kim asks.

'They have?' Mum pushes her sunglasses into her hair and looks at me. 'And how do you feel about that?'

'Why would Sophie care?' Kim frowns. 'Oh do you mean because Sophie and Ben are going to be stepbrother and sister? Actually, I don't understand, why would that matter?'

'Sophie and Ben had a fling…'

Kim turns to me. 'You did?'

'A fling in the sense that we liked each other a lot, spent time together, got on well as friends, messed about a bit.'

'You really didn't do the dirty deed with him?'

'Mum, how many times do I have to tell you, we didn't have sex.'

Mum holds her hands up. 'Okay, okay, I'm sorry, I'm just making sure. There's such an awkwardness between you and Ben and Ben and Alekos, it's easy to make assumptions.'

'Well yes, that's because I did cheat on Alekos with Ben. We kissed, we had a bit of a fumble and I had every intention of having sex with him but came to my senses in time when I found out I was pregnant with Thea. And of course there's going to be awkwardness between us all. Remember Alekos punching Ben?'

'How could I forget.'

'The whole situation was a mess but it pushed us into

sorting our lives out. Not long after moving out here Alekos told me that without really thinking he'd lose me to Ben, he'd never have had the motivation to move out from home and buy this place. My ill-fated relationship with Ben was both the worst and best thing to happen to us. I just don't know how we can all move on from this awkwardness. I mean, Ben's going to be my stepbrother, which in itself is a messed up situation seeing as though our relationship started with us fancying each other... Alekos hates him, Candy is sleeping with him...' I rub my hands across my forehead. 'I don't know how we can all get past the issues we have with each other.'

The sun beats down on us, butterflies flit around the flowers, and the sense of calm I had when I came out to the garden is rapidly being replaced by tension sliding across my forehead.

'Go on a double date,' Mum finally says.

'That is such a bad idea.' Kim laughs and leans back on her hands. 'Sophie, don't listen to her.'

'No seriously, it's a genius idea.' Mum leans forward. 'I promise you the last thing Robert and I want on our wedding day is unresolved tensions between our children. The four of you should go out, get drunk, have some fun. Maybe if Alekos and Ben got to know each other they could move past their issues with each other.'

'Mum, a minute ago you were urging me to have a romantic night out alone with Alekos. Now you're suggesting we double date with my best friend who's shagging the man I briefly considered leaving Alekos for.'

'Well, when you put it like that...'

I fold my arms. 'How about this for an idea. We could wait until Demetrius and Katrina get here and all go out together. Then we can add extra tension by Candy having slept with Demetrius too.'

'Okay, now you're getting silly.'

'Is Demetrius the one Candy had the fling with when you

met Alekos?' Kim asks.

'Yeah, he's Alekos' best friend. They were sailing a boat here when we first met them.'

'There's just too much gossip to keep up with.' Kim sighs. 'My life is so boring compared to yours.'

'Trust me, boring is sometimes good.'

'Maybe my idea of a double date is a bad one; but, Sophie, somehow you need to sort out the situation with Ben. Maybe it's a good thing he's with Candy; it can prove to Alekos that he's moved on.' Mum takes hold of my arm. 'Why are you still feeling awkward about Ben? What happened is in the past and things between you and Alekos are good aren't they?'

I nod.

'You don't still have feelings for Ben, do you?'

'No.' I catch Mum's intent look. 'No, I don't. I don't even think I had real feelings for him back when I was living with you, but…'

'But what?'

'I don't know, it's just being back in Marshton for your hen do and seeing Ben again stirred up the past. It was a weird feeling. And the things he said and did…'

'Like what?' Mum asks. 'I knew there was something odd going on.'

'He still has feelings for you, doesn't he?' Kim says quietly.

Mum sighs. 'I think you've hit the nail on the head, Kim.' She turns to me. 'There's the problem; Ben isn't over you.'

The conversation with Mum and Kim plays on my mind for the rest of the day. I'd led Ben on. We liked each other, had an easy way with each other, a friendship. He found me attractive and I'd fancied him too. He was messed up by a broken marriage and being separated from his kids, and I'd been confused by loving a man who was tied to his mother's apron strings. I'd led Ben on by kissing him, toying with his emotions, getting physical with him but not taking it all the way. Ben and I would never have worked because I'd been pregnant with Alekos' baby. I'd been relieved that I didn't have sex with Ben, but for him… what had he felt? Frustration that we'd taken our relationship only so far, that I'd teased him but never followed through. The thought that he's sleeping with Candy to get back at me pops into my head and I hope to God that's not true for Candy's sake.

Chapter Nineteen

Greek island life is a relaxed way of living, even without much time off. Running Birdsong Villas is hard work with long days but there are far harder jobs to have. Having creative people staying, often on their own, is much less demanding than if we'd gone down the route of a constant turnover of holidaymakers. Even cleaning rooms and changing bedding is enjoyable when there's only the sound of birdsong and distant waves to disturb the air. And sunshine, almost guaranteed from April often all the way into November when the air cools but the blue skies remain.

Thea is a constant source of joy and amusement, a whirlwind of energy. Now she's at pre-school for a few hours each day, I have the time to continue to build our business. There's still an outbuilding we want to restore and convert into an art studio with a potter's wheel and a screen printer.

Mum's idea of an evening out alone with Alekos is a good one. I don't argue with Despina when she insists on cooking for everyone the following evening. With Mum happy to put Thea to bed later, Alekos and I have a whole evening to ourselves lined up.

I leave Despina in the kitchen taking minced beef and a block of cheese from the fridge and rifling through the cupboards to find macaroni to make a huge *pasitsio.* I step outside and take a deep breath of fresh air, sweet with the scent of pink roses climbing up the white wall of the villa. The late afternoon sun pounds down making the courtyard and pool perfect suntraps. Laughter filters across from the pool and Thea screeches out in the garden at the back of the villa where she's playing hide and seek with Mum, Candy and Alekos. I'm about to go and join them when Robert appears on the path leading up from the beach. He waves and I stroll over.

He reaches the gate and leans on it. 'That's quite a walk back up the hill in the heat. I thought I was reasonably fit, but…' He takes a tissue from his trouser pocket and dabs it across his forehead and the sides of his face.

'The climb is a killer in the heat. To be honest, we don't often do it.'

'There's no need to when you have all of this up here.'

'That and we're usually too busy doing something either with the retreat or Thea.'

Robert tucks his tissue back in his pocket. 'Where is everyone?'

'By the pool or out in the garden. Apart from Despina who's starting to cook dinner.'

'Does she need any help?'

'You're a brave man to offer.' I laugh. 'She'll be fine. Takis is around. She doesn't much like anyone getting under her feet, so I'd stay well clear if I was you.'

'Duly noted.' He smooths the hairs on his arms and blows air over his flushed face. 'I feel like we haven't had a proper chance to talk since we got here – or when you were in Marshton for your mum's hen do.'

'It's been a bit crazy with so many people around. Anyway, it was a whirlwind visit back to the UK.'

We fall silent. I rest my arms on the wood of the gate and gaze past him to where the grass tails off and the blue of the sea and sky take over. Chatting on our own like this reminds me of our heart to heart outside The Globe when he confided to me that he loved Mum and I told him about being pregnant.

'It's good to see you looking so happy,' he finally says.

'Who'd have thought it, eh? Four years on from me being a complete and utter mess, pregnant, worried, confused and not knowing in what direction my life was going, things would have turned out like this.'

'I always had faith things would be okay, that you'd make the right choice.'

The right choice being Alekos and not your son, I think.

'And look at you, gone from wanting me to keep it a secret between the two of us that you loved my mum, to being about to marry her. You've made her so happy.'

He stands upright, away from the gate and places a hot hand on my shoulder. 'She's made me very happy too.'

'You've been good for her, I hope you realise that. She's needed a calming influence in her life, someone dependable and decent. I can't tell you how happy I am that she found you.'

Sweat beads form on Robert's forehead. I nod towards the courtyard table. 'Let's sit in the shade. I've got time for a drink before going out with Alekos if you fancy one?'

'I'd love one.'

I open the gate and we walk across the courtyard together. Robert sits beneath the olive tree while I nip into the villa and take an open bottle of white wine from the fridge and grab two glasses from the cupboard. Despina tuts as she pours macaroni into a large saucepan.

'I've forgotten, how many of us are there?' she asks.

I have to think about it, running through the names of everyone, not forgetting Arthur, a quiet presence amongst the rowdiness of the wedding party guests. 'Thirteen of us. Although remember, only eleven this evening as me and Alekos will be out.'

She nods and taps her manicured, red-painted fingernails on the work surface.

I slip back outside, sit down opposite Robert and pour us

both a generous glass of wine.

He rests back in his chair and sips his wine. 'Ah, this really is the life.'

'Not bad is it?'

He takes another sip and glances across the table at me, his eyebrows furrowed. 'To be honest, when I asked her to marry me I expected her to say no.'

'You did?' It's a pointless question because I know the reason. It's the same reason that I was shocked when Mum told me that she'd accepted his proposal.

'She's told me all about Elliot and how the situation has played out over the years. She's been brutally honest about her past, her flings, her relationship with men and how in her twenties, thirties and even well into her forties marriage or settling down with anyone was the last thing on her mind.'

He drums his fingers on the rough wood of the table and I notice his ring finger is bare. The enormity of what him and Mum are doing hits me. He's taken off his beloved late wife's ring because he's going to marry my mum. My mum, who has never wanted to get married or be tied to one man for the rest of her life. I wonder what he's done with his wedding ring. I wonder what Ben and his sister really think about their dad remarrying.

I struggle to think of what to say, biding my time by taking a long sip of wine, knowing full well what Mum was like when I was living with her back in Bristol. It feels a lifetime ago. I place my glass carefully on the table. 'People change and move on. She met you and that changed everything for her. Living in Marshton was pivotal in both our lives. We figured out a lot of things and made peace with the past. I think that's what Mum's done now she's marrying you.'

I hadn't thought about the significance of getting married from Robert's point of view and that he'd already been married to the love of his life and the mother of his children. Perhaps that's why Mum's the right woman for him, someone completely different to his late wife.

After chatting for a little longer about our plans for the rest of the week and then watching Robert walk off to find Ben and everyone by the pool, I can't help but realise that yet again I'm left with an uneasy feeling. There shouldn't be a reason for feeling like this – life is as good as it can possibly be.

Worrying is not going to make the unease go away. I head into the garden where the game of hide and seek has come to an end. Thea is curled up next to Mum on the picnic blanket in the shade of the cherry tree, reading a book together, and Candy and Alekos are relaxing in the sunshine, a bowl of cashew nuts between them.

'Mama!' Thea shrieks, giving me a grin but not moving from Mum's arms.

I lean over and kiss her forehead.

I turn to Alekos. 'Shall we get ready to go out?'

'We've really got a whole evening to ourselves?' He takes my hand and I help him to his feet. He places his arm around my waist.

'A whole child-free evening,' I say, as we stroll together to the villa, leaving Mum and Thea reading and Candy enjoying the last rays of the day.

'When was the last time we had an evening out just the two of us?' I rest back and stretch my legs out on the sandy wooden boards of the decked area which overlooks the beach in Omorfia. The fish restaurant is one of our favourite places to eat out, but we usually have Thea with us, talking non-stop and asking a million questions. Even amongst the bustle of the restaurant and surrounding bars and cafes, the beauty of the location is not lost on me. 'Can you even remember?'

'It's got to have been the last time your mum was here.'

I shake my head. 'I don't think we did go out then. I think the last time Mum was here we worked really, really hard to catch up with all the jobs that we'd never found the time to do.'

'We deserve this then.'

It's my favourite time of day with the sun beginning to set, spreading a rainbow of colour across the darkening sky. I love the grainy feel of sand beneath my toes and the sound of the surf hitting the beach, with the chatter of the people surrounding us and the beat of music from the bar next door.

'Well, *yamas*.' I knock my glass against his. 'To a much needed and long-awaited night out together.'

One of the waiters heads our way with a tray and lays out small plates and bowls filled with calamari, fried mussels, octopus cooked in lemon and olive oil, Greek salad, and feta baked in tomato.

The waiter nods and leaves us. I stab a mussel with my fork and pop it into my mouth while Alekos slices the octopus tentacle into bite-sized pieces.

'Octopus always reminds me of the beach,' he says, catching my eye and grinning.

I smile, the memory of that night flooding my thoughts and making my cheeks flush. 'Me too. Only because it was the first time I'd ever eaten octopus.'

'And not because of what happened afterwards?' Alekos reaches across the table and takes my hand in his.

'Okay, well yes, that might have something to do with it.' I pick up my glass with my free hand.

'We should go back to the beach.' Alekos holds my gaze.

'I can't believe we've been here three years and never revisited it.'

'Apparently there are steps down to the beach now; you can't reach it only by boat any longer.'

'That's a shame.' I sip my wine and gaze out at the glistening sea. The last of the sunshine catches the swell of the water as a blaze of pink and gold spreads across the horizon. 'It wouldn't be the same.' I sigh. 'It never is when you return somewhere magical.'

'Oh I don't know; I quite fancy recapturing the passion from that night.' Alekos spears a piece of octopus on his fork and waves it in my direction.

I pull it from off his fork and chew it. 'You're a tease.'

We fall silent, content to enjoy the food and the location in peace. It's true about not being able to return to a place you've loved without it feeling different. It's how I felt being back in Marshton; the memories there had been so vivid about a confusing time. They had stirred up the past and left me feeling unsettled after Cephalonia where I'd begun to feel so secure about everything.

'Are you okay with Ben being here?' The words are out of my mouth before I think them through.

Alekos glances up from his plate of food. 'Why are you asking about him?'

'Because he's going to be my stepbrother in a few days' time, that's why.'

Alekos sighs, puts his knife and fork down and leans back in his chair. 'I'd rather he wasn't here but considering his dad is marrying your mum it's not really an option.'

It wasn't, I realise. It's put Alekos in an awkward position, yet he's dealing with it way better than I thought he would. Admittedly he seems to be dealing with it by ignoring Ben completely but that's a more mature way than he would have dealt with the situation only a few years ago. Years have passed; we're all older, moved on, and with more responsibilities and maturity.

'Ben's sister is nice, and his kids. It'll be easier when they're here later in the week.'

'You really don't need to sell me on Robert's family, Sophie.' He smooths down the edge of the white paper tablecloth. 'I like Robert a lot. He's the one marrying your mum and the person who's going to be your stepfather. In my mind he's the only one who matters. Anyway, after this week, Ben's not likely to come out here again.'

It's funny, if the situation with Ben hadn't happened, I reckon Alekos would actually get on with him. They have a lot in common, not least because Ben worked in Athens for a while. Maybe it's because I've been drawn to them both that I think they'd hit it off. Once again, my fondness towards Ben makes me shudder. I have no idea why he manages to play on my mind so much. I guess we met at a time in my life when my emotions were in turmoil and rightly or wrongly, he was a welcome escape.

'I'm not sorry I punched him you know, and I'm never going to apologise for that.'

I meet Alekos' eyes. 'I wouldn't ever expect you to.'

'He deserved it.'

'Perhaps, but I led him on. It wasn't all on his shoulders.'

'He knew you were with me though, didn't he when you two…' Alekos stops and sips his lager. I can tell he doesn't want to say the words out loud. He knows everything. He'd said he didn't want to know what happened, but to me it was important to be able to put the past to rest and tell the truth so we could move on with no secrets between us.

I realise my mistake bringing Ben into the conversation during our first evening out together in what feels like an eternity. I finish the last couple of mouthfuls of calamari on my plate and put my knife and fork down. Alekos' hand clasps his lager. The dark sky and subtle lighting of the outside seating area of the restaurant accentuates his tan, his fitted blue linen short-sleeved shirt hugs his chest in all the right places.

I move the conversation on to a less volatile subject. 'I can't wait to see you in the band. I can't believe we've been together eight years and Mum's wedding party is going to be the first time I get to see you play.'

'There's just never been the opportunity.' He's dismissive of his talent and his love for making music. He sips his lager and waves his hand. 'We've had a lot of other things taking up our time over the past few years.'

'Yeah, but it's nice now you can play again, unlike when we lived at *O Kipos*.'

'Well, Cephalonia was where it all started.' He puts his

glass down, reaches across the table and takes my hand in his. 'Both music and you.'

Full of good food and a little tipsy on the wine and Greek lager, we take a taxi back to Birdsong Villas. Warm light spills from a couple of the guest rooms on the courtyard side and from Mum and Robert's room. Our villa is dark. Candy's either already asleep or in Ben's room tonight. We creep upstairs, past Despina and Takis' room, then Thea's, stifling giggles as we make it past the closed door of Candy's room and into ours without waking anyone up. It reminds me of living at *O Kipos* when we'd try really hard to be quiet, knowing Alekos' parents were asleep in the room next to ours. Still holding my hand, Alekos leads me across our room and kisses me, his hands sliding beneath my top and unhooking my bra.

It was a night like this, drunken and giggly when Alekos had led me back outside at *O Kipos* for fear of waking his parents, and we'd found the white butterfly drowned in the puddle leftover from the storm. It was the anniversary of when I'd moved to Greece and the night Alekos had proposed before our relationship had fractured and I'd escaped back to the UK to look after Mum. All that time ago and we're still not married; I'm not even sure if we're actually engaged as I no longer have the ring.

I reach my arms up and Alekos pulls my top over my head. I drop my arms back down and my bra slides off on to the floor. Alekos tastes of beer. His hands are warm and firm, sliding across my bare back and slipping beneath my skirt. I undo the button on his shorts and tug at the zip.

Thud, thud, thud. Little footsteps sound along the landing.

We freeze.

'Back to bed, Thea!' Alekos calls out in Greek.

Footsteps stop outside our door.

I fold my arms across myself in an attempt to cover my

nakedness. Alekos grins. His chest is bare, his shorts slung low on his hips. I hold my breath, hoping that Thea will stay on the other side of the door.

'*Ala*, Baba…' she whines.

'Thea, *ti kanis*?' Despina hisses from her bedroom.

'Yiayia!' Thea's footsteps retreat back along the landing. We stay rooted to the spot until we hear doors open and close and muffled voices as Despina gets Thea back in bed.

'I can't believe I'm about to say this, but thank God for your mum,' I whisper. 'And also, we really need a lock on our door.'

Alekos' hands find my bare skin again. Leaning closer his breath tickles my ear. 'All I need right now is you.'

I drop my hands from my chest and help him kick off his shorts. He pushes me down on to our bed. I close my eyes and lose myself in his warmth and familiarity. His bare skin against mine and the swirl of too much alcohol fuzzying my senses reminds me of a time gone by, a time I'm desperate to reconnect with, when there was nothing more complicated than me, Alekos and a starlit beach.

Chapter Twenty

I wake with a hangover and groan. I glance at the beside clock and groan again; I've woken up early even though Despina had offered to get up with Thea so Alekos and I could lie in. Sleeping past seven in the morning is a thing of the past, but at least I don't have to get out of bed. Alekos is still asleep next to me, snoring gently, his arm heavy where it lies hot against my hip.

There's too much going through my head to be able to get back to sleep. There are so many people to feed and look after and more arriving today. This place will be heaving by the end of the week. Alekos' snoring stops me from dozing off again and all I can think about is whether Despina is coping with Thea.

I rub my eyes, yawn and begin to swing my legs out of bed when Alekos' hand smooths across my stomach.

'Where are you going?'

'I can't sleep.'

He pulls me back into bed, so we're facing each other, his hazel eyes staring into mine.

'Mama's looking after Thea this morning, right?'

'Uh huh.'

'So why are you rushing to get up?'

Because I'm so used to it, I think. Alekos moves closer, wrapping me in his arms and kissing me. I close my eyes and relax, memories of the Alekos I first met on Cephalonia filling my head as his hands travel lower.

We're late coming downstairs for breakfast. Everyone else is already up, sitting outside on the table that's been extended in anticipation of more people arriving. There are now three tables in an L-shape surrounding the olive tree. I think it's the first time everyone's eaten breakfast together – typically on the day I'm up late.

'Mama! Baba!' Thea screeches, careering towards us and knocking into my legs.

'It's like you haven't seen us for a week.' I take her hand and walk over to the table.

Alekos pulls up a chair for me and I sit down, Thea scrambles on to my lap, and curls her fingers into my hair.

Candy catches my eye and winks. 'Good night?'

Alekos sits next to me and reaches for my hand.

'Yeah, really good thanks,' he says.

Ben's arm is draped along the back of Candy's chair and he's deep in conversation with Robert sitting on the other side of him.

'It was nice to not have to entertain this one for once.' I kiss the top of Thea's head.

'Tell me about it,' Candy says, spreading jam on a piece of bread. 'I'm missing Jake and Holly like crazy, but not the arguments, the tiredness, the never-ending questions.'

'It was good to have time alone.' Alekos strokes my hand and my cheeks burn knowing full well the alone time he's talking about was at the end of last night and first thing this morning, not our evening out.

Despina is in her element, taking charge and making sure everyone has plenty of food. Within a minute of sitting down she's placed two generous squares of *spanakopita* on plates in front of me and Alekos and has poured us both a coffee.

'*Efharisto*, Despina,' I say as she smooths out the creases in her skirt and sits back down.

She nods. '*Parakalo*.' She glances around the table and jumps to her feet again, pushing a piece of pie on to Mum's crumb-filled plate. 'You must eat, Leila.'

Mum, with a mouthful of food, shakes her head and calls across the table to Alekos. 'Your mum's doing her damned best to fatten me up. I won't be able to fit into my dress at this rate.'

Arthur, dressed in his usual smart shirt, trousers and a wide-brimmed hat, pats his lean stomach. 'No complaints from me.'

I love it, watching everyone chat and eat, munching happily on *spanakopita* and *tchereki*. Jocelyn, Kim and Pamela are in their element, all dressed for a Greek summer in floaty skirts or dresses. Takis sits quietly next to Arthur, both men eating in silence.

'Do I have to go to pre-school today, Mama?' Thea asks, her wide hazel eyes looking up at me, her lips pursed.

'There's only one more day after today and then you have the whole of the summer off. It's only for a few hours anyway and then you can come back here and see everyone.'

'And play with Grandma?'

'Of course you can play with me when you get back.' Mum beams across the table at Thea. 'Anyway, you'll have lots of fun with your friends, won't you?'

'I like Effi, she's my friend and Nikos, but Kostas sometimes doesn't like me playing with the cars.'

'Well,' Mum calls across the table, 'next time he says that, you tell him where to…'

'Mum!' I shout.

'I tell him girls can play with cars.' Thea slides off my lap and skips around the table.

'That's my girl.' Mum laughs, ruffling Thea's hair. 'Put him in his place. And don't ever let anyone tell you otherwise.'

'It's another beautiful day,' Jocelyn says, leaning towards me sounding like a broken record as that's pretty much what she's said every day since arriving. It's hard not to, I guess.

The perfect blue sky, sunshine and sparkling sea makes this location what it is – beautiful and enchanting. The reason Alekos took a chance and bought Birdsong Villas, and the reason he was sure I would love it.

'You should go down to the beach today,' I say, 'if you fancy? We've got plenty of beach towels and I can make you a packed lunch.'

'You're too good to us, Sophie.' She leans towards Kim. 'Do you fancy a couple of hours at the beach this morning?'

'Do I ever. That's the whole reason I packed my factor fifty, a sun hat and four books.'

After breakfast everyone disperses. Kim and Jocelyn go down to the beach with Pamela and Mum, while Alekos and Robert take Thea to pre-school before heading to the airport to pick up Robert's daughter and grandchildren. Candy and Ben disappear round to the pool or his room, I'm not sure which and I don't particularly care. However much I want to spend time with Candy, I really don't want to feel like a spare part with her and Ben. It's tempting to snatch a moment of quiet to myself, a bit of sunbathing in the garden with a book or a stroll along the clifftop path to clear my head, but the running of the retreat continues, even more so with so many rooms occupied.

I take clean bedding and make up the beds in the remaining empty rooms. I realise too late, that to do the beds in what will be Ben's children's room, I have to head to the pool. Holding the sheets and pillowcases to my chest, I walk round and undo the gate with one hand. The pool and sunloungers are empty. I skirt the edge of the pool to reach the room next to Ben's, unlock it and go inside. There's an unmistakable giggle from Candy from the room next door. I don't know what to do; this is just plain weird, I don't want to stay and overhear them. I should have made the beds up before now, but there's been too much going on.

Sod it. I place the bedding on the armchair and tuck a

fitted sheet over the mattress and then the camp bed. I start to stuff one of the pillows into a pillowcase when a thud, thud, thud sounds from Ben's room. I freeze with the realisation of what the rhythmic thud is. I guess with Ben's children arriving soon this is the last chance Candy and Ben will have. Blocking out the disturbing image that pops into my head with each thud, I shove the last pillow on to the bed and creep outside, closing the door silently behind me. I should have taken my book and soaked up the sun in the garden instead.

The peace is shattered long before Mum's friends return from the beach or Ben and Candy emerge from his room. Alekos and Robert pull up in the people carrier we've hired for the week and Robert's grandchildren tumble out. Ben's sister Vicky emerges from the front passenger seat, her face flushed and make-up free. She waves and strides over to me.

'Am I glad to be here. Travelling on my own with three children – remind me to never do that again.' She hugs me. 'Even if two of them are ten and eight and really quite sensible, it's my nearly four-year-old who's the problem.'

'Well done for doing the journey on your own,' I say.

Vicky nods. 'They were all great, it's just I felt tense the whole time and it's a long journey when you factor in getting to the airport, waiting for the flight, the actual flight, getting through customs and the drive here.'

'I think you need a drink.'

'I definitely need a drink. Something quite strong.'

I've only met Vicky a couple of times when I was living with Mum back in Marshton and was pregnant with Thea, but I've always warmed to her. She's less complicated than Ben, no harsh edges or sense of an ulterior motive.

'Thea's going to love having Joshua here to play with.' I link my arm in hers and we go through the gate, Joshua racing ahead of us, with Robert, Alekos and Ben's kids following behind. 'She'll be back from pre-school later.'

Ben saunters across the courtyard from the direction of the pool, hands shoved in his jeans pockets. 'Did my two behave for you?' he calls out.

'Dad!' Bella yells and runs over to her father. He holds her tight.

'Hi, Dad.' Fraser walks over and hugs his father.

I always felt sorry for Ben being apart from his kids, but although he seems to have put them first by staying in London and not moving further away to Norfolk, I do wonder if he likes the freedom of only seeing them at certain times and being able to live his life without the constant constraints of looking after children. Having sex in the middle of the day with Candy is unlikely to happen now. Maybe I'm being unduly harsh on him or maybe it's just I feel nothing's really changed in the four years since our ill-fated fling. It's good to see him with Fraser and Bella though – they always seemed to have a way of taming him.

Candy's nowhere to be seen and I wonder how their relationship is going to play out over the next few days with Ben's children here, plus the added complication of Demetrius and his wife arriving in the next day or two.

'Is Leila still down at the beach?' Robert asks as we gather beneath the shade of the olive tree.

'She'll be back soon. She knows Vicky and the kids were arriving.'

It's strange to think that my mum, my un-maternal mum, will become stepmother to Ben and Vicky in four days' time, plus take on the role of grandmother to three more children besides Thea. My mum, who freaked out at the thought of Thea, and that she was too young to be a grandma. Times really have changed. However complicated this all is, being part of a family with a father figure and siblings is what I've always wanted.

Chapter Twenty-One

Thea arrives back from pre-school and within a few minutes of meeting each other, she and Joshua are the best of friends. Whether he wants to or not, Thea takes him by the hand and shows him around, pointing out all the places they can play. She may be a few months younger than him, yet she's in her element taking charge and bossing him about. The difference in Fraser and Bella is astounding compared to the last time I saw them; no longer little kids, but sensible children, happy to sit with the grown-ups and drink lemonade in the shade next to their grandad. Robert beams, his whole family together.

Mum arrives back from the beach with the others and squeals when she sees Vicky and the kids. She rushes across the courtyard and kisses their cheeks, introducing Jocelyn, Kim and Pamela to everyone. The place had settled down since our arrival five days ago, but with new faces, there's renewed energy and excitement. Once again, Birdsong Villas feels full.

I have no idea where Candy has been all afternoon, but once Vicky and the kids have headed to their rooms with Robert and Ben to settle in, she reappears in the courtyard, freshly showered, make-up reapplied and dressed in a flattering yellow and white patterned maxi-dress.

'Where have you been?' I ask, stacking plates together and brushing crumbs from the table on to the ground beneath the olive tree.

'I had a siesta.' Candy picks up a tray of glasses and follows me and Despina into the villa.

I place the pile of plates next to the sink and Despina tuts as I pick up the washing-up gloves.

'I'll do that,' she says firmly in Greek, taking them off me. 'Go talk to your friend.'

'*Efharistoume.*'

She waves me away, so I give in and head over to the living area with Candy.

'I wish my mother-in-law had been as helpful as yours.' Candy sighs and slumps down on the sofa that faces the open doors to the garden.

'Technically she's not my mother-in-law.'

'As good as.'

I sit next to her and rest against the soft cushioned back of the sofa.

'When the hell are you and Alekos going to get married?'

'There's never really been the time…'

'Excuses, excuses, Sophie Keech. Mind you,' Candy says, rubbing her finger where her wedding ring had been. 'If things are good between the two of you why rock the boat. Getting married to Lee was the biggest mistake of my life.'

'I know you feel that way now but you already had the kids, getting married was the next natural step – do you think he'd have behaved any differently if you'd remained together but not got married? Do you think he wouldn't have had an affair?'

'I think he thought of me differently once we were married. Maybe the spark in our relationship went. We became an old married couple long before our time.'

There's no point in arguing with Candy when she's in this mood. Despina clatters behind us, stacking dishes in the dishwasher. Thea and Joshua run past the open doors, screeching.

'They're having fun,' Candy says, smiling.

'You've not met Fraser and Bella yet?' I glance at her. She's staring out towards the garden. Sunlight filters through the leaves, making patterns on the dry grass.

She looks at me. 'It's kinda weird isn't it? I mean, it feels strange to be meeting them. I know we're all here together so it's inevitable, but flipping hell, Sophie, I'm his bit on the side. I totally wouldn't be meeting his kids yet if we were back home.'

'It doesn't have to be awkward,' I say with as much conviction as I can muster. 'You're going to be introduced as my friend – they don't need to know anything more.'

Candy nods and bites her lip.

'Unless, you want to be known as more than that…' I say slowly.

'That's silly isn't it? I mean, I've only known him what, five days? Fuck, I seriously slept with him after two days…'

Despina is washing up, and even though I don't think she understands what we're talking about, I'm conscious of her in the background getting on with the jobs I feel I should be doing. I don't know what to say to Candy. I slept with Alekos after only a couple of days and committed to him in a ridiculously short amount of time, but even with our ups and downs it's worked out perfectly. And yet Candy and Ben… Both divorced, both have kids and I'm convinced they aren't really sure what they want from life right now. With the heartbreak Candy's been through over the past few months, her getting serious with a man she's only just met isn't the wisest of ideas. Especially after what happened between me and Ben in Blakeney.

'I know it's easy for me to say this, but I don't think you should worry. I'm pretty sure Ben won't say anything to Fraser and Bella. They're sweet kids. I know it's easier said than done, but try and relax. There's going to be so much going on over the next few days you won't have time to dwell on things.'

'Anyway,' Candy says with a sigh. 'His kids arriving has

pretty much put paid to anything more going on between us.'

And that they'll be sleeping in the room next to Ben's… I don't say anything. She sounds dejected but it's probably for the best, before she gets her heart broken or disappointed by yet another man.

Chapter Twenty-Two

With the wedding taking place on Saturday and the start of the week taken up with more people arriving, life is non-stop. I'm grateful for Despina's help and she seems to be genuinely enjoying looking after everyone. The night Vicky and the kids arrive, dinner is full on, the tables filled with Mum and Robert's family and friends. Despina and I work together in the hot kitchen. It reminds me once again of being at *O Kipos*. There may have been tension between us and plenty of misunderstanding, but the one thing we did do was work well together.

I'd thought it was too much hard work cooking moussaka for seventeen people, but Despina persuaded me that it would be fun. And I guess it was, making two large trays of moussaka actually wasn't that much effort. The bit that is a huge effort is all the washing-up afterwards, but then Takis and Alekos get roped into that. Our cooking is appreciated too, with every last bit of moussaka polished off and happy guests with full stomachs heading to bed.

It's a little easier in the morning, with everyone arriving for breakfast at different times, but it means we don't end up clearing away until late morning. I've lost track of where everyone is, apart from Thea who I know is somewhere with Mum, Vicky and Joshua.

Despina pulls off her rubber gloves and washes her hands,

drying them on the towel hanging on the hook next to the sink.

'Did Alekos tell you we finally have a buyer for *O Kipos*?' she asks in Greek. She pulls up a chair at the kitchen table and sits down.

'No.' I wipe down the work surface. 'When did that happen?'

'Yesterday.'

'That's great news.'

She nods and turns away, looking out across the living area towards the open double doors and the sunny garden beyond. I bite my lip, realising too late what I've said; selling their business and home was never what they wanted.

'I mean, at least after all this time you've found someone to take it on.' I backtrack, but realise I'm digging myself a bigger hole.

'It feels very odd, our life's work being passed on to strangers.'

I start to say something and then stop. I don't want to get into an argument with her, yet I don't want the blame to be passed on to Alekos and me because we have a different dream. I pour us each a glass of water from the fridge, giving myself some time to think through what to say. I place one of the glasses in front of her, sit in the chair opposite and take a mouthful of the ice-cold water.

'I get that this is hard for you. I mean really hard. I understand that, and I'm sorry *O Kipos* wasn't something Alekos and I felt we could take on.'

'That *you* felt you couldn't take on.'

I shake my head. 'That's not fair and you know it. It was never something Alekos wanted, it's just before I came into his life he felt like he had no choice. We've disappointed you, I know that. But think of it this way – you and Takis are who inspired us to create all of this.' I gesture around me. 'Less than four years ago this was crumbling and rundown. If Alekos hadn't seen you build *O Kipos* from nothing to the success it is, there's no way he would have had the guts to buy this place and for us to start our own business.'

Despina sniffs and takes a tissue out of her trouser pocket. She dabs around her eyes, being careful to not ruin her eye make-up.

'It's kind of you to say that. I always wanted to do the best for Alekos and for Lena.' She stops and looks at me through thick black eyelashes. She takes a deep breath. 'I thought I knew what was best for them both, particularly Alekos. I didn't want him to worry about his future. I honestly thought it was what he wanted.'

'You never asked him what he wanted.'

'He never told me that he wanted anything different.'

'He didn't want to break your heart,' I say. I don't add that she wouldn't have listened or believed him even if he had stood up to her, but would have instead blamed his wanting to leave on my influence. I'm surprised she allowed him to spend those couple of summers on Cephalonia, but I guess she was confident he'd return to the family business.

Outside there's an unmistakable screech of laughter from Thea, and Mum shouts, 'I'm going to get you!'

I smile; it's wonderful for Mum to have this time to spend with Thea and to enjoy a few days with her friends.

'You understand Alekos needed to step out on his own,' I say carefully, trying to find the right words in Greek without upsetting or offending her. I avoid the direct suggestion that he, and by that I mean we, needed to get away from her domineering personality.

She folds her hands together, her wine-red nails perfectly painted. 'I was not happy but I understand. Sometimes I say too much, I know. I didn't want to stay forever with my parents-in-law either, or my own parents, but then they hadn't built up a family business that could be passed down like Takis and me.' She sips her water and places it carefully back down on the wooden table. 'I understand the desire to create something for yourself, it's what I've always strived to do.

You and Alekos having that same drive is impressive, as is what you've managed to achieve here in such a short space of time.'

I think that's the nicest thing she's ever said. I wipe away a tear.

'You may have been inspired by what we achieved at *O Kipos*, but I'm impressed by *Vila Ptina*.' She leans towards me, squeezing my hands and kissing me on both cheeks. 'Truthfully it's a relief to know that the restaurant is off our hands, that the hard work is over *and* both our children are happy and successful. Now we only have to decide where we're going to retire – close to Lena or to you.'

She leaves me with another kiss. Her heels clack across the tiled floor, then disappear through the open doors and out into the courtyard and sunshine. I rest my head in my hands and take a deep breath. What the hell just happened? A future with Despina and Takis living next to us, breathing down our necks flashes before me. I'd never considered that they'd move anywhere but to a smaller place in the town close to *O Kipos*. Now I realise with the restaurant gone there's nothing to keep them there any more but they have every reason to up and leave and start a new life in Athens or here on Cephalonia.

Chapter Twenty-Three

I step out of the kitchen into the sunshine, wanting to rid myself of the worry that Despina has managed to ignite. However much of a help she's been over the past few days, there's a difference to her being here for a holiday as opposed to forever… I shade my eyes and squint across the courtyard. Mum's friends are sitting at the table in the shade.

'Have you seen Alekos or Candy?' I call across.

'Not Alekos,' Jocelyn replies, 'but I think Candy's by the pool.'

I presume Mum and Thea are still playing chase out in the garden and Alekos is with them too. I pace across the courtyard, the difference in the warm sunshine stark compared to the coolness indoors. I probably shouldn't mention anything to Alekos about where Despina and Takis will potentially move to. I know it's a toxic conversation and one that's better left until after the wedding.

Robert's in the pool with Fraser and Bella, hitting a blow up ball between the three of them. Candy and Ben are sitting together on the edge of a sunlounger, watching and cheering the kids on. I almost turn around and walk back the way I've come, but Candy waves me over.

'You okay?' she asks when I reach them.

I nod.

'You're frowning.'

Ben glances at me.

'I didn't realise I was,' I say and sigh. 'But I've been chatting to Despina so that's probably why.'

'You want to talk about it?' Candy asks.

Ben stands up. 'Here,' he says, offering me his spot. 'I'm going to get a drink. Either of you two want anything?'

'No thanks, babe,' Candy says.

'No thanks,' I echo.

He runs his hand across Candy's shoulders as he goes, brushing past me. I sit down on the still warm spot on the sunlounger and watch Robert throw a ball across the pool and Fraser catch it.

'Things are still fine between you two then, even with Fraser and Bella here?'

'Yeah.' Candy smiles. 'You were right, they're lovely kids. To be fair, they want to spend all their time with Robert. Ben's hardly had a look in, so I still feel like I've got him to myself.'

I look at her watching Fraser and Bella splashing about in the pool with Robert. 'You really like him, don't you?'

'Yeah, I do. And it's weird, the last thing I was expecting from these couple of weeks was to meet someone. I was kinda hoping for a bit of time to myself, to spend time with you, relax and recharge. I'm sorry if we've not spent as much time together as we should have.'

'Hey, it's fine. I wasn't expecting you to be here at all, so what time I do have with you is a bonus.'

A blast of a car horn cuts short our conversation.

'Who's that?' Candy asks.

'Should be the band,' I say, touching her arm. 'Don't worry, it's not Demetrius – he won't get here until later.'

'Uh huh. I'm really not bothered even if it is him.' She stands up and helps me to my feet. 'But I do want to meet Alekos' famous band.'

Together we walk back to the courtyard. A van is parked outside the main gate, the back doors open, and a long-haired bearded Greek man is dragging out a guitar case from the back. The passenger door of the van opens and slender tanned legs in sparkly open-toed heeled shoes swing out.

Candy nudges me. 'She's the singer Alekos played in the band with? She looks like Monica Belluchi. She's stunning.'

Raven black hair tumbles in waves on to the toned and tanned shoulders of the woman. She slams the van door shut. Her strapless cream dress clings in all the right places, but is long enough to remain classy.

Candy takes out her iPhone. 'What's her name?'

'Aphrodite.'

Candy looks up from her phone, eyebrows raised. 'Seriously, Aphrodite?'

I nod.

'That's got to be a stage name.'

'I don't think so.'

Candy grunts and taps the name into her phone and presses enter. She clicks on a link and a black and white photo of Aphrodite appears. Candy scrolls to the top and clicks on 'About' and whistles under her breath.

'Shit, she's forty-six. No way does she look forty-six. She doesn't even look like she's in her forties.'

Mum's never looked her age either, but then she's always had a fun and quirky style that's defied her age. Aphrodite is glamorous and seductive. Kim, Jocelyn and Pamela are still sitting at the table beneath the olive tree, sunglasses shading their eyes, pretending they're not looking at her but they blatantly are; Ben appears from the guest lounge, a mug of coffee in his hand, and falters when he catches sight of her, almost doing a comical double take; Mum is by the gate, shaking hands with the man holding the guitar, but her gaze follows Aphrodite. Alekos jumps from the back of the van and lifts out a large speaker, heading after her.

'Did you know she was the singer?'

I nod, my eyes following Alekos into the house after Aphrodite. 'I've seen photos of the band but I've not seen her in real life before.'

'I don't remember Alekos mentioning much about her, which seems odd when he obviously…' Candy stops, frowning briefly.

'When he obviously what?'

'Nothing.' Candy wafts a hand in front of her face. 'Flip, it's hot today, isn't it?'

'Don't change the subject.'

'It was nothing, I wasn't thinking through what I was saying.'

'Seriously, Candy, tell me.'

Candy sighs. 'He played in the band with her for a whole two summers, right? But never really mentioned her. She doesn't seem like someone you'd not talk about again. I mean apart from being beautiful she's got that quality about her, you know, the kind of person everyone notices when she walks into a room.' She waves her hand again. 'I'm being silly, maybe they had a falling out, that's why he doesn't really talk about her. Anyway, I'm looking forward to a day of relaxing before the celebrations properly begin.'

A sudden chill runs through me. I know exactly the reason why Alekos has rarely mentioned her. It's the same reason Candy doesn't talk about Demetrius and why I feel uncomfortable at the mere mention of Ben's name.

I see myself through Alekos' eyes – his pale English wife tired from looking after a young child and working non-stop, compared to a glamorous older Greek woman, tanned and beautiful, younger than her years, single and exciting and talented. No wonder Candy didn't want to put the thought in my head of why Alekos has rarely talked about Aphrodite.

While we were sailing on *Artemis* with Alekos and Demetrius, I had a pretty good idea that we weren't the first girls they'd seduced. They lived the perfect life those two summers before meeting us. Two young, single handsome men, earning lots of money taking tourists out sailing, enjoying the attention of attractive foreign women. And then

Alekos got to spend sultry late nights playing guitar in the band with its glamorous and seductive lead singer. How naive I've been.

'I'm going to have a dip in the pool – you coming?'

I shake my head, my thoughts still filled with Alekos and Aphrodite playing music in Retro night after hot night, the summer before I even knew Alekos existed.

'You okay?' Candy asks.

I pull my sunglasses out of my hair and over my eyes. 'You go; I need to find Thea anyway.'

I stalk across the courtyard, veering away from where the van's being unloaded. Alekos and Aphrodite disappear into the guest living area. They even have delicious Greek names that sound perfect together. I hate these doubts that have invaded my head. I've been so happy and content, the three of us living here, Alekos and me raising Thea and working hard to build our retreat. Now, with all these people from our past arriving, that control and satisfaction is ebbing away.

I hear Thea's laughter from the garden and my heart skips. Being away in England was the longest amount of time I've spent away from Thea and I know I've not been paying her enough attention since I got back. I shouldn't berate myself really; Thea's getting to spend time with her grandma and yiayia and papou, while I can take a break from the full-time responsibility of an inquisitive three-year-old. It's been good to spend time with Candy, talk to Robert and reconnect with Mum's friends. Maybe I'm letting my imagination run away with me over Alekos and Aphrodite. He wouldn't be so stupid or blatant to invite her and the band here if there'd been something going on between them? Would he?

Chapter Twenty-Four

Thea brings me firmly back to reality with a game of chase in the garden, zipping between the trees, hiding behind bushes, her shrieks carrying into the air. I'm hot by the time I manage to catch her and swing her up into my arms. I pretend to nibble her neck like a dinosaur. She shrieks even more and I land her back on to her feet.

'Baba!' she yells.

I turn and shade my eyes. Alekos walks across the grass, Aphrodite alongside him, matching his pace.

'We could hear you all the way from the other side of the house.' Alekos bends down and kisses Thea. He turns to me. 'We were wondering where you were.'

'I thought I'd better take Thea off Mum's and Vicky's hands.'

Alekos turns to Aphrodite. 'Sophie, this is Aphrodite; Aphrodite, Sophie.'

'It's good to finally meet you,' she says in Greek, kissing me on both cheeks. She smells as good as she looks, a light floral scent. She's about my height in her heels and when she steps away I can see her tanned smooth skin, her eyes hidden by large sunglasses. 'And this must be Thea.' She bends down and cups Thea's cheeks in her hands. 'You are beautiful. You have your baba's eyes.'

Alekos steps towards me. 'We're going to go in a bit and

set up for the gig tonight.' He takes my hand and glances towards Thea and Aphrodite. 'You're all coming, aren't you?'

'Yeah of course, everyone's looking forward to it.'

'Great, see you later.' He kisses me and leans down to kiss Thea.

'*Ta lema agotera*,' Aphrodite says to me. She smiles at Thea and waves. '*Ciao*.'

'Mama, who's that lady?' Thea asks as we watch them walk back across the garden, Aphrodite's hips swaying. They reach the open doors of the villa. Alekos reaches out his hand and places it on the small of Aphrodite's back to let her go inside first.

I look away and down at Thea. She has a red lipstick mark on her cheek.

I crouch in front of her and rub away the lipstick with my thumb. 'She's the singer in the band that Baba used to play with.'

'She smells funny.'

'She smells expensive, that's why.'

Katrina has been my closest friend since moving to Greece. Not only did I leave behind my home and job in Bristol but I left Candy and all my other friends. A new start in Greece where I didn't know anyone apart from Alekos, meant his friends ended up becoming my friends. It wasn't even like I had the opportunity to make friends of my own because working at *O Kipos* meant my work colleagues were Despina, Alekos and Takis, along with a handful of waiters and waitresses who I didn't get to know well. Katrina was warm and friendly from the start and I think I'd have become friends with her even though she was Alekos' best friend's girlfriend. She's now Demetrius' wife and I miss seeing them since we moved to Cephalonia. I remember being insanely jealous of them moving to Thessaloniki into an apartment of their own while I felt stifled living with Despina and Takis, longing for our own space and freedom.

They arrive later that afternoon and with thoughts still swirling around my head about Alekos and Aphrodite, seeing Katrina's beaming face stops me from feeling sorry for myself.

'*Yasou*!' she squeals and hugs me.

'*Ti kanis*, Sophie?' Demetrius asks, kissing my cheeks.

'*Kala, kai ici*?'

We've not seen each other for a while, our lives so busy with work and kids, us on Cephalonia, an island on the opposite side of the mainland to where they live in Thessaloniki. I love how we slip back into a comfortable friendship, much like it is when Candy and I see each other even if months or even years have gone by.

'I can't wait to meet your mum,' Katrina says. The taxi leaves and we walk across the courtyard towards the villa. Katrina has heard the whole story with my mum, both the good and the bad. I was beyond angry with Mum when I first moved to Greece so there was no sugar coating my feelings about my relationship with her.

'The kids are okay?' I ask.

'They're fine, looking forward to a few days with their yiayia and papou being spoilt.'

'Much like Thea is now with everyone here. She's in her element. Come and meet everyone.'

Candy has made herself scarce. There's never been any reason to tell Katrina about Candy's brief fling with Demetrius, and I didn't think they'd ever meet, but now… knowing they're here together it feels a bit strange introducing them. I remind myself that it wasn't Katrina who Demetrius cheated on with Candy, so there's no reason to stir anything up. Plus from everything Katrina and I have talked about over the past few years and what I've gleaned from Alekos, Demetrius has changed his ways since then.

It's only Despina and Takis who don't speak English, but I think Despina understands more than she lets on. The living area of the villa is packed. Pretty much everyone who's staying is enjoying a drink, even Arthur. Despina is playing host once again, keeping everyone's drinks topped up. Thea and Jacob are centre of attention, messing about in the middle of the room making everyone laugh as only cheeky three-year-olds can. Aphrodite, the band and Alekos have headed off to rehearse for the gig this evening.

With the introductions done, everyone is happily chatting and laughing. The worry I had after the conversation with Candy earlier about Aphrodite is easing. Candy looks relaxed even though she's in the same room as Demetrius. I don't think they've said more than a polite hello to each other. Candy is sitting shoulder to shoulder with Ben – together but not quite together. I take a deep breath and a slurp of wine as Thea takes Jacob's and Bella's hands and tries to get them to dance.

Aphrodite and her band, Melani, are playing an acoustic set at a live music venue just up the coast. They're in demand and Aphrodite is making the most of the few days they have here, squeezing in playing at Mum and Robert's wedding in-between three or four other dates at various locations including Retro, the old bar they used to play at in Fiskardo, the one where Alekos and I first kissed.

It takes me forever to decide on what to wear. Everything I try on, I discard the moment I look in the bedroom mirror, deciding I hate myself in it. Nothing I own will make me look as glamorous as Aphrodite. Since when have I, the tomboy, ever been bothered about what I look like compared to someone else? I decide not to fight it. I can't compete in the glamour stakes next to Candy or Despina, let alone Aphrodite, so I'm not even going to try. There's a mountain of skirts and dresses on the bed that I've already tried on and discarded. I pull on white skinny jeans, a fitted longline silky grey top with a low, V-neck cleavage, paint my toenails a burnt orange and leave my hair tousled and natural on my sun-kissed shoulders. I look in the mirror again and breathe deeply. I look like me.

The thought of Aphrodite and Alekos won't shift from

my head though. Did she say yes to playing at the wedding as a favour to Alekos? Or maybe it was an excuse to see him again and to get him to play the gigs while on the island. I need to shut out these thoughts or else they'll drive me crazy. And I know the sensible thing is to simply talk to Alekos to clear up any misunderstanding and rid myself of these worries. As soon as we get a chance and some proper alone time, I'll tackle the subject. Too many times in the past I've bottled up my feelings and worries, making a bigger problem than there was to begin with.

Not one for loud music or a late night, Despina happily offers to stay and babysit Thea, while Vicky is content to have an early night and get Joshua and Ben's kids to bed. Even knowing that Joshua is going to be at the retreat doesn't pacify Thea about staying home, wanting to go and see Baba play instead. Even by Greek standards I know it's going to be too much of a late night for her. I leave her in tears having a tantrum at the top of the stairs with the firm thought that I really, really need a drink.

Alekos looks at ease on stage. It's the same as he does when he's playing volleyball or when I first met him sailing on *Artemis*. Confidence envelops him, the Alekos I first knew, who disappeared when we lived back at *O Kipos* and who's reappeared while we've been working together building Birdsong Villas.

Aphrodite's voice is sultry and seductive. The beat of the music, the heat and vibe of the venue, and the good looks of the band is a winning combination. She sashays across the stage, smiling at the bass player and sliding her hand across Alekos' broad shoulders. I shiver and imagine that's the reaction her touch has on Alekos too. She oozes sexiness. And so does Alekos. I can sense the chemistry between them even from the crowd and I wonder if anyone else has picked up on it.

I glance sideways at Candy but she's talking to Ben, their

arms entwined, their faces inches away from each other. Am I the only one who noticed that touch? Mum and Kim with their arms across each other's shoulders are swaying in time to the music, Jocelyn and Pamela are next to them clapping their hands; even Robert's foot is tapping as he sips a beer, looking completely out of place, yet like he's loving it at the same time.

I don't quite feel in the moment; it's like I'm an outsider looking in, noticing the details that everyone else seems oblivious to, fuelled by alcohol, the heat and music. Maybe that's the problem, I've not drunk enough. Although my head spins and the beat thumps like a headache that won't shift.

I put my drink down and make my way through the throng and outside into darkness. It's a warm night and yet it feels cooler outside, fresher than the stuffiness of the bar. I lean against the wall and take a deep breath. Away from the town it's dark. Moonlight reflects off the water. The air smells of Greek summer: the tang of sea air, the sweetness of corn on the cob grilling on the stall further down the road, the heady scent of roses, and the smoke from the bar.

Katrina joins me outside. She leans against the wall next to me.

'Everything okay?'

I nod. 'Too hot in there.'

I'm in two minds whether to ask her this question or not, because I know something about Demetrius' past that she doesn't, but we've been friends for long enough for her to not take it the wrong way. 'Has Demetrius ever talked to you about the summers he worked on Cephalonia with Alekos, and what they got up to?'

She frowns and waves her hand. 'It was before he met me, I don't ask.' She leans closer and lowers her voice, even though there's no one else outside the bar. 'I was well aware of his reputation when we got together, but he's changed. It's never been worth dragging up the past – what good would it do?'

I nod and take a deep breath, knowing she's right, but me and Alekos *have* talked about our pasts and yet Aphrodite has never really been mentioned…

'What's bothering you, Sophie?'

'Nothing.' I push myself away from the wall. 'I'm being silly, that's all. Come on, let's go back inside.'

Voicing my worries to someone else would make them real. What I'm even more worried about is that Katrina will suspect that there was something between Alekos and Aphrodite all those years ago and fuel my concerns.

'Well?' Alekos finds me straight after their set finishes. I'm the first person he talks to. He puts his hands on my waist, tugging me close. 'What did you think?'

'I thought…' I don't quite know how I can put into words how I feel. 'I knew you'd be good, but you're better than I even imagined.'

He cups my face in his hands and kisses me. 'You look beautiful tonight.'

Aphrodite is looking at us. Our eyes meet and she turns away and beams at Mum who's just walked over.

I want to ask Alekos about her. I want to know if there was ever something between them, but I can't. I can't take away his enjoyment of playing music again; I can't risk stirring up the past, the idea of mistrust, particularly if there wasn't anything between them apart from friendship and the band.

I need to switch off. I need to stop thinking. I need to not read too much into things that might never have happened.

Alekos is in demand. Strangers come up to him for a chat and to buy him a drink. Even if I want to talk to him, there's no opportunity. When he does get a chance, he spends time with Demetrius and I let him have their time together. I've got Katrina, Mum and her friends. Everyone is enjoying themselves, even Jocelyn who is on the wine tonight rather than being teetotal. Ben's chatting to Robert, so Candy sidles over and perches on the bar stool next to me.

'He's really bloody good,' she says, a slight slur to her words, nodding towards Alekos chatting to Demetrius and a couple of local Greeks. 'I didn't think it'd be possible for him to get any hotter, but…'

'You're talking about Alekos right, not Demetrius?'

'Of course I am. I'm so over Demetrius.' She knocks her glass of wine against mine. 'Him and his wife look good together. She seems nice.'

'She is.'

She sips her wine. 'Does the name of the band Melani mean anything?'

'It means ink.'

'Why did they choose that?'

'Alekos explained it to me once – the band always went by Aphrodite's name but they wanted something that showcased their music better. Ink or *melani* is about literally writing the songs in ink – creating the music.'

'That's really quite beautiful. Who chose it?'

'I don't actually know.'

There's quite a lot I don't know about the band and Alekos' time with them and Aphrodite. I feel a need to know more now, even if I'm not going to like what I find out. Candy has put so much doubt in my head that I can't shake off.

I'm glad they're not staying at the retreat. With everyone else, there's not enough space for the band to stay too, so they're at a local hotel and leaving their equipment with us. We all pile back, a little worse for wear after a night of music and drinking. Everyone calls out 'good night' and '*kalinikta*' to each other across the dark courtyard.

I'm longing for sleep. I climb the stairs with heavy legs, creep into Thea's room and kiss her warm, smooth cheek. Tumbling into bed next to Alekos, I will sleep to take over, to wake in the morning, my worries about Alekos and Aphrodite little more than a bad dream.

Chapter Twenty-Five

I can't remember the last time I woke up twice within the space of a week with a hangover. Thea's awake, I can hear her singing in her room. I sit up, rub my eyes, feeling hot, sticky and in need of a shower. My hair stinks of smoke. Alekos is snoring next to me, taking up most of the bed. I lean down and kiss him, my head throbbing.

I wonder if I can make it to the bathroom without Thea hearing me. I creep out of our room and along the hallway. Candy's door is closed, Despina and Takis' is open and I can hear someone clattering about downstairs. I push the bathroom door and it squeaks open. Thea stops singing. Footsteps thud across her bedroom and her door creaks open.

'*Kalimera*, Mama!'

I place my hand against my forehead. '*Kalimera*, Thea. Please talk quietly.'

'I am,' she says, in a three-year-old's normal voice, which is ten times louder than an adult's.

'Then please whisper,' I say, not even wanting to raise my own voice my head hurts that much. When did I start feeling so old? Too much to drink, a smoky atmosphere and loud music has done me in.

Thea's still talking but I realise I've not listened to a word she's saying.

'Can I?'

'Can you what?'

'Mama!' She stamps her foot. 'Can I watch telly?'

'Thea, it's only seven in the morning.'

'Yiayia lets me watch telly.'

'Not in the morning she doesn't.'

She stamps her foot again, folds her arm and gives me her best evil glare.

I try not to laugh.

'It's not fair.'

'No, it's not, but then being up this early in the morning feeling the way I do isn't fair either.'

'Aaaghhrr!' she shrieks.

'Thea, shush, you're going to wake everyone.'

Despina appears at the top of the stairs, tutting. She holds her hand out to Thea. '*Ela*,' she says. 'So much noise. Let your mama get up and come downstairs with me and have breakfast.'

'Thank you,' I mouth, grateful for a few quiet minutes to myself to wake up and shower before another full-on day begins. Thea stomps along the landing but takes Despina's hand. I need another hour or so to sleep, but I'm up now and conscious of Despina getting everything ready for breakfast and keeping an eye on Thea without any help from me. I envy Alekos' ability to sleep regardless of what's happening around him.

I shut myself in the bathroom and run the shower until it's lukewarm. I step in and let the water pummel my body. If only it was as easy as this to wash away worries… I shampoo and condition my hair, rub myself dry, clean my teeth and return to my bedroom and a still snoring Alekos.

Everyone who's coming to the wedding has now arrived. Breakfast has been cleared away, all the guest rooms occupied and Thea is on her last day at pre-school before breaking up for the long summer. I take the opportunity to relax and head to the pool with my book. It seems it's the same idea that pretty much everyone has. Mum, Jocelyn, Kim, Pamela and Candy are relaxing on the sunloungers along one side of the pool.

'Finally,' Mum says, pushing her sunglasses down her nose to look at me. 'I was wondering when you were going to take some time out.'

'Thought I'd best take the opportunity while I can.' I settle myself on a sunlounger alongside Kim and Pamela and facing Candy, Mum and Jocelyn. 'Where's Robert and everyone else?'

'He's taken the kids to the beach with Ben and Vicky.' Mum unscrews a pot of nail varnish and starts painting her nails fuchsia pink. 'Where's Alekos?'

'Rehearsing with the band in the guest lounge.'

'Ah yes,' Mum says, glancing up from her toenails. 'We invited Katrina to join us but she said she was going to go with Demetrius to listen to them.'

I settle back and open my book. I start reading, blocking out the conversation. I catch occasional snippets, something about Kim never believing Mum would ever get married. The book's a light-hearted romance set in Cornwall and marketed as a perfect beach read. Perfect for reading by a pool beneath blue skies and the Mediterranean sun. Mum says something about never having trusted men until she met Robert. I realise how much she's changed and how much happier she is now thanks to him and finally letting go of Elliot. I return to my book and its picture-postcard perfect Cornwall cottage setting, missing the gist of Jocelyn's reply.

'I don't trust men any more,' Candy says. I glance up again from my book. She stretches her long tanned legs out on her sunlounger and her red-painted toenails gleam in the sunshine. 'I've been burnt too many times and refuse to make the same mistake again.'

'Why sleep with Ben then?' Mum as always gets straight to the point. I drop my sunglasses down over my eyes and pretend to read my book, not wanting to get involved in what

I'm sure will be a heated conversation, but too distracted and intrigued to stop listening.

'There's nothing wrong with having some fun, but getting married and having kids with someone without really knowing them first wasn't such a great idea.'

Jocelyn smooths down the towel covering her sunlounger. 'Oh I don't know. My husband and I met when we were in our early twenties and got married after only a few months. We're still together and happy after forty-two years. It can work.'

'I think it's probably a generational thing,' Mum says. 'I mean in the sixties and seventies it was less usual than it is now for couples to live together. You were expected to get married first. Not that I ever heeded that advice, much to the disappointment of my parents.'

'That and the fact you had an affair with their married best friend.'

I nearly drop my book. I can't believe Jocelyn just said that.

Mum laughs it off. 'Thanks for bringing that up, Jocelyn. Always nice to be reminded of my failures as a daughter.'

'Leila, I didn't mean it like that. I don't know where that came from…'

Mum waves her hand. 'I'm teasing you. Don't worry, it's the truth, and it wasn't the last affair I had either. But hey, I've grown up, moved on and settled down. This is the all new me. But Candy, back then, unless you were a rebel like me, you were expected to get married, so people married young. I think you settling down with Lee when you were what? Twenty-four? Twenty-five?'

'Twenty-five.'

'Is unusual for nowadays. I say, have fun but don't go rushing into anything serious without being sure it's what you want and it's *who* you want.'

'Also,' Jocelyn says, rubbing sunscreen on her arms. 'Back then people worked harder at their marriage than couples do now.'

I know Candy's going to snap before she even opens her mouth.

'Are you seriously suggesting I should have stuck with my husband and worked on our marriage while he was cheating on me with another woman?'

'Well no, I wasn't commenting on you, Candy, and an affair breaking apart a marriage is completely different to someone filing for divorce because they've grown apart. Marriage is hard; there are arguments, difficult times; disappointing times. But there's the tendency nowadays that if things get tough, people take the easy route and walk away instead of really trying to make it work.' Jocelyn reaches across from her sunlounger and lays her hand on Candy's arm. 'Honestly, I wasn't meaning you, Candy.'

'I know.' She wedges her sunglasses into her hair that looks even blonder in the sunshine. 'Trust me, if it was anything other than him having an affair, I would have worked my arse off to make our marriage work for Jake and Holly. But him screwing around for months and having absolutely no intention of ending the affair when I found out was unforgivable.'

'I couldn't agree with you more.' Mum picks up her glass of Prosecco and takes a sip. 'Once that step's been taken I don't think there's any way back from an affair. I'm only saying this from the other side, being the other woman. If they can cheat like that, then their wives are well shot of them. Or vice versa if it's the woman who's the one who's having the affair. That's why I'm proud of you, Sophie, working so hard to make your relationship with Alekos work.'

Without wanting to be, I'm drawn into the conversation, one that I don't really want to be a part of, particularly after the way things have been playing on my mind since Aphrodite arrived.

I glance at Mum over the top of my book. 'Mum, I know what I did was wrong but I didn't cheat on Alekos in the way that Lee cheated on Candy.'

'Really, Leila,' Candy says, turning on her side to face Mum. 'Ben and Sophie didn't even get to third base, they hardly cheated.'

'What's third base?' Jocelyn frowns.

I put my book down and look at Candy. 'You and Ben have been discussing me and him? I told you I messed around with him but I didn't tell you exactly what we did. He told you, didn't he?'

I can hear Mum and Kim's hushed voices explaining to Jocelyn about third base and Jocelyn's surprised, 'Oh, well, I never knew that.'

Candy scrambles to sit up. 'Sophie, I'm sorry… After you told me you and Ben had a thing, I just kinda felt a bit odd about being with him knowing that you had too.' Her cheeks flush. 'Or rather not knowing exactly how you'd been together.'

'So you asked him if he'd had sex with me?'

'I wanted to be sure, that was all.'

I pick up my book and stand up. 'So neither of you,' I say, looking between Candy and Mum, 'trusted me when I said so many times that we didn't have sex. And no, we didn't get to third base – it was hardly even second base.' I look at Jocelyn. 'Ask the others to explain what that involves.'

I scoop up my towel and walk away, around the edge of the pool, Candy calling out, 'Sophie' as I go and Mum saying, 'Leave her to calm down for a bit.' I turn the corner, past Arthur's end guest room and out through the gate until I'm in the courtyard. I head towards the villa.

'Afternoon, Sophie.'

Arthur makes me jump; I hadn't noticed him quietly sitting in the shade of the olive tree, a notebook and pen on the table in front of him, a frappé in his hand.

'It's unusual to not have seen you all day; you must have been busy,' he says.

I stop and walk over to him. 'I was, but I've just been by

the pool.'

'Is everything okay?'

'Yes.'

He frowns. 'Really? You seem a little... stressed.'

'I probably am.'

'It's a lot of people to host for ten days.'

'It's not just that,' I sigh. 'The past is being dragged up and I'd quite like it to remain where it is – in the past.'

'Ah, I can understand that. That's the problem of being surrounded by family and friends for any length of time, tensions begin to bubble up. Anything you want to talk about?'

'Not really.' The midday sun beats down on me, the backs of my bare legs taking the brunt of the heat. 'I made a bad decision a few years back and it seems to be haunting me. Everyone can't stop talking about it and assuming there was more to it than there really was.'

'Man trouble?'

'Isn't it always?' I say. 'I'm okay though; just got a little annoyed with the assumptions the people closest to me were making. I guess I'm also embarrassed by what I did. I was in my twenties, frustrated with my life in Greece, frustrated with Alekos not standing up to his mother, not taking any initiative.' I wave my arms around the courtyard towards the villa and guest rooms. 'What a difference a few years makes.' I neatly fold the towel I'm holding across my arm. 'There you go, you managed to get me talking after all.'

Arthur laughs. 'I'm a good listener, that's why.'

'Well, I'm going to do something else for a bit, clear my head. If you're not going to your room, I'll change your bedding and towels.'

'Thank you, Sophie. I think I might go and sit out in the garden, so please, my room will be free of me for a couple of hours at least.'

'Great, I'll do that now before Thea gets back from pre-school and I get distracted.'

'As long as you're okay.' Arthur picks up his fountain pen.

'Don't go writing anything I've said down in that notebook of yours.' I grin.

He holds his hands up. 'As if I would.' He taps his fingers on the side of his head and winks. 'I just store everything up here for possible future use. You never know where inspiration can come from.'

I leave Arthur, feeling less annoyed. Maybe I'm being oversensitive and shouldn't worry about what anyone else thinks happened between me and Ben. It is in the past after all. That kiss in Norfolk took me by surprise, but I know how I feel about him now, and I also know the truth about what happened between us. There's no need to defend myself. And so what if Candy asked questions? After all, she's the one who's now sleeping with a man who once had a thing for her best friend, and according to him still does.

Chapter Twenty-Six

As I reach the villa, music filters into the courtyard from the guest lounge. Alekos is strumming his guitar and Aphrodite's melodic voice blends with it seamlessly. I head in the opposite direction, into the villa, which is blissfully quiet. I like how the retreat is just big enough to lose yourself in even when it's filled with people. I go into the utility room off the kitchen, take bedding from the airing cupboard and slip back outside.

Arthur has the guest room closest to the edge of the retreat, with the pool on one side and the main courtyard on the other and uninterrupted views of the Ionian Sea. He's headed out to the garden, to no doubt write in his favourite spot on the bench beneath the apple tree. I pull the sheet off the bed and put on a clean one, then bundle up the old one and leave it next to the door. I pick up a used coffee mug from the desk by the open window and hear voices talking in Greek – and Alekos' name.

Something stops me from leaving Arthur's room and walking out into the courtyard. I hover by the side of the door, hidden in the shadows of the wall, but I can see the back of Demetrius' head as he talks to Aphrodite. Her profile is stunning. Sleek and shiny black hair frames her face. Her cheek bones are emphasised with blusher and I can't stop watching her full lips as she talks.

'I fell in love with him on this island,' she replies to

Demetrius. They're not whispering but they are talking quietly.

'It was a good summer that first one. I always thought you and Alekos would...' Demetrius lowers his voice and I don't catch the rest of what he says.

'I thought so too.' Aphrodite turns from Demetrius and gazes in the direction of the sea. 'Especially after that night on the beach... I'll never forget it...'

I back further into Arthur's room. Still clutching the used coffee mug, I sit on the end of Arthur's bed and breathe deeply. I had an idea that the night at the beach with Alekos wasn't the first time that Alekos and Demetrius had taken girls to a secluded beach, but to hear it confirmed by Aphrodite makes it all too real.

They're still talking, their voices lowered, so I can't make out what they're saying. My Greek is good, but I'm not able to pick up words said in hushed tones. I catch sight of Aphrodite's silky black hair as she walks back up towards the room where they'd been rehearsing.

I wait a moment longer until I'm sure she's out of sight and Demetrius is on his own. I place the mug back on the desk and walk out of the room just as he's heading from the courtyard towards the pool.

'*Yasou*.' The cheerfulness of his voice is betrayed by a faltering smile.

I take his arm. 'Walk with me.' I steer him away from the guest rooms and across the courtyard to the gate. I release his arm and turn to him.

I breathe deeply, trying to prepare myself. 'I need to know something and I want you to tell me the truth. Were Alekos and Aphrodite together during the summers you two worked here before you met me and Candy?'

'They played in the band together, yes.'

'Together, Demetri – you know exactly what I mean by that.' I fold my arms and look at him. 'Were they sleeping together?'

'Did you hear us just then?'

'Demetri, answer the question.'

His eyes shift away but he nods. 'They had some fun and then he met you and that changed everything.'

'Why has he never told me about her? He knows about my ex-boyfriends; I know about his ex-girlfriends.' I pause and frown. 'I heard what she said, about falling in love with him. Was it the same beach they went to that you took me and Candy to? Was he in love with her? I actually know nothing about what he got up to on Cephalonia before he met me.'

Demetrius shrugs. 'I don't know, Sophie.'

'You don't know if he was in love or you don't want to tell me?'

'All I know is there's nothing to worry about. She's in the past. Until this week he'd not seen her for nearly four years.'

I'm about to accept that I'm reading more into this than there actually is, when the significance of Demetrius' words sink in.

'Wait, what do you mean he hasn't seen her for nearly four years? The last time he played in the band was before he met me. Eight years ago. Four years ago was before I was living here, when he was doing this place up…' I turn away and lean back on the gate. The view up the driveway is blurry through tears. 'Oh my God, I'm so stupid. All those months when he was here alone, he was far from lonely, was he?'

Demetrius' hand is on my shoulder. 'I wasn't here, Sophie, I don't know. But I know Alekos would never cheat on you.'

'Even though at the time he wasn't sure if I'd cheated on him?'

Demetrius holds up his hands. 'Sophie, I don't know.'

'But you were talking to her just then about the time you all spent on the island during those two summers. I heard, Demetri.'

'Sophie, it's really not what you think.'

'Don't go defending him. And anyway, how can I believe you? You spent those two summers here cheating on your girlfriend. You had a girlfriend back on the mainland yet still had sex with my best friend and treated her like shit. Why should I believe anything you say?'

I don't wait for him to answer. I storm off across the courtyard, putting as much distance as I can between myself and Demetrius and the blatant lies he's telling on behalf of Alekos.

Chapter Twenty-Seven

I go into the guest lounge and walk right up to Alekos strumming his guitar. 'I need to talk to you. Now.'

The drummer and other guitarist are here, plus Katrina's still in the room, lounging on the sofa watching them play. I catch the concern on her face as she looks between me and Alekos.

'We're in the middle of a rehearsal,' Aphrodite says.

I don't look at her, but keep my gaze firmly focused on Alekos. 'If you had time to stop and talk to Demetrius then Alekos has time to talk to me.'

It's Alekos' turn to frown. He unhooks his guitar from his shoulder and leans it against the sofa.

He turns to Aphrodite. 'Give me a minute.'

Without waiting for him, I turn and stalk from the room, back into the courtyard and sunshine.

'That was rude,' he says, joining me, his arms crossed, still frowning.

'So is not being honest about your real relationship with Aphrodite.'

His eyes momentarily leave mine. 'It was in the past; I didn't think it was important.'

He takes my arm and leads me further away from the open door where the rehearsal has gone quiet. I'm sure they're all trying to listen to our conversation. The courtyard remains empty, with only the sound of splashing, laughter and screeches filtering across from the pool.

Alekos perches on the edge of the table in the shade of the olive tree. I stand facing him, my whole body tense, anger and confusion coursing through me along with annoyance at why I didn't realise the connection they had long before now, and guilt for the mistakes I've made. Alekos is as handsome and sexy as the day I first laid eyes on him. As for Aphrodite… how could he not have fallen in love with someone as beautiful and alluring as her?

'Sophie, once I met you and asked you to come live with me in Greece, it never seemed important to tell you that I'd had a relationship with the lead singer of the band. It was in the past. As far as I was concerned I was with you and I wasn't returning to Cephalonia.'

'You told me about other girlfriends though.'

He wafts away an insect. 'I didn't mean to not tell you, it just never seemed important. Anyway, how do you know?'

'I overheard Demetrius and Aphrodite talking. I asked Demetrius. He was adamant you and her are in the past, except the past isn't that long ago, is it?'

Alekos' frown deepens.

'I get that you and Aphrodite were together during those summers you and Demetrius worked here. I have no problem with that, I just wished you'd told me. What I have a problem with is you being with her while you were over here alone, working on this place.'

He holds my gaze. 'I did see her during that time, but we were never together, not in the way you're assuming we were.' He steps towards me and takes my hands.

'How do you expect me to believe that? I mean look at her.' I tug my hands away from his. 'She's beautiful, she oozes sexiness. The chemistry between you two when you were playing the other night was obvious. How can I believe you weren't with her in the months before me and Thea came over?'

'And how do I know you didn't sleep with Ben?'

'Because I told you everything – the whole truth. I've always been upfront with you about what happened.'

'Exactly like I'm telling you the truth about Aphrodite now.' He folds his arms across his chest, his biceps bulging from beneath his T-shirt.

'You can go ask Ben if you still don't believe me. Shall I go and ask Aphrodite the same thing?'

He sighs and looks down. And in that moment, I know. 'You did, didn't you? Oh my God, Alekos; I may have made bad choices in the past but this… I was pregnant with Thea. You'd bought this place for *us* to be a family.'

He moves closer to me again and I take a step back, needing to put a physical distance between us.

'Sophie, it's not what you think, really it isn't. I just don't trust that she'll tell you the truth – and by the truth I mean that we were together once but not together during those months I was alone here. Not in that way.'

'How convenient for you – a woman who won't tell the truth either way.'

'He is telling you the truth.'

She makes me jump. We both turn to see Aphrodite standing halfway between us and the villa. Her feet are bare, a long ankle-grazing skirt wafting in the gentle breeze. Her silky top with spaghetti straps is low cut, clinging in all the right places, showing off her tanned skin and toned shoulders to perfection. I feel unbelievably inadequate compared to her.

She walks across the paving and joins us beneath the tree.

'And how am I supposed to believe you?' I meet her deep brown eyes framed by long black lashes.

'What have I got to gain by lying to you?'

'Oh, I don't know,' I put my hands on my hips, 'the possibility of breaking us up.'

'And why would I want that? Why would I want to be with a man who's madly in love with someone else?'

I open my mouth to say something but stop, as the

meaning of her words filters through. Alekos is quiet, listening to Aphrodite but watching me.

Aphrodite moves closer and brushes her fingers against my arm. 'Walk with me. Please.'

She's not someone you can say no to. She's the type of person everyone notices, everyone looks at. I've seen the way people have been drawn to her over the past couple of days – men and women alike. With a glance at Alekos, I follow her across the courtyard in silence. She opens the gate, avoiding the gravel and sidestepping on to the grass. I follow her on to the sandy path.

Before Birdsong Villas disappears, I glance back. Alekos remains perched on the edge of the table, resting back on his arms. I wonder what he's thinking as he stares upwards into the branches of the tree. I focus on my footing as the path curves downwards.

Aphrodite doesn't walk far, but heads off the path to sit on a grassy ridge. She stretches her legs out, her bare feet crossed, the deep red of her painted toenails bright against the sand and dried grasses. I sit next to her, the grass scratchy against my bare legs.

'I love this island,' she says, gazing out to the sea that glints in the sunshine. 'Despite travelling so much for work, Cephalonia will always have my heart. It's where I grew up, where my home is,' she glances at me, 'when I get the chance to come back here, that is.'

I pull my legs up and tuck my hands around my knees. It's peaceful, and apart from occasional shouts and laughter from the pool, the only other sounds are the buzz of bees or the squawk of birds.

'Alekos has never told me about the two of you,' I say after a while. 'And the only reason I can think of is because there was something going on between the two of you after we got together.'

She sighs and leans back on her hands. 'I have memories of me as a thirty-something woman and Alekos as an eager twenty-something man. Pretty sweet memories. There was a time when we were together romantically, but the moment Alekos set eyes on you that changed. We've written songs together about love, but the love he now writes about is between you and him, no one else. I understand and respect that.' She tucks a loose hair behind her ear. 'It doesn't mean I've been happy about it or didn't try and lead him astray, but trust me when I say he's a decent man. He's never cheated on you despite me giving him every opportunity to do so.'

I have a lump in my throat, tears threatening to spill. 'So, when Alekos was here on his own four years ago…'

'Nothing happened. And I wanted it to, that's the truth. We did see each other and I kissed him, but he stopped me. And then we talked. He talked about you and I came to accept I no longer had a chance with him, that he was yours and always will be.'

A tear trickles down my cheek and I wipe it away. Regardless of what I put him through when I was in Norfolk, and an ex-lover and woman as beautiful as Aphrodite chasing him when he was here alone, he never faltered.

Aphrodite sits up and brushes off the dried grass stuck to her palms. 'I've never wanted to settle down and have children. My life is too good and maybe I'm too selfish to give up my freedom and all the things I enjoy. If the right man comes along then I wouldn't say no to getting married, but he'd have to be someone very special.'

'Was Alekos the right man?'

She looks at me through long eyelashes. 'There was a time when I hoped he would be. But no, he wasn't because he was never properly in love with me. We were thrown together through a love of music and enjoyment of playing together. He was never serious about me. We had fun, hung out, made music, had sex. It was me who chased him. He was young, single, having the time of his life…'

'And you're beautiful.'

'He loves you, Sophie. I know this because I tried my

hardest, trust me, to seduce him when he was here on his own. And he kept saying no. If I can one day find a man half as decent as Alekos who wants to be with me, then I'll be a happy woman. Even if we'd had an affair, he'd never have truly been mine. His heart has always been yours.'

Chapter Twenty-Eight

I leave Aphrodite sitting, looking out at the view. My cheeks are tight from crying, yet I feel calmer than I have for days, the tension and worry dispersed by Aphrodite's words. All I want to do is find Alekos, put my arms around him and tell him how sorry I am for ever doubting him.

He's is no longer in the courtyard, but Mum is, striding across from the gate by the pool the moment that she sees me, a floaty kaftan covering her bikini, sunglasses wedged in her hair.

'I've been waiting for you. Alekos said you were talking to Aphrodite.' She reaches me. 'Everything okay? Alekos seemed worried.'

'Everything's fine. It will be fine.'

'Alekos said to meet him at the top of the drive. I'm going with Takis to pick up Thea later and I'll look after her this evening.'

'Okay great,' I say slowly, my head still spinning with the revelations of the past couple of hours. 'Where am I going?'

Mum shrugs. 'No idea, but Alekos said he's taking you somewhere special.'

I turn to go but Mum catches my hand. 'By the way, I'm sorry about earlier, around the pool. I'm sorry I doubted what you'd told me about you and Ben. As you well know, I can be a dick at times.'

'I know; you don't have to tell me that.'

She kisses my cheek. 'Go find Alekos. Get out of here; I'll look after Thea.'

Mum walks back towards the pool. I put my hands on my hips and gaze up at the deep blue sky. I have no idea where Alekos intends for us to go and I don't really care, I just want time alone with him. I smooth down my short summer skirt. I pace across the courtyard, nip into the villa, take my bag from the sideboard in the living area and head back outside.

I'm glad I don't bump into anyone on my way out of the retreat; even with so many people staying, it's been blissfully quiet today with everyone hungover from the night before, chilling out, sleeping, keeping to themselves. I walk up the driveway and spot our car at the top. Alekos is leaning against the side. He pushes away from it when he sees me, shoving his hands into the pockets of his knee-length shorts and strolling to meet me.

'Hey,' I say as we stop in front of each other.

His eyes search my face and I know in that moment, more so than even Aphrodite explaining things to me, that every word she said was true.

'I'm sorry I ever doubted you.'

He pulls me to him and I rest against the top of his chest, his strong arms enveloping me. I never want him to let me go. I never want to feel doubt again – either for the way he feels about me or how I feel about him.

It's a nearly two-hour drive to the beach. *Our beach.* The place where it all began. It's fitting really to be going back there after the conversation that's just played out. We don't talk much on the way, content to watch the scenery pass by: late spring flowers a riot of colour on the grass verges, lush green hillsides, and pretty houses with red-tiled roofs.

We park the car on the side of the road at the top of the cliff. Alekos takes a bag and his guitar from out of the boot. The boot slamming shut echoes loudly in the stillness of early evening.

'This is a bit different to arriving by boat,' I say, peering down the craggy cliff where steep wooden steps have been built into the cliff face, winding down to the beach at the bottom.

Holding the wooden rail, we slowly make our way down, Alekos leading. It was so much easier sailing to the beach without the thought of having to climb back up. The boat was utterly romantic. I remember we dropped anchor a little way from the shore and waded through the clear shallow water to the beautiful and desolate crescent beach.

We're not alone this time. A family are camped under the shade of an umbrella at the foot of the cliff. The two children, a few years older than Thea, splash about in the shallows with a blow-up lilo. We reach the pebbly sand and lay our towels out close to the sea, towards the middle of the beach and away from the family. The mother calling to the kids in Greek floats towards us and I presume they're locals or perhaps over from the mainland for a holiday.

We haven't brought much with us, only a bottle of chilled sweet red wine, a simple picnic tea of leftovers packed by Despina, and Alekos' guitar. We don't even have an umbrella, but the heat of the day has dispersed and although it's still warm the sun is beginning to dip making it pleasant to catch the last rays of the day.

Being with Alekos back on the beach is the same and yet not the same. I watch him skim a stone into the sea, his broad shoulders tensing. I still adore him as much and find him as good-looking and sexy as I did when I first laid eyes on him aboard *Artemis*. The difference now is we have years of getting to know each other behind us – back then I knew so little about him and he knew virtually nothing about me. I had no idea what the future held for us, that I'd drop everything in the UK and move to Greece to be with him. If I'd known how challenging and frustrating those first few years living with his parents at *O Kipos* would be, would I have done something as drastic as quitting my job, leaving my home and life behind for a man I barely knew? If I'd have known how different Alekos was going to be back under his parents' roof, would I have found him as attractive as when he was a free spirit on Cephalonia? Who knows. Perhaps we needed to go through the tough times to really appreciate what we have now? A beautiful home and successful business, an unexpected but much loved daughter and our freedom back. The second I saw Alekos at the airport when Thea was a few weeks old, I knew he had his spark back, he'd found his place and freedom away from the influence of his mother.

Even with the occasional shrieks from the Greek children, it's peaceful on the beach, with only the surf lapping the shore and the call of birds flying overhead. Birdsong Villas has been filled with people, chatter and laughter. The relative peace and quiet is refreshing. It's why I love running the creative retreat, it's the best of both worlds. The place always has interesting people staying but it retains a calmness with guests coming to enjoy that peace and quiet, to find time to write, paint, draw or whatever else they want to do. Having a couple of communal dinners each week is the perfect balance.

The family pack up, nod and say '*yasas*' as they walk past us and struggle up the steps with bags, umbrellas and lilos. The expectation of finally being alone weighs heavy in the air, particularly when Alekos returns from splashing in the shallows and grins at me. The sky is dusky. I switch on the torch and wedge it against a rock so the light spills across the sand and on to our towels. It's not quite the same as having a bonfire with flames flickering soft light across tanned skin.

But sex on the beach is not yet on the agenda. Alekos takes out his guitar and strums it while I pour us each a plastic cup of sweet red wine. I rest back on my hand and take a sip. As Alekos starts playing guilt floods through me about how I doubted him. My mistakes come crashing down around me and it's always because I've been hoping for something else, something better: whether it's been a real father instead of an imagined one when I was a child, or the desperation of a place of our own when I was living with Alekos at *O Kipos*. I even remember being in my early teens longing for a mother who didn't embarrass me like Mum did. I've always been fighting my life rather than simply enjoying each moment for what it is.

I close my eyes and listen to Alekos play. It's beautiful and melodic and his voice and the soulful guitar drifts into the air. I listen to the words, so meaningful, a beauty about them being sung in Greek. It's rare to hear him sing, only occasional snatched moments when he's working on a song out in the villa garden or sitting under the olive tree, his legs resting on the wooden table. I don't remember him playing a song just for me. The music ends. The rush of the waves on to the sand is once again the only sound. I open my eyes and we sit for a moment, him with his guitar in his lap, me facing him.

There are no words to describe the moment and the overwhelming love I have for him, so I don't say anything. I reach forward and take his guitar, laying it carefully back in its case. I move closer until our thighs are touching. I kiss him. Everything that's happened in the years since our first night together on this beach flashes through my mind, a snapshot of our life together, both the good and the bad. He tastes of the sweet red wine. His fingers dance across my bare back, sliding beneath the string of my bikini top and around to the front.

'I didn't think that family were ever going to leave,' he whispers, making his way with kisses from my lips down to my throat.

'As long as no one else turns up.' I caress my hands across his taut back, his skin hot against my fingertips.

'They won't, not now it's dark.'

These past few days have reignited something between us. The happy monotony of day-to-day life looking after Thea and running Birdsong Villas has been interrupted by time apart, faces from the past and fresh misunderstandings. We've been forced to confront and question once again how we feel about each other. Our relationship has always been both very simple because we've loved each other from almost the moment we met, yet it's been complicated by other people. This past week has proved that once again.

I'm still kissing him but my mind is wandering like crazy. All I want to do is lose myself in the moment.

Alekos pulls me on to his lap, so my legs are crossed behind him, and kisses the tops of my breasts.

I lift his chin with my finger until he's looking at me. 'Are we being silly trying to recapture that night? It can't be repeated that spontaneity, that passion.'

'It might be fun giving it a try.' He slides his hands up my thighs, tucking his fingers in the top of my bikini bottoms. He leans forward, gently pushing me down until I'm lying on my back. He tugs my bikini down and I shift position, half on half off the towel, the hard grains of sand digging into my bare skin.

'Ouch,' I say, wriggling to get comfortable, my skirt up round my waist and my bikini bottoms around my ankles.

'*Ti?*' He stops, his hands splayed in the sand on either of side of me. 'What, Sophie?'

'I've got stones digging in my back and I have a sandy bum now.' I hold my hands over my mouth to stifle a giggle.

Alekos laughs and sits down in the sand next to me. 'We're not drunk enough.'

'Or drunk on the excitement of it being our first time.' I sigh and pull my bikini bottoms back up, brushing off the sand stuck everywhere. 'We can't recapture that.'

I know we're both thinking about that night, our stomachs full of seafood cooked in the embers of the fire, the lamps on the boat casting shimmering light on to the dark still water of the Ionian Sea. It must have been uncomfortable lying down on the beach, but I don't remember anything about that apart from desire for Alekos and being totally and utterly lost in the moment.

Alekos reaches for my hand and takes it in his.

'I'm sorry I never told you about Aphrodite.' He rubs his thumb along the side of my hand. 'I didn't mean to not say anything about her, it's just I was never sure what our relationship was and then I met you. It was easier to not bring her up, but I get how it seemed like I was hiding something.'

I look at him, his face shadowed, the torch light on the sand rather than us. We've been foolish in the past and guilty of not being open and frank with each other, hiding our feelings and letting the worries, distrust and paranoia build and build until we made an issue bigger than it really needed to be. It's about time we learnt from past mistakes.

'Did you ever bring her here? Aphrodite?'

Alekos shakes his head. 'No.'

'She mentioned a beach when she was talking to Demetrius…'

'We slept on a beach near Fiskardo after a party not long after we got together.'

'But there were other girls you brought here…'

'Yeah, there were. Like there were other guys for you.' He holds my gaze.

I can't argue with that, although the other men in my life – and there really weren't that many of them – were mostly long-term boyfriends. The girls Alekos is talking about I know were mostly flings. Pretty young tourists he and Demetrius took out on the boat.

'Me and Demetrius had fun and Aphrodite liked me and I liked her. We messed around a bit…'

I glance at him.

'Okay a lot… but it was nothing like the connection we had.'

'Not for you maybe, but it was for her.'

He turns away. 'I was twenty-four, away from home for the first time, and me and Demetrius enjoyed ourselves. Aphrodite swept into my life, offered me a place in the band, was sexy and seductive.' He glances at me. 'There was no reason to say no. I didn't want more than a fling and I figured she didn't either. I know she's older than me but I got the impression she wasn't looking for someone to settle down with either, she was simply up for having a good time. Maybe I was wrong.'

From my conversation with Aphrodite, I know Alekos is wrong and she's hidden her true feelings from him. Even if she didn't want to settle down, she still wanted a boyfriend who was faithful, who hadn't fallen in love with someone else. I look out over the darkening Ionian Sea, the gold and pink of the setting sun reflecting on the water. I see things from Aphrodite's point of view. She may be an independent woman with no burning desire to settle down or have children, a woman who wants to maintain her lifestyle and freedom but that didn't mean she hadn't fallen in love, or didn't want someone to commit themselves to her. Alekos was perfect – young and carefree, seemingly not wanting a serious relationship either. They played and wrote music together; there was the possibility of them sharing a life touring, making music, a casual relationship, the perfect man for Aphrodite. Until he met a younger woman, fell in love and within a few days of meeting asked her to move to Greece to live with him.

'You never actually told her that you and her were over, did you?'

Alekos shakes his head and releases my hand. 'No and I was wrong to not be upfront with her. It always seemed so casual – we hooked up over two summers and the couple of times the band played in Thessaloniki when I was back at *O Kipos*. We got on, we had fun, played gigs, had sex…' He stops and looks at me. 'You really want me to talk about this?'

'Yes, I do. I'm okay with you and her being together – it was you not telling me the extent of your relationship that made me fear you'd been messing around with her behind my back while I was pregnant with Thea.' It's my turn to pause. 'It was a messed up and confusing time for both of us. I did things I regret but I always loved you. I was frustrated by circumstances and you being so different when we were living with your parents to how you were when we first met here.'

'I felt guilt over Aphrodite and the way I ended our relationship with no explanation. Those months I was here getting the villa ready for you and Thea, I purposefully reconnected with her but to apologise and move on from her guilt-free. She wanted a lot more.' He pulls me closer and takes my hands, squeezing them tight and looking at me with an intensity that sends a shiver through me. 'I didn't want more. It's always been you. Only ever been you.'

I rest my forehead against his. 'I know, she told me. I believed her and I believe you.'

The sun has disappeared completely by the time we pack up and puff our way up the uneven steps by torchlight to the road at the top. I glance back. The beach has been swallowed by inky blackness, but memories of our time remain. We put everything into the boot and get into the car. Parked up on the grass verge on an empty road far from the nearest town or village, the stillness and darkness is all encompassing. The clear black sky is decorated with stars. I love how there are no street lights to taint the night.

Alekos turns the key but doesn't start the engine.

He turns to me. 'We might not have recaptured our first night together but we needed this time alone. I'm sorry for causing so much confusion.'

'I'm sorry for doubting you.'

His hand clasps the back of my neck and he kisses me. I kiss him back, the uncomfortableness of our embrace on the beach replaced by overwhelming desire. He reaches beneath his seat and pushes it backwards to make space. Still kissing him I scramble over the gear stick and slide on to his lap, my legs tucked either side of him, squashed against the door. Alekos lifts my top up and over my head, dropping it on to the passenger seat. I undo the button and zip on his shorts and he slips his hands beneath my skirt.

'You have sand everywhere.'

I laugh and kiss him. It doesn't matter that we were unable to recapture a moment from the past when all we need to do is make new memories.

It's late by the time we arrive back home. Aphrodite and the band have left ages ago, back to their hotel in the village and I'm glad there's no chance of bumping into her. I have no desire to parade what Alekos and I have in front of her, especially after she was so generous and open with me. I assume Thea's in bed and probably Despina and Takis have called it a night too. The air is filled with a thudding beat floating across from the pool. It sounds like nineties Brit-pop; I can only imagine that's Candy's and Mum's influence.

With the car parked on the grass on the edge of the lane, we shut the gate behind us. Alekos catches my hand in his as we walk together.

Robert wanders across the courtyard towards his room but heads our way when he spots us.

'Your mum said you'd gone out,' he says, smiling. 'You had a good evening?'

'Yeah, it was great, thanks.' I clasp Alekos' hand tighter.

'Your mum's still round by the pool with her friends – Vicky, Ben and Candy too, and your friends, Alekos. Quite the party. Somehow, despite the noise, all the kids are in bed – think they're exhausted after a day of fun and sunshine.'

'You're heading to bed now too?'

'Oh yes, I'm feeling my age – Leila has a fair few years on me. Plus we're getting up early tomorrow and I'm taking her out to the winery Aphrodite recommended. Need to be up early.'

'Well, good luck getting Mum up on time. Have a lovely morning.'

'Night, Sophie.' He kisses me on the cheek and clamps a hand on Alekos' shoulder. 'Night, Alekos.'

We watch him walk off, back across the courtyard and up

the stairs to his room.

'I know I've always had my reservations about Ben, but Robert's a decent guy.'

I nod. 'He really is.'

'You want to go round and join them?' Alekos motions towards the direction of the pool.

I shake my head. 'No, I don't really fancy seeing anyone. I want to spend the rest of the night with you.'

Chapter Twenty-Nine

I'm in the kitchen preparing some of the salads for the wedding party tomorrow when I hear a car crunch down the drive. I wipe my hands on the towel, surprised that Mum and Robert are back this early. I step outside into the sunny courtyard, glad of a break and thinking how much I could do with a chilled glass of wine.

A taxi stops in front of the closed gate. The driver gets out, opens the boot and takes out a small suitcase. A neatly dressed woman with sunglasses tucked into the neckline of her blouse, emerges from the back seat.

She's achingly familiar, even though I don't know her. I have seen her before though, years ago and only from a distance, yet I still recognise her. Even out of context and thousands of miles away from home, I recognise her. It takes a moment though, to register first confusion of exactly who she is and then shock at why on earth she's here.

I stalk across the courtyard as the woman closes the gate behind her and the taxi drives away. She turns and I stop in front of her, my arms folded. We don't say anything for a moment – it's hard to find words as I take in her long red hair that falls in waves around her shoulders like mine does, the same green eyes and freckled skin, hers paler than mine but then I've been living in Greece for years. She's a little shorter than me and I know she's twelve years older, evident in the laughter lines around her eyes. She looks like our father and I look like her.

'Hello, Sophie,' she says, in a quiet voice laced with a northern accent like Elliot's. 'I'm Amy.'

I didn't know her name, in fact I know nothing about her apart from what I'd secretly witnessed when Candy and I had driven up to Elliot's house on the edge of the Peak District and I'd seen her with him. She'd had a toddler with her at the time, so I know she has at least one child but that's the extent of my knowledge of her. She's someone I'm related to, someone I look very much like but who I know nothing about.

'I only found out about you recently,' she says, stepping forward and taking my hands in hers.

I snatch my hands away.

'Why are you here? How… I don't understand?'

The sun beats down on my shoulders; it's midday and the hottest part of the day and I should be inside preparing food for tomorrow. There's still so much to do and now this. This person's walked right into my life, someone I thought I'd never meet.

'I didn't know what else to do.' Amy shifts her handbag higher on her shoulder. She has a small wheeled suitcase next to her, as if she's planning to stay for a while. 'After Dad admitted the truth about his affair with your mum, and your grandma said she was getting married, I knew I had to try and see her.'

'Woah, slow down.' I rub my hand across my hot forehead. 'You know about the affair? I didn't think anyone did apart from my bloody grandparents.'

'The whole truth came out after my mum left Dad.'

I frown, thinking I've misheard her. 'Wait, your mum's left him?'

'Dad's been living a lie his whole married life. He didn't think Mum had a clue about his affair, but she did. She stuck around for us, maybe hoping that one day he'd give up on loving your mum. He never did. So she looked elsewhere for the kind of love Dad has for Leila, and she found it.'

Tension courses through my body, rooting me to the spot. Panic builds from the pit of my stomach mixed with a desire to punch the lookalike stranger standing in front of me. Ben is up a ladder on the far side of the courtyard stringing lights along the roof of the guest accommodation; Kim walks across, a book in one hand, a frappé in the other as she makes her way towards the pool. Even from this far away I can see her frown as she does a double take, falters as if to say something then decides against it and carries on walking until she's out of sight.

'Say something, Sophie.'

'I think you need to leave.'

'I'm not going anywhere until I've spoken to your mum.'

The panic rises higher, relief that Mum's out with Robert, yet I know that she'll be back soon and I need this woman gone. 'You have a fucking nerve.'

'Mama, Mama, Mama!' Thea skids around the corner of the villa from the garden, running full pelt across the courtyard. Despina's puffing behind her yelling '*sega sega*', telling her to slow down. Thea careers into my legs, hugging me tight and nearly knocking me off balance.

She looks up at the woman and frowns. 'She looks like you.'

My half-sister meets my eyes. Despina reaches us, breathing deeply, her fully made up face gleaming, her cheeks flushed.

'*Signomi*,' she says, smiling at us both. She takes Thea's hand, bends down and scolds her. She stands back up and is about to walk away when she lowers her sunglasses and looks again at the woman.

'*Poios einai aftos*?' Despina asks, her perfectly plucked eyebrows creasing even more.

'Nobody,' I reply in Greek.

Despina's nostrils flare but she gives a small nod. She's

not a person to back down easily, but maybe for once she senses that I don't intend to be argued with.

'*Ela*, Thea.' She takes her granddaughter's hand.

'I'm Amy, Sophie's half-sister.' Amy holds out her hand and Despina shakes it, her frown creasing more.

Despina turns to me. 'Sophie?'

'It's a long story and one I'm not going into right now.' I say in Greek, fixing her with a look, daring her to question me further. She doesn't.

Thea tugs on Despina's hand, trying to pull her away, not really listening to what's going on.

'Yiayia, Mama, play with me,' Thea whines.

'This is your daughter?' Amy says, smiling down at Thea.

Apart from forcibly trying to remove her from the retreat, what choice do I have? Ben's out of earshot but he's securing the end of the lights and will be down soon. I don't want him to meet Amy and have to explain to him what her relationship is to me and Mum.

'Come inside and we'll talk.' I turn to Despina and switch to Greek. 'Can you please look after Thea for a bit longer?'

'*Fysika*,' Despina says, with a forced smile. She turns to Amy and says in thickly accented English, 'Nice to meet you.'

'Mama, can you come and play?'

'Not right now, Thea,' I say. 'Go with Yiayia and I'll find you in a bit.'

'Please, Mama.'

'Thea, not now, be a good girl please.'

I walk towards our villa, Amy following. Thea trails after Despina back around the villa towards the garden, her lips pinched. The house is empty. Everyone is either having a day out visiting the local winery, are down on the beach or, like Alekos, getting some last minute bits for tomorrow's wedding. Only Kim, Jocelyn and Pamela stayed behind to relax by the pool and Ben offered to help put up some extra lights. I'm supposed to be cooking while Despina and Takis take turns helping me and looking after Thea. Meeting my half-sister for the first time was not on the agenda for the day before my mum gets married.

'You have a beautiful place.'

'We really don't have to make small talk.' I close the doors leading to the courtyard behind us. I lean against the shiny white kitchen island that has views both ways towards the courtyard and through the living area to the garden, and wait for her to say something else.

She leaves her suitcase and bag by the patio doors and walks across the kitchen, her eyes flicking around the room, taking it all in. She runs a hand along the back of the sofa that faces the garden, turns to me and leans against it.

'I only found out you existed less than a month ago.' She holds on to the edge of the sofa as if to steady herself. Her nails are neat and painted a dark red and I like her knee-length skirt and navy capped-sleeve blouse that looks like it's from FatFace. 'I'm forty-four and have only now discovered I have a half-sister. Our whole lives – my younger brother's and sister's included – have been turned upside down in the last few weeks because of what our father did thirty-three odd years ago.'

I remain rooted to the spot, anger simmering inside me as I watch Amy, waiting for her to continue. She grew up with the father I longed for, but he'd chosen his wife and children over Mum and me, the daughter he was too ashamed about to tell his family the truth.

I push away from the work surface. 'The first and last time I met him he was adamant that you and the rest of your family was never to find out about me or his affair with my mum. So how the hell do you all know?'

'You've met him?' Amy frowns and sits down on the back of the sofa. 'I had no idea.'

'Just the once, actually that's a lie, apparently he met me when I was a little kid at my grandparents' house but I was too young to remember.' I step towards her. 'But you're not answering my question. How did you all find out? I think as far as your father was concerned he was going to take his dirty secret to his grave.'

'Mum's always known. She's not stupid. She's best friends with your grandma. She knew about the strained relationship your grandma has with your mum. She knew Anna had a granddaughter who she never saw – no photos about the place of you either. I think she was content enough having a relatively happy and stable life with Dad and brushed any doubts she had about his relationship with your mum under the carpet. Until she fell in love with someone else and started her own affair.

'She met someone two years ago, they became friends, then more. He's widowed, adores Mum and so she decided to leave Dad after nearly fifty years of marriage. When Dad confronted her and tried to stop her from leaving, she turned it on him and everything unravelled. Everything. His affair, your mum, you.'

I shake my head, turn away from Amy and look out of the closed doors to the courtyard where Ben is putting the ladder away.

'Leila is the love of his life, not my mum.'

Amy's words hit me hard. I turn back to her.

'And you're okay with that?'

'I wasn't, but I've grown to understand why she is, plus his reasoning to do the decent thing and stick with us and Mum.'

'Oh the decent thing, what a charmer he is. Yeah, such a decent man after screwing an eighteen-year-old, getting her pregnant and deciding to wash his hands of her to protect himself. It was never about you or your mum, it was all about him.'

'Sophie, I understand you're angry.'

'Fucking right I am.'

'But you don't know my dad…'

'And why do you think that is?' I storm over and stand in the middle of the room, glaring at her. 'I know enough to know he's only ever had his best interests at heart to the detriment of my mum, and to the lesser extent me. Why you thought it was a good idea to come out here and stir things up, is beyond me.'

Amy runs her hands down the front of her skirt and holds my gaze. 'I know he wouldn't have come out here himself, so I came on his behalf. I'd never have forgiven myself if I didn't at least try.' She moves closer to me. 'He loves Leila and this is the last chance he has of making her realise what she means to him. She didn't move on from him for so many years…'

I point outside to where everything's set up for tomorrow's wedding party. 'What do you think all this is if it isn't Mum moving on? She's getting married tomorrow to the first decent guy she's ever been with. Your father cheated on his wife and didn't have the guts or decency to be honest to your mother or true to his heart, so why the hell would my mum give him the time of day now?'

'Because I think she still loves him,' Amy says quietly.

I take a deep breath and fight back tears. 'You don't even know her. *He* was the one who made her promise to never come back into her life and she's kept that promise. Yet it's always been him interfering in Mum's life, never allowing her to forget about him, to get over him. How is any of this right or fair? My mum is getting married tomorrow – what the hell do you think you're playing at? You know nothing about my mum or what she's been through. He screwed around with her and has messed about with her emotions for long enough and now he's doing it through you. He's a coward, you know.'

'Maybe.'

'There's no maybe about it.' I put my hands on my hips. 'I've seen the emotional hell he put her through for years. She never let anyone get close because she was still hung up on your father. Instead she went for men who meant nothing, men who she knew wouldn't want a serious relationship. She's finally with someone decent and loving who treats her right and loves her despite her flaws, and that bastard is still interfering with her life. You're interfering. You don't understand the pain you're going to cause her if you stay.'

'And you don't understand the pain my father's dealing with.'

'No.' I shake my head. 'You don't get to do that – whatever pain he's feeling doesn't count. He made his choice a long time ago and neither of you are going to get to mess things up for Mum now.'

'Well, if you feel that strongly about your mum, then understand I feel just as strongly about my dad. I love him and I can't stand to see the pain he's going through and the regret he has for making the wrong choice all those years ago.'

'What about your mum? If he'd left your mum for mine, how'd you have felt about him then? Seems this is a no-win situation for anyone. He cheated. My mum was well aware she was messing about with a married man. For fuck's sake he was a much older married man and a friend of the family. Both of them were in the wrong and have had to live with that decision ever since. Mum has washed her hands of him, as have I.'

'Don't you think your mum should be the one to make that decision? There was a time when she loved him, and Dad rightly or wrongly has always loved her. He still loves her – he's blatantly said so and isn't even fighting for his and mum's marriage. You honestly believe that your mum doesn't love him?'

I clench my fists and turn away from her, yank open the fridge and pour myself a glass of cold water. I take a mouthful wanting to calm down and cool the rage burning in my chest.

'Sophie?'

I spin round, knocking over my glass of water as I do, splashing it on to the work surface. It drips on to the tiled floor.

I meet Mum's eyes. She closes the door to the courtyard behind her.

'Where's Robert?' My heart thuds at the thought of him

walking in.

'Gone up to our room. I came to find you.' Her eyes travel from me to Amy and she falters, her frown intensifying as she steps further into the room.

'Sophie, what the hell is going on?'

Amy turns to me. 'Will you please let me talk to your mum?'

'Oh my God,' Mum says slowly. 'You're Elliot's daughter, aren't you?'

I can see no way out of this besides letting them talk. I'll leave it up to Mum to tell Amy where to go and then I'll have the pleasure of watching Mum send her packing.

'Mum, I'm so sorry, she turned up wanting to talk to you.' I take Mum's bag from her and place it on the counter. She looks in shock, her sun-kissed skin pale. I turn to Amy. 'You can go upstairs – no one will disturb you up there. My room's the last one on the right.'

Without saying another word, Mum steps past me and walks up the stairs.

Amy turns back and says, 'Thank you,' before following Mum.

'You've given me no choice,' I mutter to her retreating back.

Chapter Thirty

There's no sign of Robert when I emerge into sunshine, so I presume he's still up in his and Mum's room, hopefully having a siesta – a habit he's happily taken up over the past few days. I glance up at my bedroom window and wonder how on earth Mum will react to what Amy has to say. The feeling of panic remains in my chest, particularly when I realise the time. Not only do I still have food to prepare but I need to go and collect the wedding cake from the village. I have no idea what to do, what to make of her turning up unannounced like this. Her timing is beyond awful.

The courtyard is empty; Ben's cleared away the ladder and has no doubt gone to find Candy. I don't think Alekos is back yet with Demetrius and Katrina, and I'm sure Arthur is either tucked away somewhere quietly writing or having a snooze in his room. I'm thankful it's quiet and there aren't many people around. So far I can't hear anything from my room – no shouting from Mum at least.

I glance at my watch and curse. I jog across the courtyard and around the corner of the guest rooms only to find the pool empty. The door to Ben's room is closed, so I assume he's in there with Candy, but I can hear voices coming from Jocelyn's room. I knock on the open door and step inside.

Kim and Pamela are perched on Jocelyn's bed while Jocelyn is showing them the bottles of wine she brought back from the morning's trip to the winery.

'Hello, Sophie,' Pamela says, patting the space on the bed next to her.

'We have a problem.'

'Oh?' Jocelyn says, putting the wine on the bedside table.

I sit down on the bed between Pamela and Kim but look at Jocelyn.

'Elliot's eldest daughter has just turned up out of the blue dropping a bombshell that Elliot's wife has left him for another man and the whole family knows about me and his affair with Mum…' the words tumble out.

'Wait, what?' Jocelyn frowns.

'Oh my goodness.' Kim places a warm hand on my arm.

'Elliot being Leila's long-time ex and your father?' Pamela says slowly.

'The very one.'

Kim's hand tenses on my arm. 'What on earth does she want?'

Jocelyn catches my eye. 'You can't seriously mean she's here because that bastard of a man wants Leila back?'

'She's talking to Mum now; I didn't want her to. Mum came back before I could get rid of her. Mum will tell her where to go, it's just Alekos is still out and I've got to go and pick up the wedding cake. In case things kick off while I'm gone I need you all to be here for Mum and make sure Robert doesn't find out a thing about Amy turning up.'

'Oh my goodness,' Kim says again.

'We're on it,' Jocelyn says, 'don't worry. Go and get the cake. Ladies, let's sit out in the courtyard. That way we can keep an eye on everything.'

'Thank you.' I stand and smile at Jocelyn.

'Don't worry, Sophie, everything will be fine, I'm sure.' Jocelyn hugs me. 'You know your mum, she'll tell Elliot's daughter in no uncertain terms where to go. Now go get out of here.'

I leave them grabbing their sunglasses and sunscreen, and

I shoot back to the villa to get my car keys. I hover by the bottom of the stairs, straining to make out voices from upstairs, but I can't hear anything. I'm not sure if that's a good or bad thing, Mum not screaming at Amy… Maybe a civil conversation before Amy leaves might be the best and easiest way of resolving a toxic situation. I jog back outside, waving at Jocelyn, Kim and Pamela, then slip out of the gate and get into our car parked on the grass verge.

I drive the few minutes to the village on autopilot, then revert to Greek as I chat with the ladies behind the counter at the cake shop. I place the boxed cake next to me on the passenger seat, strap it securely with the seat belt and drive carefully back, my fingers drumming on the steering wheel. I park up in the same spot beneath the shade of the trees outside the gate. I'm unnerved by how quiet the place remains, and also that Kim and Pamela are still sitting at the table beneath the olive tree but Jocelyn is missing.

I leave the car doors open with the cake in the shade on the front seat, and walk over to Kim and Pamela, pulling up a chair opposite them.

'They're still upstairs talking?' I frown and glance up at my bedroom window.

'They must be, no one's appeared yet,' Kim says.

'Where's Jocelyn?'

'Popped back to her room to get something.'

'And Robert hasn't come down?'

'Only people we've seen are Alekos, Demetrius and Katrina who came back from the beach a little while ago, waved at us and went round to the pool.' Pamela pats my hand. 'All is calm.'

It does feel calm but my pounding heart suggests otherwise. It's too calm. Mum's not one for tackling a situation like this peacefully. I'm surprised they haven't seen Amy frogmarched off the property.

I go inside the villa. Thea's cross-legged on the floor in the living area making ice cream sundaes from different coloured play dough spread out on the coffee table.

Despina's in the kitchen, slicing pita into small pieces.

'Have you seen my mum?'

Despina doesn't look up but shakes her head. 'No, but we've only been inside a little while.'

Amy's handbag and small suitcase remain next to the patio doors and it's still quiet upstairs. With a glance at Thea, I take the stairs two at a time and head along the landing. The door to my bedroom is open and neither Mum nor Amy are there or anywhere else upstairs. The pounding in my chest intensifies as I jog back downstairs, past Thea and Despina and head back outside.

'They're not upstairs,' I say, reaching the courtyard table, out of breath.

'What?' Kim says. She looks at Pamela. 'We'd have seen them if they'd come out, wouldn't we?'

'Of course, there's no way we'd have missed them.'

'Well, they're not there now.'

'Maybe Leila went out the back and is with Jocelyn?' Pamela says.

'Stay here.' I walk around to the pool. Laughter comes from Demetrius' room. The door to Ben's room is still shut.

I knock and poke my head around the door of Jocelyn's room. 'Shit, Mum's not here.'

Jocelyn's sitting on the bed doing her sandals up. She looks up and frowns. 'As far as I know she hasn't left your room.'

'Somehow she's managed to without anyone seeing her.' I step into the room and close the door. 'I was hoping she'd be here with you.'

'Do Kim or Pamela not know where she is?'

'No. She's seemingly disappeared and Amy wasn't up there either. Shit.'

Jocelyn's door bangs open and Kim flies into the room, panting.

'Apparently,' she says, catching her breath, 'Alekos saw

Leila get into a taxi at the top of the drive when they were coming back from the beach about twenty minutes ago. He's taken the cake out of the car and up to the house.'

'He saw my mum, not Amy?'

Kim breathes deeply. 'Definitely Leila.'

'Going where?' Jocelyn asks.

Kim shrugs. 'No idea. He thought it was odd. We didn't see her come out of the villa – at least not out of the front otherwise we'd have been able to stop her.'

'Oh shit, this really isn't good.' I rub the sides of my face with my hands, wondering where the hell Mum would have gone. To the airport? With the revelations maybe she's seriously thinking of calling off the wedding. My heart thuds faster.

Jocelyn takes my hands. 'It'll be alright. She can't seriously be thinking of leaving Robert for *him*.'

'I wouldn't be so sure. He was the love of her life. She's tried to stay out of his life and even told him in no uncertain terms where to go. I thought she was over him because of Robert. With Amy turning up, who knows?'

Jocelyn shakes her head. 'That bastard has always had an emotional hold over her. Always. I remember meeting Leila for the first time at an antenatal class. She was the youngest one there and although she seemed confident and sure of herself on the outside, she had a vulnerability about her. We stayed in touch and met up after you and my daughter were born and she told me the whole story. He's a good-for-nothing weak and selfish man who should have known better than to seduce a teenager who happened to be the daughter of his best friend. I'm sorry, I know he's your father but he's screwed with her life enough and to ruin things now…' She shakes her head, anger and frustration simmering through her clenched fists and flushed cheeks.

'He's my father in name only. If he'd had the bloody guts to have come here himself, I'd have told him where to go too.'

Jocelyn grips my hand tighter. 'We can't let him ruin this. He can't destroy Leila's life again or the one good man and relationship she's ever had.'

'I'll go find her,' I say.

'Have you any idea where she's gone?' Kim asks from where she's still hovering in the open doorway.

I shake my head. 'Not really, no.' I look between Mum's two oldest friends. 'I'll find her. Can you tell Alekos where I've gone? And can you please look after Thea – she's in the villa playing. Despina's trying to get the food finished for the party.' I falter on my way out of the door and turn back to Jocelyn. 'And find Amy. I'm pissed at her for turning up here like this but we need to make sure she's okay. And *please* make sure Robert doesn't find out about any of this.'

'Don't worry, we won't.' Jocelyn says, firmly. 'That bastard of a man will not mess any of this up.'

'What will you tell Robert?' I ask.

'I'll figure something out. Go find your mum and bring her home.'

Chapter Thirty-One

I sit in the car at the end of the driveway with no idea which direction to take. Where would Mum have gone? What would her thought process have been? I call her mobile and for the eighth time it goes straight to answerphone. I throw my phone down on the passenger seat. With the engine whirring and the air-con only just beginning to take effect, I can't think straight in the heat. I haven't a clue. I take a deep breath and attempt to calm the panic rising in my chest. I drum my fingers on the steering wheel. Everyone is here. Everyone who matters to witness Mum and Robert getting hitched. I've known for days now that Mum's nervous about getting married, not because she doesn't love Robert, because it's evident she does, but because I know she has doubts that she's a suitable wife for him. In her own words 'suitable marriage material'. Now, with the unexpected arrival of Amy, my half-sister and the daughter of the man who broke Mum's heart, I wouldn't be surprised if it's torn her apart.

Sitting at the end of the drive, my hands gripping the steering wheel, my feet hovering over the gas, I have three choices: go back and hope Mum needs some alone time to think things through and will come back when she's ready; head down the coast to Omorfia or up the coast to Poros.

I put my foot on the gas and skid in the gravel, turning the car left. The only place I can imagine she will have gone to suddenly pops into my head. It's walkable but quite a trek in the heat of early afternoon to one of the beachfront cafe's in Omorfia that Mum and I have been to each time she's visited. It's the only place I can imagine she would think of going, unless of course heading to the airport was her initial reaction. Calling for a taxi was a calculated decision and that worries me even more. I still the unwavering panic with the reasoning that she can't simply get on a plane like she can a taxi or a bus. At the very least she's still on the island.

I park on a quiet street leading down to the beach and walk the rest of the way past pastel coloured villas and hotels that edge the tree-lined road. The promenade buzzes with tourists making the most of the afternoon heat instead of retreating inside to cool off and sleep like the majority of the locals.

There are a couple of cafes I've taken Mum to a few times so I make a beeline for them, my canvas shoes pounding the pavement as I weave between couples strolling hand in hand and families carting beach bags, umbrellas and blow up rubber rings in the direction of the beach. I reach the first cafe and scan the outside tables but can't see Mum anywhere.

That all too familiar tightness in my chest is back. What if Mum doesn't want to be found and has gone somewhere I wouldn't think of? I walk on, determined that this isn't the way her time on Cephalonia is going to end. The next few cafes are all busy but there's no sign of Mum. I'm beginning to lose hope when I walk past our favourite fish restaurant and catch sight of a woman with over-sized sunglasses, tousled dyed blonde hair and an eye-catching burnt-orange coloured sleeveless top. She's staring out to sea and I manage to walk right up to the table, pull up a chair and sit down before she even notices me.

'You found me then,' Mum says quietly, finally turning from the view to look at me.

I reach my hands across the table and take hold of hers. 'Mum, what happened with Amy? We thought you were still talking to her, not run off somewhere.'

Mum's laugh is hollow. 'If only I could run away. There's no point you being here, Sophie.'

'I've spent far too long fighting against my family. Don't push me away, not now.'

Our surroundings are at odds with the desperateness of our situation. Cloudless blue sky, shimmering turquoise sea, achingly clear and inviting, combined with the scent of salt-air and grilled lemony seafood from the surrounding tavernas. Everything is accentuated, both the beauty of the location and the turmoil oozing from Mum, making my panic build and build.

'You told Amy where to go I presume?'

Mum pulls her hands away and pushes her sunglasses into her hair. Redness circles her eyes where she's been crying. 'She gave me the news I've been waiting for since I was eighteen years old. That Elliot is finally single, divorcing and still loves me.'

This is everything I was dreading the moment I saw Amy standing at the gate of Birdsong Villas. 'Don't revisit the past, Mum. There's a reason it's in the past. He's not worth it. He's certainly not worth losing Robert over.'

'He was the love of my life, my soulmate.' She stares out towards the sea and the white and blue painted boats bobbing on the gentle swell of the water splashing against the harbourside further down. 'He was the wrong person for so many reasons and I shouldn't have touched him with a bargepole, but I fell in love and he encouraged me. I may have hated him over the years for abandoning us but I never stopped loving him.'

'So you don't love Robert?'

'I do love Robert.' Mum picks up her drink and takes a sip.

I lean back and rub my forehead, unable to see a way through this to salvage the wedding or to save Mum's relationship with Robert.

Mum places her drink carefully on the blue and white chequered paper tablecloth. 'You don't understand how I can love two men, do you?'

'Not when four years ago you effectively told Elliot to go fuck himself.'

Her eyes leave mine and she takes a deep breath. 'And that was the hardest thing I ever did.' She rests her elbows on the table and leans forward. 'What if that was the wrong decision?'

'What if it was the right one? It took guts to do that. It enabled you to move on. It allowed you to have a proper relationship with Robert, something you'd never had before with meaningless boyfriends you had fun with but were never really serious about.'

One of the waiters pauses next to our table. 'Can I get you a drink?' he asks, smiling at me.

'*Ohi efharisto*,' I reply, barely glancing up from Mum.

'Sophie, for the first time in my life I really don't know what to do.'

I move to the chair next to her and wrap my arms around her. Sobs wrack her body. She buries her head into the crook of my neck. The sun pounds down on us as her tears drip on to my skin. All around us I can hear laughter, snatches of conversations in Greek and English, the roll of the surf breaking on the sand. I wish I'd been able to protect Mum from the turmoil she's going through and the choice she's going to have to make. I wish I'd sent Amy away the moment I realised who she was. I let her into our life and look where we've ended up. A week that should have been filled with so much happiness has ended up being a confusing time for both of us.

'Oh Mum, I really don't know what to say. Your friends loathe Elliot because of how he's treated you, and I know what I think you should do, but only you can make that decision. You have to go with your heart or your head or a combination of both.'

She moves away from me, tears streaking her cheeks, leaving my shoulder damp. She drops her sunglasses back over her eyes. 'But my goddam heart is pulling me in two different directions. Part of me wants to fly back to England right now and run into Elliot's arms, the other half, well… It's Robert, the loveliest, kindest man I could ever have asked for and I don't think I deserve him. How can I ever live up to his wife?'

'Is that what you're worried about? You don't have to live up to her. You're you and he loves you because of who *you* are. He's not comparing you to his wife. I'm sure from everything that he and Ben have said about her, she'd want to see him happy, settled down and married again.'

Mum shudders, actually shudders.

'I don't think I can get married,' she says quietly. 'I'm not the marrying type. I'm the screw-around with married, much younger than me, inappropriate men type of woman. That's not who Robert wants or deserves.'

'You don't think a person can change? That you can change? So what if that was you twenty years ago?'

Mum shoots me a dark look over the top of her sunglasses. 'More like five years ago.'

'You're missing the point; it doesn't have to be who you are now. We all change, move on, grow up. Four years ago I was tempted to sleep with someone other than Alekos and I did cheat on him with Ben even if we didn't take things as far as I wanted to. And Alekos hadn't told me the truth about his relationship with Aphrodite until now. Ben kissed me a week ago when we were in Norfolk. Mum, we all have secrets and have done things that we want to forget ever happened. At the same time, they make us who we are.'

'I can't hurt Robert and I'm scared to death that marrying him when I shouldn't would hurt him far more than walking away now.'

Her hands clench her drink, her knuckles white with tension. The tightness in my chest remains. It's absolute fear that everything is falling apart around us: Mum's happiness, our relationship with Robert, the stability and love with Alekos, the confusion with Ben and Candy, my new-found half-sister suddenly showing up the way she did, the re-emergence of a father… The confusion erases the comfort I've recently felt with my love for Alekos back on track and the father-figure in Robert I've longed for all my life. Perhaps my real father remaining a nameless, meaningless one-night stand that Mum had once led me to believe was the truth, would have been for the best.

'Mum, you're risking so much. Trust me, I've come close to losing Alekos twice now through stupidity on my part, for thinking there's a better life for me with someone else instead of working through the problems we were facing. For making massive assumptions about his past without really knowing the facts. These last couple of days I've questioned his love for me, doubted him, assumed he's having an affair. I've been swept up in theories from well-meaning but blinkered friends because they're dealing with their own relationship shit and are so resolved into thinking that all men cheat.'

'My situation is different.'

'Maybe. But what if Robert is really your soulmate? What if *you're* being blinkered by the past and the love you felt as a young, impressionable teenager, pregnant with a much older man's child? If you hadn't got pregnant, if you hadn't been tied to Elliot forever through me, don't you think you might have felt differently about him?'

'He's not with his wife any longer…'

'But that was *her* choice, not his. Mum, I'm begging you, don't throw your life with Robert away over a man who never had the guts to leave his wife. He didn't even come out here to try and win you back. His daughter's here on his behalf because he's hurting too much. Well boo fucking hoo. I'm only telling you what you'd tell me if it was the other way round.'

Mum stands up, scraping her chair back on the wooden

boards of the restaurant's deck. 'I need time alone.'

I shake my head and hold out my hands. 'What am I supposed to tell Robert?'

'I don't know. Tell him I need time.'

'Mum, you're getting married tomorrow. Everyone's here, your friends, family…'

'I need time alone to think, Sophie.' She takes her shoulder bag from the back of the chair. 'This is the biggest decision of my life.'

'Where are you going to go?'

'I don't know. For a walk. Somewhere to clear my head.'

She strides away, a picture of summer in her white gypsy skirt and sleeveless orange top. She looks half her age and free as she walks, and I suddenly get it. The free spirit that she is, that she always has been, doesn't want to be contained. Even though she loves him, I know she feels stifled by the prospect of marrying Robert. But isn't that exactly what would happen if she went running back to the UK and into the arms of Elliot? Wouldn't he ensnare her in complicated emotions, just like he's had her heart caged in empty promises for the past thirty-three years? I remain sitting and watch her until she disappears into the crowd of holidaymakers. I put my head in my hands and wonder what on earth I'm going to do.

I can't be the one to tell Robert that Mum's about to break his heart.

Chapter Thirty-Two

I drive back. What the hell should I tell Robert? What has Jocelyn already told him? To tell him Mum isn't sure about going ahead with the wedding will break his heart and I can't do that, plus there's still the chance that she'll come to her senses and make the right decision. If Mum wants time alone, I need to give her that time. With a deep breath I put my foot down and accelerate along the winding road that leads back to Birdsong Villas.

Jocelyn and Kim are sitting outside Kim's room but they're on their feet and heading across the courtyard before I've even closed the car door. I can read the disappointment in their frowns when they realise I'm alone.

'You didn't find her?' Jocelyn asks, reaching me.

'I did and we talked, but she wants some time alone to think things through.'

'She can't possibly be considering throwing away everything she has with Robert for *him*,' Jocelyn says under her breath. 'Can she?'

I sigh. 'When has my mum ever done what's expected of her?'

'I'm so mad at Amy turning up like she did.' Kim puts her hands on her hips and blows air over her flushed face.

'You and me both,' I say.

'The nerve that family has.'

'Talking of Amy, where is she? Did you find her?'

Jocelyn nods. 'She was at the end of the garden crying her eyes out. I think coming out here and finally talking to Leila did her in. I don't agree with what she's done but I do understand her reasoning. She's had a bombshell dropped on her with the truth about her father's affair coming out the way it did while her mother was divorcing him. She may be well into her forties but she's taken it pretty badly. She's with Pamela in her room under strict instructions to stay there until we know what on earth is going on with Leila. Speaking of which, what are we going to do?'

'We're going to give Mum the time she needs and hope that she comes to her senses.'

'And if she doesn't?' Kim says.

'I have no idea what happens then.'

Jocelyn places a warm hand on my arm. 'Are you going to say anything to Robert? He's awake now, by the pool I think.'

'He doesn't need to know what's going on. I am going to speak to Ben though.'

'What do we say to Robert?' Kim frowns. 'I mean if he starts wondering where Leila is?'

'Tell him she decided to go and have a massage and facial after all. That might buy her a bit of time. But only say so if he asks. Please don't make it obvious.'

The worry etched across Kim's and Jocelyn's faces doesn't give me much hope that they're not going to completely stress about it and give Robert the impression that something's up. I breathe a sigh of relief when they head towards Pamela's room. At least I don't feel obliged to go and comfort Amy. She's got three friendly mother figures with her, so I'll let them deal with her emotional mess.

I take a deep breath and stride across the courtyard. The sound of laughter and kids screeching gets louder as I round the corner and go through the gate. All the kids are in the pool with Alekos, Demetrius, and to my relief, Robert. Katrina, Vicky, Ben and Candy are relaxing on sunloungers watching the commotion in the pool as Alekos and Demetrius take it in turns to hit a blow up ball to the children in the shallow end. I make my way round the edge of the pool and lean across Candy, my shadow falling over her tanned stomach.

'Ben, can I talk to you.'

He turns his head from the pool to me. 'What, now?'

I nod. 'Yes, now.'

Candy slides her sunglasses down to the end of her nose and gazes up at me. 'Everything okay?'

'It will be; I just need to talk to Ben.'

Whether it's my tone or lack of explanation, Candy nods and Ben gets up off the sunlounger, slips his feet into his flip-flops and follows me away from the laughter, screeches and splashing. Neither of us say anything until I close the gate to the pool behind us.

'If you're worried about Candy, things are fine between us,' Ben says. 'I like her.'

'I really don't care what's going on between you two; it's Mum and Robert I'm concerned about.'

The place is filled with people, and I know nothing's going to stay a secret for long, so I decide to tell Ben the truth. I motion for him to follow me across the courtyard, out through the main gate and on to the path that winds its way down to the beach, where no one can overhear us.

'What's up?' He stands with his back to the sea, his arms folded across his bare chest. 'What's with the secrecy?'

'Mum's having second thoughts.'

He frowns and shakes his head. 'What do you mean?'

'Second thoughts about marrying your dad.'

'You're kidding, right?' He laughs.

'I'm dead serious.' My head thumps from the strain of secrets and worry. 'Luckily your dad was out at the time, but the woman who arrived earlier is my half-sister.'

'That's who she is? I thought she looked like you.'

'Well, she turned up to tell Mum that my good-for-nothing father is no longer with his wife and is still in love with her. I'm telling you because Mum's emotions are shot to pieces. She needs time to think things through – it's knocked her for six.'

Ben grabs my arm. 'Wait, you're seriously telling me she's reconsidering marrying Dad? It's the day before their goddam wedding.'

'She's thinking things through. I honestly don't think she'd ever seriously consider leaving your dad for *him* but…'

Ben releases his hand from my arm and starts as if to head back towards the retreat.

'Where the hell is this sister of yours?'

I stalk past him and block the way back. 'For God's sake, Ben, I met her for the first time today. She's my half-sister in name only. I had no idea about any of this any more than my mum or you now do. Help me out could you? This isn't just a nightmare for you, you know.'

'You bloody Keech women, leading men on, screwing us around or not as the case may be…'

'This has got absolutely nothing to do with what happened between us. My God, how can you even bring that up right now? We have a way bigger problem than us having fooled around a few years ago.' I look at him, pleading with him to not storm off and make an unnecessary scene. 'Ben, I'm trying my best to contain the situation and not worry your dad over nothing.'

He looks down at the ground then back to me. 'You really think it's nothing?'

'Honestly, I don't know, but giving Mum some time to cool down and think things through is the only thing I can do, so please help me out. She needs some time – she's always been so independent she's struggling with the idea of being married after all these years of being on her own.'

'There's more to it than that. She's still in love with him, your bastard of a father?'

'All I want you to do is not get Robert worried. There's no

need for him to know any of this. Tell him Mum's having that facial and massage they were talking about and she's decided to sleep in our villa tonight. After all, it's traditional for the groom to not spend the night with his bride-to-be the night before the wedding.'

'Fine. I'm doing this for Dad. You sort this whole mess out with your mum. For what it's worth Dad loves Leila with all his heart. I never thought he'd find anyone he could love as much as he did Mum. Don't you dare let her break his heart.'

He stalks back up the path, his thigh muscles straining on the hill, tanned shoulders hunched forwards. I sit down on the scratchy grass at the side of the path and hug my knees to my chest. How has everything got so complicated in such a short space of time? I know Mum, I know the hold Elliot has over her, I know her reluctance to commit, and here she is, the day before her wedding facing that commitment or a potential new life with the man she's loved since she was a teenager. The choices she made then still affecting her life more than thirty years later.

It's nearing the end of the afternoon and I've done nothing towards dinner. With so many people staying here now the place feels stifled. I'd love to escape like Mum, to enable myself to think straight, to hold everything together. It's what I've always done in the past and look what trouble that got me into. Escaping to Norfolk to look after Mum when things got tricky with Alekos. Escaping a strained relationship with Alekos by running into Ben's arms rather than working things through by simply talking.

I have to be the one who pieces everything back together if there's any chance of a happy ending tomorrow. The place is divided into two groups of people: those oblivious to what's played out over the course of the afternoon and those who are stressing over what the hell's going to happen, myself included. Clarity about what I need to do dawns on me – taking Amy and everyone who knows what's going on away from Birdsong Villas. That way there shouldn't be any possibility of Robert finding out what's really happening.

I had planned to cook something decidedly un-Greek like a huge chilli con carne with rice, but I've done nothing towards it. Knowing after a day of either sightseeing or playing in the pool stomachs will be rumbling, I suggest to Alekos we pick up a couple of roasted chickens and chips from the local grill place instead.

'I did think you were mad to cook the night before the wedding when there's so much to do anyway,' he says. 'What made you change your mind?'

'The shit-storm that's gone down this afternoon,' I reply in English, unsure how to vent my frustration quite so powerfully in Greek.

Alekos frowns. 'What are you talking about?'

I take a deep breath and fill him in on the Amy and Elliot situation.

'*Ti malaka*,' he swears and hugs me. 'Are you okay?'

Enveloped in his strong arms, I shrug. 'I have to be. I'm going to sort this. I'm going to take the girls for an evening out. Get everyone who knows what's going on out of here – Amy included. She can't hide away in Pamela's room all evening and I can't risk her causing a scene if I try and send her away.'

'Fuck, this is messed up.'

I place my hands on his chest and look up into his hazel eyes. 'Tell me about it. Yesterday everything seemed so perfect, and now…'

He wipes away the tears on my cheeks with his thumbs. 'It'll be okay. Your mum will make the right choice, I'm sure.'

'That's what everyone keeps saying.'

But what if the right choice for her is the wrong choice for everyone else? I know how Mum ticks; I know how much hold Elliot has had over her for more than three decades; I know how she was unable to hold on to a long-term relationship, until Robert, and how her choices in men – too young, married or total nut jobs – was down to her not wanting to commit to anyone. I've always believed she's held on to the unhealthy thought that one day Elliot would leave his wife and choose her.

Well, Elliot's wife has now left him and his daughter is saying that he still loves Mum. But if that really was the case, if Mum is honestly the true love of his life, then why the hell isn't he here proclaiming his love instead of his goddam daughter.

Chapter Thirty-Three

With Alekos in charge at Birdsong Villas and aware of the Leila and Amy situation, I stride across the courtyard, knock on Pamela's door and push it open before anyone has a chance to answer. Jocelyn and Pamela are sitting in the armchairs by the window and Kim and Amy are perched on the bed. Their conversation stops the moment I appear in the doorway.

'Goodness you scared me,' Pamela says, holding a hand to her chest. 'I had a horrible feeling you were Robert.'

'You lot can't stay holed up here all evening, so we're going out.' I look at Jocelyn, relying on her to get on board with my decision.

'Okay,' she says slowly. 'Where are we going?'

'To Omorfia for a girls' night out to meet Mum.'

'You've found her?' Kim asks.

'No, but that's how we're going to cover for her this evening.' I turn to Amy sitting on the edge of the bed, her hands clasped in her lap. 'You too, you're coming with us.'

'Right then, ladies,' Jocelyn says, standing up. 'Let's get ready to go out.'

'Alekos has ordered a taxi to pick us up in thirty minutes. We'll meet on the lane.'

I close the door behind me. I turn to head to the pool when my heart feels as if it slams against my ribcage at the sight of Robert walking across the courtyard towards me.

'Hello,' he says, reaching me. 'I've hardly seen you all day, or your mum for that matter since we got back from our lunch out.'

I clear my throat. 'She decided to have that massage and facial after all.'

'Oh really? She was commenting last night about how much she hates the thought of a stranger messing about with her. I told her a massage would be relaxing…' He frowns.

I hate lying to him. He's everything I thought Mum wouldn't want in a man but he's turned out to be everything she needs.

I take his warm dry hand in mine. 'You know what she's like, always impulsive. That's not going to change simply because she's getting married. She also wants us to meet her in Omorfia and have a girls' night out.'

'Yes, Ben did say that she's going to sleep in your villa tonight.'

I'm sure he knows something's up, but he's too damn nice to say anything.

He nods and lets go of my hand. 'Have fun tonight. Tell Leila I love her and I'll see her in the morning.'

'I will.' I can barely hold back my tears. From my initial opinion of Robert all those years ago in the hospital after Mum had her accident, when he infuriated and annoyed me in equal measure, I've grown immensely fond of him. He doesn't deserve to have his heart broken but neither does Mum, not by someone who's messed her around her whole life. Elliot has no place forcing himself back into Mum's life in such a cowardly way. And as for Amy, the thought of her stirring up all this unhealthy emotion in Mum makes me want to slap her.

I watch Robert stroll across the courtyard, hands shoved in his trouser pockets, seemingly oblivious to the chaos that has ensued this afternoon. I need to make this right. With a deep breath I march in the opposite direction, around the corner and through the gate to the pool.

Candy and Ben are the only ones still there, lying on adjacent sunloungers, their hands clasped in each other's.

'Candy,' I call across the pool. 'We're having a last minute girls' night out, you coming?'

'Another hen do?'

'Kind of.'

'You know I'll never say no to a night out.'

'Where's Dad?' Ben sits up and removes his sunglasses.

'Gone to his room.'

'He's okay is he?'

I nod. 'He's fine, I promise.'

Candy glances between us, frowning. She picks up her towel, book and sunscreen, bends down to kiss Ben and follows me to the villa. Before we reach the open door leading to the kitchen she hooks her arm in mine. 'What's really going on, Soph? You're stressed; Ben's been acting weird since you chatted with him earlier, I've not seen your mum and what the hell's going on with Jocelyn and Kim, they seem flappy.'

I pull her into the villa and check that no one's downstairs.

'Long story short, Elliot's eldest daughter turned up, told Mum Elliot still loves her and is now separated from his wife. Mum's freaked out and my half-sister has been bawling her eyes out in Pamela's room. I talked to Ben earlier because I needed him to help make sure Robert doesn't find out what's really going on.'

'Robert's not stupid.'

'I know, that's why I want all of us out of here, before Jocelyn or Kim or bloody Amy say or do something stupid.'

'Shit, Sophie. You're really not joking are you?'

I shoot her a look. 'I couldn't even make this shit up, Candy. Going out tonight is purely covering for Mum, to give her time to get her head straight.'

'Okay, let's do this; I'll go and get ready.'

We climb the stairs together. Candy disappears into her room and, hearing voices coming from Thea's bedroom, I push open the door and find Thea and Alekos sitting on the floor playing together.

'Mama, Mama!' Thea pretends to fly a plastic dinosaur towards me and roars in my face.

'Hey there, baby girl.' I put my arms around her.

'You still going out?' Alekos asks, eyebrows raised which I take to mean 'is everything okay?'

'Yep, all the girls. You sure you're going to be alright here on your own with everyone?'

'Of course.' He pulls me down to him, stroking the back of my neck. 'Baba's gone to get the roast chicken and we've got so many leftovers, dinner's sorted. Mama's here to put Thea to bed and I can entertain everyone else. We might have a boys' night in – a beer, game of cards.'

'Great.' I breathe a sigh of relief, knowing Alekos will have everything under control. I kiss him. 'If Mum does come back, phone me straight away.'

'She's still not answering?'

'Nope. I've left her a message so she knows we're covering for her and giving her the time she needs. Please hold it together here. Once we're out it's only you and Ben who actually know what's going on. Please keep it that way. And don't say anything to your mum about my mum because she'll completely freak out and that's the last thing we need.'

I kiss him, hug Thea, and go back downstairs.

Going out, even if it is a pretence, would not be high on my list of things to do the night before the wedding, yet I do feel relief at escaping Birdsong Villas and no longer having to lie to Robert. We sneak Amy from Pamela's room while the courtyard is empty. Everyone else has had a chance to change or get ready. I realise too late I'm still wearing what I've been in all day: cropped trousers, a vest top and canvas shoes, decidedly un-dressy for an evening out in Greece. I'm too tired to care.

I choose a bar where we can talk – it's busy, as everywhere

is, but the music is low enough to give the place a chilled out atmosphere and allow us to hear each other. It's set a little way up on the hillside and has a terrace with views across the town, the darkness pinpricked with lights from the multitude of other bars and restaurants dotting the hillside. The location suggests a carefree night out yet every part of me is tense, worrying about Mum, wondering where she is, what she's up to and what the hell she's thinking.

Apart from the conversation I had with Amy when she first arrived, I've barely spoken to her. She talked to Mum and then spent the rest of the day holed up in Pamela's room. My mum's friends have actually spent more time with my half-sister than I have.

We manage to find an empty table on the terrace that can squeeze all six of us around it. A waiter takes our order and comes back with a tray of drinks and nibbles. I sip my lemonade, wanting to keep a clear head. I take my mobile from out of my shoulder bag and text Mum:

Hope you're okay. We're in Omorfia at Hydra bar on the hillside. Please join us and come home with us later. Xx

I leave my mobile on the table in hope that she'll reply.

Jocelyn leans towards me. 'She's actually very nice, Amy is.'

I glance across the table to where Amy is chatting to Pamela.

'I'm sure she is,' I reply. 'But I don't appreciate her turning up the way she did and giving Mum that kind of news the day before she's getting married.' I can feel my voice rising and a pressure returning to my chest.

Jocelyn places her hand on my arm. 'I'm not trying to defend her, Sophie, it's just she seems a decent person making a misguided choice.'

'I think she's got more guts than her bloody father has. I might have been less angry about the situation if it was actually Elliot who'd turned up professing his love for Mum. In my mind he's a spineless waste of space.'

Candy places her bottle of lager on the table with a thud and jabs a finger across the table at Amy. 'You do understand the shit storm you've caused by turning up here?'

Amy flinches and leans back in her chair. She swallows and it's obvious she's fighting back tears. My arm pressed against Jocelyn, I feel her flinch too.

Everyone has their eyes down, focused on anything but Candy and Amy facing off. I don't have the energy or desire to attempt to diffuse the situation. After all, this evening out was never really going to be an easy-going one.

'I know, and I'm sorry for that,' Amy finally says. 'But I would never have forgiven myself if I hadn't tried and given Leila all the facts.'

'Fuck the facts.' Candy shakes her head. 'You're messing with the rest of someone's life.'

'You wouldn't do the same if you were in my position?' Amy grips her drink and locks eyes with Candy. It's unnerving how much we look like each other.

'I've no idea what I'd do in your position, but I hope I'd have been able to do the decent thing and left well alone. Either way,' Candy says, stabbing a finger in Amy's direction. 'I don't have a shit of a cheating dad to make that decision in the first place.'

The tension around the table is palpable. On the eve of Mum's wedding, her friends shouldn't have been put in this position, to be made to feel so uncomfortable and helpless with no way of making the situation right.

I lean forward and look at Amy. 'Why didn't your dad come out here instead of you?'

She opens her mouth to say something but stops. 'He wanted to… it's just…'

'He told you not to meddle, didn't he? Yet here you are anyway.'

She meets my gaze. 'He loves her. He loves your mum more than he's ever loved mine. I'll forever be grateful for the way he put me, my sister and brother before his happiness…'

'His happiness? Are you for real? He had his fun, screwing around with my mum when she was a goddam teenager. He got to have an affair with the much younger daughter of his best friend *and* keep his marriage and family life intact. I'm so pleased that you had such a lovely childhood with a mother and a father in that beautiful house…'

'I know how this must sound to you…'

'Seriously, do you really have any idea?'

Everyone else remains silent, drinks clutched in tense hands, our conversation at odds with our surroundings.

'My mum went through hell. She's only eight years older than you. While your fucking dad enjoyed his life everything changed for mum. She lost her family, her home. She moved to a strange city so your pathetic excuse for a father could maintain the pretence of being a happy family man while my idiot grandparents kept the peace and didn't have to face the public embarrassment of their teenage daughter being knocked up out of wedlock with a married man who happened to be their best friend. And even though Mum's stayed out of everyone's life, here we are again. Your fucking family meddling with mine.'

'He's your father too,' she says quietly.

'Oh go to hell.'

Candy takes my hand. 'Let's take a walk, Soph.'

She pulls me to my feet and leads me past the neighbouring tables, people glancing at us as we walk by.

'The nerve she has,' I say once we reach the pavement. My hands are clenched, my heart racing and I want more than anything to make Amy and Elliot and my bloody grandparents feel a tiny amount of the hurt that Mum has for more than three decades.

'I know.' Candy walks me to the wall that overlooks the red-roofed whitewashed buildings that lead down to the seafront. 'Quite frankly I want to punch her but that would do no good. She's here, she's spoken to your mum. The damage is done.'

Candy and I walk; I'm too tense and we're both too angry to go back and sit at the table while Amy is there. Jocelyn, Kim and Pamela will just have to deal with her without us. I don't want to be this angry and frustrated at someone I don't know, yet have such a connection to. The fact that we look like each other, and in turn I look like Elliot, incenses me.

The evening is sultry and hot for mid-June, adding to the intensity of the last few hours. We stroll along the quieter back roads, catching snippets of conversations in Greek and English, the beat of music from a bar floating into the night, the tang of lemon and seafood in the air from the fish restaurants when we get closer to the waterfront. It's nice to have companionable silence, something Candy and I have always been able to do and be comfortable with. I don't know how long we've walked for when we find an empty bench at the quiet end of the beachfront, away from the bars and restaurants and throng of people enjoying their evening out. We sit down and watch the dark water foam white as it reaches the beach. Lights twinkle out on the open sea and I think back to the night on the beach with the boat lit by lamps bobbing up and down on the black water. There's something magical about being by the sea at night-time; the endless space, the openness, the freedom. I sigh, lean back against the wooden bench and will my head to stop thinking.

'I wonder what it would be like to have a normal family,' I say after a while.

'You can't think like that,' Candy says. 'I mean, what's normal anyway?'

'Your family.'

'Normal in the sense my parents are married, still together and I have a sister.'

'Yeah, that's normal, not the messed up crap I've got.'

'Every family's different, Sophie. I can't tell you how many times growing up I wished my mum was more like Leila. I loved your mum. I still do.'

'And I envied you with the normality of a mum who

didn't embarrass you the whole time.'

'Trust me, my mum embarrassed me plenty of times.'

'Not by flirting with a hot twenty-year-old at the garden centre. Not that kind of embarrassment.'

'Well, no.' Candy sighs. 'It's funny isn't it, how we always want what each other has and are never happy with our own life. Nothing like enjoying it for what it is. You have the coolest mum and didn't need a father figure.'

'And you have the loveliest mum. I adored coming over and having dinner with you and sitting around the dining table with your family.'

'You know what I loved, drinking Peach Schnapps and watching *Thelma and Louise* when we were underage at your house. And remember the art student lodger you had?'

'Which one?' I laugh.

'The fit one, who always used to walk around the place with his top off.'

'Oh yeah, can't remember his name, but yeah, he messed with my head. Always made me blush whenever I passed him in the hallway.'

'Was your mum shagging him?'

'I think she shagged them all. Apart from Stinky Pete.'

Candy smiles. 'Ah yes, Stinky Pete. He was the one growing pot in his attic bedroom?'

'That's the one.'

'Seriously, my teens sucked compared to yours – maybe that's why I rebelled and you didn't. You were allowed to drink, smoke, bring guys back and your mum wouldn't have batted an eyelid, and yet you never really did. I came home stinking of alcohol and cigarettes with a love bite on my neck and my dad grounded me for two weeks.'

'I guess for me there was no real excitement in doing those things because Mum wouldn't have punished me. She was up to no good most of the time.'

My phone pings. I reach into my bag, take my mobile out and read the text message. I look up at Candy. 'It's Mum.

She's going to meet us at the bar.'

Mum sits down in the free chair that Pamela's pulled up. It's evident from her bloodshot eyes and smeared mascara that she's spent a lot of the past few hours crying. No one says anything, watching and waiting for her to speak. This has felt like the longest few hours of my life. Whatever Mum's going to tell us, I already know that it's one of those pivotal moments – like it was when I did that pregnancy test in Mum's bathroom in Salt Cottage; or when I finally made that phone call to Alekos to tell him I was pregnant with Thea. Those moments changed the direction of my life. Mum's decision won't just affect her, but me too. I've waited my whole life for a father who lives up to his name, yet only one of the two men Mum is making a decision over has ever been a father-figure to me. I'm scared to death that we've come this close only to lose him and for Mum to make, what is in my mind, the wrong choice.

Mum looks across the table at Amy. The rest of us are frozen, waiting to hear what decision she's reached. I feel like I can't breathe and the earlier tension in my chest returns.

'I phoned your father and we talked.' Mum holds a scrunched up tissue in her hands. 'It's the first time I've spoken to him since Sophie and I drove up to see him before Thea was born. And it's only the second or third time since Sophie was born that we've actually had a proper conversation. That's insane, isn't it? Sophie's father, the man who turned my life upside down, the man who has continuously been there in the background for the last thirty-odd goddam years. We had a hell of a lot to talk about…' Mum rubs her hands across her forehead and places them back on the table, her fingers clenched around the tissue, knuckles white with tension.

Amy is the only one capable of breaking the silence and asking the question that's on everyone's lips. 'What have you decided to do?'

Mum looks first at me and then at Amy. She unlocks her hands and slides them off the table into her lap. 'I've decided that I'm not going to marry Robert tomorrow.'

Chapter Thirty-Four

Birdsong. It's the only sound as dawn breaks. The faintest of breezes filters through our open bedroom window. I lie still, waiting for the darkness to slowly turn to daylight. I struggled to get to sleep, feeling too hot with too many thoughts swirling about to relax. Even with the lack of sleep, I'm wide awake now. The events of the last twenty-four hours play over and over in my head like a bad dream.

Alekos is still sleeping, the sheet wrapped around his legs, his chest bare, his breathing gentle. As far as I can tell, I'm the only one awake as apart from the birdsong, the place is silent. Perhaps Mum and Robert are awake – that's if they managed to get any sleep to begin with last night.

It's no good, there's absolutely no chance of drifting off again. I slip out of bed and pad over to the window. The sky is brightening fast, casting a magical glow across the courtyard and the shimmering sea beyond. I put one of Alekos' T-shirts over the top of my vest and pyjama shorts and creep out of our room, closing the door quietly behind me, hardly daring to breathe in the stillness on the landing.

I go downstairs, glad to be the only one up, not even hearing Thea stirring in her room. I need this moment of quiet, before the craziness of the day begins, people wake and questions are asked. It's going to be another perfect day. The forecast is for a pleasant thirty-two degrees, sunshine and cloudless blue skies. I throw open the doors on to the patio and the thin see-through curtains flutter in the light breeze. I switch the coffee machine on and take out a mug from the cupboard.

With every room occupied the night before the wedding, Candy offered Amy her room to sleep in. It was no hardship for Candy to spend yet another night with Ben. It's weird to think of my half-sister up there now, in our house, just one of many blood relatives I've never met. For a stranger she's caused one hell of a lot of commotion in a short space of time.

I pour myself a coffee, spoon in a heaped teaspoon of sugar, slip on my canvas shoes and go outside. The advantage of being up so early is the heat of the day hasn't yet developed, and with the breeze, it's a beautiful temperature.

There are now six long tables set up in the courtyard, the olive tree the centrepiece, decorated with fairy lights for when it gets dark later. Bunting and more lights hang just below the roof of the guest rooms and the bay trees in pots outside the villa have lights entwined in them too. The scene is set for a wedding that's not going to happen.

I sit down at one of the tables and take a deep breath, relishing the fresh sea air. We were a sombre group arriving back last night. Mum refused to say anything else to us at the bar, insisting she needed to speak to Robert first. As soon as we arrived back, she left us and headed up to her room to face him. I wonder if anyone got much sleep last night. Ben's going to go mental with us 'Keech women' when he finds out. I blow on the coffee and regret not having put milk in it to cool it down.

The sight of Robert emerging from his room makes my heart thud. What am I supposed to say to him to make things better? How can I even find the words to apologise enough on behalf of my goddam mother.

He sees me and raises his hand, clatters down the steps and comes over to join me at the table. His eyes look tired with dark rings below them like he's been up all night.

Fighting back tears, I lean forward and rest my arms on the table. 'I'm so sorry for what Mum's put you through.'

'Why are you apologising, Sophie? You're not responsible for your mother's actions.'

'I feel like I should have seen this coming. That man…' I can't even bear to say his name or refer to him as my father, 'has messed with Mum's life enough times and now this…'

I stop talking when Mum appears, closing the door to the room behind her and walking carefully down the steps. She crosses over to us, pulls up a chair next to Robert and sits down, her hands resting on the silvery grey wood. Robert reaches across and takes her hand in his, sliding his fingers between hers. My eyes can't leave their entwined hands. I frown and look up, first at Robert and then Mum.

'I don't understand?'

Mum rests her head on Robert's shoulder.

'Last night you told us that you'd decided you weren't going to marry Robert.'

'She did decide that,' Robert says. 'And we're not getting married today, that's true.'

Mum lifts her head off Robert's shoulder, strokes the side of his face and turns to me. 'I'm not marrying Robert but not for the reasons you think. I'm so sorry to have left you all confused and upset last night – I needed to get back here, I needed to talk to Robert without anyone trying to talk me out of anything.'

'What the hell's going on, Mum?'

I realise now she's still wearing her clothes from yesterday, her make-up is faded, her mascara is smudged below her eyes.

She takes a deep breath. 'I'm not marrying Robert today, but it's not because I don't love him, because I do, more than I've loved any man ever and that includes Elliot. Honestly, I'm not in love with him any more. I actually fell out of love with him a long time ago. I think it was more the idea of us one day becoming a family unit, you having the father you've always longed for – it was that idea I was in love with. Are you drinking that?' She motions towards my mug of coffee.

I shake my head and push it across the table to her.

She takes a gulp and places it carefully back down. 'In a weird way Amy turning up the way she did clarified everything for me. My whole life I've never wanted to get married – Sophie, you of all people know that. These past couple of weeks I feel like I've been going through the motions of what's expected from a bride-to-be but I've never truly embraced it. I've loved the partying, the excuse to see old friends, have you over from Greece, but I've shied away from the practicalities like the idea of changing my name, making a decision on where we're going to live, really thinking about what marriage entails.'

'All I can say, Sophie, is what a shame and waste of all your hard work.' Robert motions around us and shakes his head. 'This mother of yours…'

Mum hooks her arm in his and kisses his cheek.

'I'm a nutcase, I really am. Trust me, it's probably a wise idea to not be married to me.' She laughs.

'Wait.' I frown, unable to quite get my head around Mum's words compared to how still in love they look. 'You're not getting married but you are still together?'

Mum nods. 'Elliot can go to hell.' She holds Robert close but continues to look at me. 'Like I said, I love Robert, more than I've ever loved anyone. And I mean that. He was married to a wonderful woman and I can never live up to her or would want to. She'll always be his wife, but I know he loves me and wants to be with me as much as I want to be with him. What Amy's done by coming here has given me the chance to think things through in a way I never did before. Up till now there was never any chance of being with Elliot because he was married and would never have willingly broken up his marriage, but knowing he's now single, I was able to really think about what that meant. I realised I have no desire whatsoever to be a part of that man's life any longer. He may say that I'm the love of his life, but I've felt like an afterthought and someone he's wanted kept hidden. He can go to hell for all I care, because that talk with Amy and then with him, gave me clarity about who my soulmate truly is.' She kisses Robert's hand.

Tears roll down Mum's face and Robert is choked up too. I can hardly keep myself from breaking down; the way Robert's looking at her just melts me.

'But you're not getting married today?'

Mum shakes her head. 'We were up talking about this most of last night. I know what's been bugging me this whole time, this feeling that getting married is because it's the expected thing to do. Marrying Robert isn't going to make me love him any more than I already do. I like being me and I love being me and Robert, a proper grown-up couple.' She laughs. 'But I don't want a marriage certificate or the show of getting married, I want to continue as we are. I can't explain it any clearer than that, but Robert being the wonderful man he is understands. I'm not going to replace his wife but I am utterly committed to being with him.'

'Oh my God, Mum, I don't know what to say.'

Going from believing not only the wedding but her whole relationship with Robert was off to realising they're still together leaves me feeling rather emotional.

Mum scrapes her chair back and walks around to my side of the table. I stand up and we hug, tears running down our faces. It only takes a moment for Robert to join our embrace and wrap his arms around us both.

'If I wasn't a blubbering wreck before, I certainly am now,' I laugh through tears.

Mum pulls back and wipes away my tears.

Robert puts his arm across my shoulders. 'Thank you, Sophie, for everything.'

I nod, unable to say anything. Instead I bury my head against his chest, making his shirt damp with fresh tears. He's the father I've always wanted and the perfect person for Mum to settle down with, even if they're not actually tying the knot.

'So,' Mum says. 'We were thinking. Today might not be about getting married, but it is about celebrating, so are you still okay if we have the party?'

'Am I okay with that? Are you kidding me!' I pull Mum to me again, taking her hand in mine. 'Nothing has to go to waste. It was a party and a celebration of your union – the official bit wasn't happening until tomorrow. It doesn't matter if there won't be a legal bit of paper involved. Love is all that matters.'

'Bloody hell, Soph.' Mum laughs and wipes away her own tears. 'Now you're sounding like you've just stepped out of a cheesy romantic comedy.'

Robert squeezes my shoulder. 'I'm going to go and talk to Ben, let him know what's going on.'

'Make sure you knock first,' I call after him.

He turns and frowns.

'Candy…'

He raises his hand. 'Ah, say no more.'

Slowly, one by one, people emerge and drift to the courtyard for breakfast. Alekos, Despina, Takis, Demetrius, Katrina, Vicky and all the kids, bringing laughter and energy to the morning, oblivious about what's been going on over the past twenty-four hours. Those of us who went out last night in a bid to find Mum, arrive a little later, tiredness showing on frowning faces.

'I couldn't sleep for worrying.' Jocelyn reaches me and gives me a hug.

'You and me both,' I say, as she steps away from me. 'But it's not as bad as you think. In fact, things may have worked out for the best all round.'

Jocelyn frowns.

'What's going on?' Kim says as she and Pamela reach us. 'Your mum looks… well, happy, and are they holding hands?'

I follow her gaze to where Mum and Robert are deep in

conversation with Vicky, their hands clasped.

'Are they still together?' Kim's voice is full of disbelief.

'By some small miracle, yes.' I'm about to explain how when I spot Ben and Candy, the last to appear in the courtyard, wandering across, looking like they've only just got out of bed. Ben catches my eye, looks towards our parents then back to me and nods.

I can't believe the relief I feel. Mum and Robert have got through such a testing time. Still together, their love intact.

'It's true what Robert said?' Candy joins us, running a hand through her messy blonde hair.

'It's true.'

'What's true?' Kim asks.

A wolf whistle pierces the air. Mum's standing on a chair, hands on her hips, a smile on her face. The chatter dies down as everyone turns to her. The whistle even stops the kids in their tracks, where they're running up and down along the edge of the courtyard.

'Now that everyone's here together, Robert and I have something we want to tell you all.'

I glance around at the courtyard packed with friends and family. Even Arthur's sitting on a chair at the edge of the scene, his usual notebook and fountain pen clasped in veiny hands. I scan the familiar faces and realise there is one person missing.

I look up to the spare room where Amy stayed last night. She's not yet appeared but the curtains and windows are open so I presume she'll be able to hear what Mum's saying. I sigh. I can't ignore her and she can't hide away up there all day. Today might not be exactly what we've been planning for months, but it's still going to be a celebration even if Mum and Robert aren't making their love legal. I slip away and walk across to the villa, passing Despina on her way out with a large plate of croissants.

'Get Alekos to translate what Mum's saying,' I say in Greek, leaving no time for her to question me further.

I cross the kitchen and take the stairs two at a time, pausing outside the spare bedroom door. I knock.

'Come in.'

I push open the door. Amy's standing by the window, looking out. Mum's voice carries across the courtyard and I can hear snatches of what she's telling everyone.

'We love each other… want to be together… it was the wake-up call I needed to at last put that man and his influence behind me…'

Amy turns to me. Her eyes are red from crying. She's dressed in cream linen trousers and a floral blouse, her flame-red hair pinned up off her shoulders. Her small suitcase is packed and leaning against the wall by the door.

'Your mum made her decision then,' she says quietly.

I nod.

'I saw you talking to them out there earlier, saw how happy your mum and Robert looked. I've booked a taxi – it should be here in a few minutes.'

I walk across the tiled floor and take hold of her hand. 'You're welcome to stay, if you'd like to.'

'That's very kind of you, Sophie, and incredibly generous after what I've put you and your mum through. Thanks for letting me stay last night, but I don't think it would be right to stay any longer.'

She releases her hand from mine, brushes past me and picks up her small suitcase.

'I've asked the taxi to meet me at the top of the drive; I didn't want your mum to have to face me this morning. Is there a way out through the garden?'

She's adamant, suitcase clutched in her hand, standing by the door. I now feel bad that she's upset about upsetting my mum and disappointing her dad, but I know it's futile to argue and make her stay. To what end? She's an outsider to everyone here – most of whom she's not even met yet, least of all Robert.

'I hope you understand that I meant to give Leila the

chance to choose my dad if that was what she wanted. I also wanted to know that I'd done everything in my power to ensure that Dad had a chance of happiness. It wasn't meant to be and I'm fine with that. It was never my desire to break up your mum and Robert's marriage. And now we know where her heart lies that can only be a positive thing. We can all move on.'

I follow her out of the bedroom, along the landing, down the stairs and into the living area.

Laughter and the sound of people talking floats in from the courtyard. I know Mum's said her piece and seemingly put everyone's mind at rest that even though the wedding isn't taking place, there's still cause for celebration.

I feel sorry for Amy and sense that she's holding it together, wanting to get away from here as quickly as she can.

A car beeps.

'That'll be my taxi.'

I open the doors into the garden, and together we walk out into sunshine to the gate at the far end. Bees and butterflies buzz and flutter around the flowers. In the shade of the trees the grass remains green but the large expanse where the sun pounds down is already beginning to look parched.

We reach the gate and see a silver Mercedes parked at the top of the driveway.

Amy stops and turns to me.

'Can you tell your mum sorry from me, please. Sorry for everything.'

'I will. But honestly, if I was in your shoes I would probably have done the same, tried everything I could to make Mum happy, same as you've done for your dad. You do understand that he's the one who needs to apologise for what he's put her through for so many years. As Mum said, you turning up and forcing her to question her love for Robert and her history with your dad may have been the best thing. She has no doubts now. Mum may be the love of Elliot's life, but Robert's the love of hers. Without her having to face that and decide, she might never have realised. It means she's truly let go of Elliot for good.'

'But I've ruined the wedding.'

I shake my head. 'We're still having a party, plus I think Mum and Robert will be happier together not being married. Living in sin kind of suits my mum – that's if she'll ever bloody move in with him.'

The taxi waiting on the driveway beeps again.

'I should go.'

I nod and open the gate. Amy drags her suitcase across the grass.

'When's your flight?' I ask as we reach the taxi.

'Not until Monday. I didn't know how things would play out, so I wanted to give myself some time. I'll find a hotel to stay in, it's only for two nights.'

The taxi driver takes Amy's suitcase off her and heaves it into the boot of the car.

'Despite what I've put you through and the circumstances that made me turn up here, I've loved meeting you, Sophie. I'm so glad I finally know that you exist.'

The driver opens the back door of the taxi and Amy turns to go.

'I'm glad too.' I grab hold of her hand and hug her to me. 'I have no desire to have any kind of relationship with your dad, but I'd like it if you want to stay in touch.'

Amy hugs me back, pulls away with tears welling and nods. She doesn't say anything else, just gets into the car. With a wave I watch the taxi head up the drive until they reach the road and disappear. My half-sister. And I have another half-sister and half-brother I have yet to meet back in the UK, along with Amy's children, which technically makes me an auntie. It's a bizarre thought considering it's just been me and Mum for all this time. And now there's Robert and Ben with his children and Vicky with her son. Family in spirit even if not officially in name. How things have changed in a space of a few years. Plus there's Alekos, Thea, Despina, Takis, Lena and the rest of my crazy extended Greek family. I walk back towards Birdsong Villas, closing the garden gate behind me.

Chapter Thirty-Five

The stress of the last couple of days has dispersed by the time I return to the courtyard. Any confusion about Mum and Robert having decided to not get married has been replaced by relief and excitement because the party is still going ahead.

Apart from cancelling the person who was initiating the ceremony and apologising profusely, the original plan for the day with me and Despina making packed lunches for everyone and sending them off while the caterers and band arrive goes ahead.

Only Mum and Robert are still hanging around by lunchtime, helping Thea lay out the little presents that Mum has bought for everyone along with handwritten name tags. Alekos manages to persuade them to take a break and have a wander along the coastal path. I catch sight of him talking to them by the gate, while I'm running after Thea chasing balloons that have blown away. We give up as the balloons zip higher in the air, making a bid for freedom towards the Ionian Sea.

'Never mind.' I catch hold of Thea's hand as we watch the balloons getting smaller and smaller until they're tiny dots of white and blue. 'We have plenty more.'

We turn and walk back towards the villa. Mum has her arms around Alekos and laughs as she hugs him. Robert's standing next to them, watching and smiling.

'Mama,' Thea says, swinging our arms.

'Yes, *moro mu.*'

'I like wedding day.'

I laugh. 'It's not exactly wedding day any longer, but we are going to have so much fun, aren't we?'

'I like my new friends. I want them to stay forever.'

'Well, unfortunately they can't stay forever but we will see them all again soon.'

Mum and Robert start walking along the path in front of the retreat that leads away from the beach and up the coast towards Poros. Alekos closes the gate behind him and grins at us.

'What was that all about?' I ask as he joins us, taking Thea's free hand and walking with us to the villa.

'Oh nothing. Your mum's a bit emotional today.'

She's not the only one; it's been a hell of a couple of days. A lump forms in my throat at the sight of the decorated tables and balloons and bunting flapping in the breeze. The band are setting up by the stone wall that runs the length of the courtyard and continues along by the pool. Their backdrop is sea and sky, although by night-time it will be pitch black out there with only twinkling stars and the lights they're setting up around a small raised stage.

'How's Mama coping with the caterers taking over?'

'To be honest, after doing so much this week with everyone here, I think she's quite relieved to have someone else take over. She said her and your dad were going to have a siesta before the festivities start.'

'You know, that's not a bad idea, a little sleep. What do you think, Thea?'

'No! I want to play chase!'

Guests drift back by mid-afternoon to shower and change, and when they re-emerge into the late afternoon sunshine, two waiters greet them in the courtyard with a tray of Pimm's and lemonade – a slice of British summertime brought to

Greece at Mum's request.

In our room Alekos changes into a smart pair of grey fitted trousers and a white linen shirt, and Thea wears the new dress that Mum brought with her. It's grey with pink flamingos on it. She kneels on the chair looking out of the window. I slick on pink lipstick and smooth down the front of my dress. It's knee-length but strapless in pale-grey and even I think I look reasonably elegant – even Greek.

'You look gorgeous as always.' Alekos dabs aftershave on his cheeks and puts his arms around my waist, tugging me to him. 'Well done, for everything, for organising all of this.' He motions out towards the courtyard.

'I couldn't have done it without you.' I kiss him.

'Mama, Baba, Mama, Baba, Mama!' Thea screeches across from the chair. She stops in front of us and does a huge gesture with her arms. 'There's an uggler outside,' she says in English.

'A what?' Alekos frowns.

'An uggler.'

I look at Alekos and laugh. 'She means a juggler. *O tachydaktylourgos.* It's so much easier in English, and it's not even that easy in English for a three-year-old to say.'

'Come on, Mama, let's go outside.' She removes Alekos' hands from my waist, takes me by the hand and leads me from the bedroom.

'Is Joshua outside already?'

'He's watching a lady make balloon animals!'

'Nice.' I turn and grin at Alekos following behind. We clatter downstairs and through the kitchen where the caterers have taken over. The juggler is beneath the shade of one of the trees by the side of the villa with Fraser and Bella watching. Thea lets go of my hand and runs across the paving to where Joshua jumps up and down in front of the lady who's just finished making him a balloon lion.

One of the waiters appears in front of us with a tray of Pimm's and we take a glass each.

'It was a good idea getting entertainment for the children.' Alekos places his arm around my waist. He sips his drink and pulls a face.

I laugh. 'There's plenty of beer, you don't have to force yourself to drink that.'

Everyone is dressed up yet still summery, and it's easy to forget this now isn't an actual wedding. God knows what the Greek caterers make of the last minute change or the lady who helped me arrange all the legal bit. As Mum pointedly said earlier, 'who gives a flying fuck!' She's never been one to hold back her feelings. I'm just glad that Robert has embraced that side of her.

Mum's decision to not wear a white wedding dress has proved to be a good one. Maybe she really had known deep down that getting married to Robert was not the right thing, although being with him is. In a saffron-yellow dress, she's centre of attention beneath the olive tree, a glass of bubbly in one hand, Robert's hand in her other one, chatting to Despina and Takis with Katrina translating. It's lovely to see Despina relax with other people looking after her for once. It's always been her stressing about making sure family gatherings are perfect. I remember all the trouble she went to organising her birthday party the night I got that phone call from England to say that Mum was in hospital. She spent pretty much the whole of her birthday in the kitchen at *O Kipos* cooking. It seems that the passing of time may well have mellowed us all.

As dusk begins to settle and the fairy lights come on, Birdsong Villas reminds me of *O Kipos*. It's strange how desperate I was to escape that place and yet we've created our own version of it here.

The kids are entertained by balloon animals, the juggler and face painting until the sun begins to go down and the steady flow of drinks is replaced by food. Everyone is seated at the tables round the olive tree at the heart of the courtyard. The caterers bring out plates of grilled seafood and skewered chicken with bowls of Greek salads, *meletzansalata*, fries and hot feta.

I realise absolutely nothing has changed. Apart from cancelling the blessing and the legal registry office bit that would have taken place the following day, Mum and Robert's wedding day has played out exactly as planned. Glancing around at the familiar faces surrounding me, tucking into food, chatting with each other, it couldn't be a better feeling.

We move on to ice cream sundaes. Thea jumps off her chair and clambers on to Mum's lap. Mum spoon-feeds her strawberry and vanilla ice cream until she has yellow and pink smeared all the way around her lips.

As the last of the sundaes are finished, Robert gets to his feet and a hush descends over the courtyard. 'I didn't actually prepare a speech and after the events of last night and this morning, I'm relieved I didn't. For a wedding day without an actual wedding, it's been perfect…' he pauses and catches his breath and I can tell he's fighting back tears. 'After losing Jenny I never dreamed I would ever find someone I would want to spend my life with, let alone love as much. But Leila, you are so very special. I love you.'

A sigh goes around the courtyard. I know I'll lose it if I give in to my emotions.

For once Mum is lost for words. She takes Robert's hand in hers, kisses him and whispers something in his ear. He smiles and turns back to everyone. 'Now, before the band get their chance to play, Alekos, I do believe you have something you want to ask?'

Still looking at Robert and wiping away a tear, I hear Alekos' chair scrape back.

'I have no idea how I can follow that, except to say… Sophie Keech.'

There's an audible gasp from Candy and Mum's friends. I turn and the chatter around me fades. Alekos is down on one knee looking up at me.

'*Po po*,' Despina says from her seat next to Alekos, her

manicured hand pressed to her chest.

He has the ring in his hand, the damned engagement ring that seemed to be a part of all the issues four years ago. Now, it feels like a symbol of commitment and love and perseverance, that after all this time Alekos is still willing to commit, to marry me.

'*Ti kanis*, Baba?' Thea calls out from Mum's lap.

Laughter filters around the tables. Despina puts a finger to her lips and says 'shush'.

'I've done it properly this time, Sophie,' he says in English, 'and asked your mum and Robert this morning if they'd give me their blessing to ask you to marry me.'

'And I said we'd be delighted!' Mum calls out. Whoops and the thumping of feet fills the air.

'So, Sophie Keech, for not the first, but hopefully the last time, will you marry me?'

Chapter Thirty-Six

'Yes.'

One word, so simple, so perfect.

We were on our own in the garden at *O Kipos* when Alekos first proposed. I remember hesitating, but not because I didn't love him, because I did, but because of the situation we were in. It felt like I'd be marrying his family as well as him.

Now, there's no hesitation and instead of being alone we're surrounded by all the people who matter in our lives, even the ones who have caused us pain and confusion and nearly cost us our relationship. Like Mum and Robert, we've weathered the past and know without a doubt that we want to spend the rest of our lives together.

Alekos stands, pulls me to my feet and places the ring on my finger. He catches my hands in his, rubbing his thumb against the ring.

'Back where it belongs,' he whispers in my ear.

I swallow back tears as a rush of love, hope and peace floods through me. The thought once again of how close we've come to losing each other flashes before me. I rest my head against his. The courtyard is silent, even the kids are quiet and I have no idea if anyone else besides Alekos can hear me, but I don't care. It feels as if Alekos and I are the only ones here. I look into his hazel eyes. 'I've loved you from the moment I first set eyes on you,' I say. 'In my wildest dreams I wouldn't have been able to predict how our lives turned out. The moment I saw you on *Artemis* was the start of my life. If Candy hadn't gone back for that necklace, if I hadn't been standing where I was at that very moment, none of this would have happened.'

Looking around me at the place we created together filled with our family and friends, I let tears roll down my cheeks. I look up into the branches of the olive tree, through the small silvery leaves to the darkening sky beyond. Closing my eyes, I hear only the sound of waves and birdsong. There's always birdsong here, from the dawn chorus to the sweet call of birds as they fly over. It's the soundtrack of our lives.

I open my eyes and look first to Thea, wide-eyed and snuggled against Mum, then Alekos standing in front of me, silhouetted against the backdrop of twinkling fairy lights and glowing lanterns.

'I promise I will always love you,' he says.

'And I'll love you. I always have done, even the times when we've been apart.'

Alekos takes hold of my hands, his touch warm and firm. He leans closer.

'I fell in love with you on that beach,' he whispers. 'When you took the photo of me with that octopus – you were so happy, carefree and adventurous. I adored you from that moment.'

We cling to each other, tears streaming down my face. I want to stay like this forever, lost in the moment, surprised and shocked by his proposal. Thea clasps her arms around our legs bringing me back to the moment. Alekos and I bend down and envelop her into our embrace.

'Maybe now,' Despina calls out in English with a strong Greek accent. 'You give me another grandchild.'

'Mama!' Alekos says, turning away from me and Thea.

'Hear, hear!' Mum shouts, raising her glass.

Despina raises her glass to Mum and blows us a kiss.

Candy comes over and hugs me. 'She never lets up, does she?'

'Nope, not when it comes to her children, her children's partners, grandchildren, marriage or food.'

'You do realise, by marrying Alekos, she's officially going to become your mother-in-law…'

'He's worth it. And you know what, I'm going to embrace that. She cares about Alekos, she cares about Lena, she's only ever wanted what's best for them even if she does have a tendency to smother.'

'That's an understatement,' Candy says under her breath.

'We've got past that though,' I say, motioning around us at the villa.

Mum climbs on to her chair and rattles her fork against her glass until everyone's attention is on her. 'Right, now we've got all that lovey-dovey stuff over and done with, let's please have some music and get this party started!'

Everyone laughs. Alekos lets go of my hand and walks up on to the stage. Aphrodite avoids looking at him as he picks up his guitar. I flush as she faces us all and looks directly at me.

'I think this is an appropriate song to start off with,' she says in English.

The other guitarist strums the first chord. It's the song that Alekos played and sang to me on the beach the other night, the song he said he'd written for me.

Mum comes and stands next to me and puts her arm around my waist as we watch Alekos play. 'Congratulations,' she says. 'About bloody time too. I can't think of a better way for what was supposed to be my wedding day to end.'

Laughter and music fills the air for the next hour with dancing and more drinking. The kids are in their element. Even Jocelyn joins Kim and Pamela on the makeshift dance floor in front of the band. Alekos has a permanent smile on his face, playing music at our creative retreat with his old band on the night he proposed to me for the second time. Life can't get much better.

The band take a break and instead of seductive Greek music, a Justin Bieber song fills the air and the kids bounce around. I take two glasses of Prosecco and walk over to the shadowed wall where Aphrodite is looking out over the dark sea. Her hair is the colour of the clear night sky, sleek against her shoulders. Her long black dress clings to her, showcasing her hourglass figure.

I don't say anything for a moment. I stand next to her and gaze out at the darkness, soaking up the magic of the lights glinting along the coast and breathing in the warm sweetness of the night air.

'I can't even begin to comprehend how hard that was for you. I'm sorry.' I hand her one of the glasses.

I turn to face the party and lean against the wall.

'You have nothing to apologise for, Sophie,' she replies, still staring out at the sea. 'I came to terms with Alekos being in love with you a long time ago. I've sung the songs he's written about you, remember. We've sung them tonight.'

'Well, either way, I'm sorry and I'm also thankful for you being so understanding and kind.'

She turns and rests her back against the wall. 'Admittedly I doubt I would have said yes to singing if I'd known it would be your engagement party rather than your mum getting married, but there we go, it's strange how things turn out.'

'It is indeed, strange and unexpected.'

'Not so unexpected.' She sips her drink, leaving a red lipstick mark on the glass. 'He should have married you a long time ago. Tonight's given me closure – it's what I've needed for a very long time.' She downs the rest of her Prosecco and hands me the glass. 'I think there's enough time for a couple more songs before we call an end to tonight. We can make do without Alekos for these. It's time you two had a dance.'

She saunters off towards the stage, her hips swaying as she joins her band. How I misjudged her. I understand why Alekos fell for her that first summer she worked here. Apart from her looks, there's a warmth about her that I only now appreciate.

I leave Aphrodite's empty glass on the wall, take my drink and head back towards my friends and family. The drummer taps his drum sticks together and a jazzy beat once again fills the night air. I search for Alekos but catch sight of Arthur instead. He's sitting at the end of a table at the edge of the party, his foot tapping, a contented look on his face as he watches Despina take Mum's arm to begin a circle for Greek dancing.

I pull up a chair next to him and sit down. 'You'd better not be getting any ideas of turning any of this into a book.'

He gives me a sideways glance. 'Sophie dear, if I wrote family dramas I'd have had plenty of inspiration over the past few days. So unless a mutilated body turns up, then your friends and family are perfectly safe from being turned into fiction.'

'Well, after the few days I've had, the last thing I need is for a dead body to appear. It's been a rollercoaster. I think no drama and peace and quiet is in order, for a while at least.'

He takes my hand in his wrinkled veiny one. 'I can't thank you enough for allowing me to stay and be a part of your celebrations. Since my darling wife passed, family gatherings back in England haven't been the same. Our sons, their wives, the grandchildren all miss her terribly, and so there's always a melancholy when we're together. Here, well, I've felt part of your family but the sadness my own family's feeling isn't here. I've experienced real happiness and celebration for the first time in a very long time.'

'Oh Arthur, you've been most welcome. I'm glad you feel that way even with all the tension and misunderstandings going on.'

'I think that passed me by. For once, I was focused on all the positives. It's hard not to enjoy oneself in a place like this where the sun shines every day. Edith would have loved it here.'

I wipe away a tear. 'I'm sure she's looking down on you. From what you've told me about her, I imagine she'd be delighted to see you enjoying life again.'

He pats my hand. 'I'm sure she would be too. And I for one am immensely pleased to see you looking so happy. And engaged!' He lifts my hand and my engagement ring glints beneath the fairy lights. He kisses it.

I am happy. I *have* been happy for a long time but that happiness had taken a knocking over the past couple of weeks. To come out the other side, with everyone happy and settled feels right.

I kiss Arthur's cheek. 'I've been told to have a dance with Alekos, if I can find him. Do you fancy joining in?'

'Oh goodness no,' he says, shaking his head. 'I'm quite content to watch. You go ahead though and find that lovely man of yours.'

I leave him in the shadows on the edge of the courtyard and walk towards the light, heat and thumping feet where Despina is leading the circle. I stand beneath the olive tree and finally catch sight of Alekos sandwiched between Kim and Candy as they sidestep past in a whirl of colour. Thea is holding Mum's and Robert's hands, a massive smile plastered across her face.

'So, we never were destined to become stepbrother and sister, were we?' Ben appears next to me.

Everyone's clapping, feet tapping in time to the music as it gets faster and faster and faster.

'No we weren't. It doesn't mean that it wasn't the right thing for us to not, you know…'

'You can say it, Sophie, for us to not have had sex.'

I turn my attention away from the dancing and look at him. 'Ben, seriously, after what's happened tonight you really want to bring this up again?'

He holds his hands up. 'Slow down, Sophie. See, we'd have made a great brother and sister with my ability to tease you so easily.'

I huff and playfully punch his arm.

'No seriously, I want to call a truce. I've said and done stuff that I really shouldn't have considering what your mum and my dad are to each other. Also, I really like Candy. I mean really like her.'

'You do?'

'You have a good choice in friends.'

'Have you told Candy that you like her?'

'I'm going to; I wanted to know that you're okay about me and her first.'

'All I want is for Candy to be happy and to be honest us to be okay with each other. No weirdness between us. You and me moving on is absolutely the best thing ever. And yes, as long as you only have good intentions towards Candy then I'm happy for you both.'

'Do you think she likes me?'

I laugh. 'Go talk to her. But between you and me, yes. I've seen the way she looks at you. She may jump into relationships pretty quickly but it's easy to tell when she's not serious about someone. With you, well, deep down you're a nice guy, so she can't go wrong really.'

'I think that's the nicest thing you've ever said to me.'

'Well, don't get used to it.' I laugh.

He nudges my shoulder. 'See, we make perfect non-siblings.'

I take a mouthful of Prosecco and together we watch the dancing in companionable silence. All the tension of the past couple of days has disintegrated as if a physical weight has been lifted from my shoulders.

As the dancers circle again, Candy and Alekos catch sight of us. When they reach us, drinks are swiftly taken from our hands and we're pulled into the circle. Alekos' hand is warm and firm in mine, and Candy holds my other hand with Ben on her other side. God knows what he'll make of this as the last thing he'll be comfortable with is making a spectacle of himself Greek dancing. I laugh as my feet automatically fall in step with Alekos' and the beat takes over. The music gets even faster until it feels as if my feet are no longer able to keep up. Opposite me, Thea's feet are no longer touching the ground as most of the time she spends in the air with Mum and Robert lifting her. The song dramatically stops and cheers go up. Our circle disperses as people drift away to catch their breath and find their drinks.

A soulful guitar takes over from the beat of the drum and Aphrodite's smooth voice fills the air. Melodic Greek washes across the courtyard as the mood changes and only couples remain dancing; Mum and Robert, Despina and Takis, Candy and Ben, Demetrius and Katrina, me and Alekos. I wrap my arms around him and rest into his shoulder. He holds me close, slowly swaying together.

'A perfect end to a perfect day,' I say after a while.

'I know what really will make the perfect end to the day,' he whispers in my ear.

He takes my hand and we slip away from the dance floor, smiling at Kim, Jocelyn and Pamela as we go past and into our villa. The caterers are clearing away and we giggle like schoolchildren as we zip past them, taking the stairs two at a time.

Alekos closes the bedroom door behind us and spins me around until I'm leaning against it, his body pressed against mine. A huge grin makes his dimples visible through his stubble. 'I thought we could do with some alone time.'

'Oh did you now?'

'Mrs Kakavetsis,' he says and kisses me.

I waggle a finger in front of him. 'Not yet, we're only engaged – again – and we've sort of had an engagement-come-wedding party, but we've got to do all the official stuff first.'

'Technicalities.' He runs his hand across my back, reaching my bare skin where the back of my dress dips. 'We could still count tonight as our wedding night though?'

'Well later, when the party's finished.'

'That is too long to wait…' he says, kissing my neck.

'When did you decide to propose?'

'After seeing how happy your mum and Robert were this morning. After all we've been through this week, it felt like the right thing to do.'

'It was.'

'Sophie, I've wanted to marry you since almost the moment we met, this,' he lifts my hand so we can both see the ring, 'is long over…'

Bang, bang, bang. The knock on our door makes me jump.

'Sophie? Alekos?'

Alekos shakes his head before leaning in to kiss my neck. 'Not now, Mama,' he says, his voice muffled where his lips are pressed against my skin.

I clasp my hand to my mouth to stop myself from giggling.

There's a slight pause and Despina says, 'We're going to cut the cake in a minute.'

I rest my head back against the door and close my eyes, enjoying the sensation of Alekos' lips tickling my skin.

'Now's really not a good time,' I call out. My mother-in-law-to-be never has been good with her timing.

I imagine Despina on the other side of the door, putting her hands on her hips in annoyance.

'We can't cut the cake without you,' she says.

Alekos' head shoots up. 'Mama, not now. The cake will have to wait.' He looks at me and grins. 'We're trying to make babies.'

I bite my lip and shake my head in disbelief at his boldness of effectively telling his mum where to go.

There's silence from the other side of the door and it feels like eternity before Despina's footsteps tap a retreat along the hallway to the stairs.

'Making babies are we?'

Alekos leads me over to our bed. 'It's about time Thea

had a little brother or sister, don't you think?'

I wrap my arms around his waist. He takes my face in his hands and leans his forehead against mine.

'I love you, Sophie Keech.'

ACKNOWLEDGEMENTS

The Birdsong Promise has been a long time coming. Initially I intended *The Butterfly Storm*, the first book that follows Sophie's story, to be a standalone novel. It took nine years between starting to write *The Butterfly Storm* in 2004 and publishing it in 2013, and then another five years to complete *The Birdsong Promise* after lots of readers commented about wanting to read what happened next to Sophie and Co. From thinking I'd only write the one book, I've loved revisiting the characters from *The Butterfly Storm*: Sophie, Alekos, Leila, Despina, Candy, Robert and Ben, and it was great fun to introduce new ones and fast forward the story to three years on from when *The Butterfly Storm* finishes. I enjoyed writing it so much that there's another book in the pipeline which will tell Leila's story, plus a spin off series of novellas set at Birdsong Villas.

My lovely beta readers, Judith van Dijkhuizen and Elaine Jeremiah helped me shape the book from an early draft to the finished published version with their honest assessment, encouragement and suggestions. Judith once again managed to pick up an incredible amount of repeated words and phrases including lots of 'shivering despite the heat'. I mean, who even does that!

Helen Baggott was thorough in her editing and proofreading of the book at two different stages, picking up all the issues and errors I'd missed despite countless self-edits and read throughts. Thank you Helen!

Getting the cover designed is one of my favourite parts of the publishing process and Jessica Bell is a joy to work with, creating a beautiful cover that I think captures the tone of *The Birdsong Promise* to perfection.

It's been quite a journey from when I started to write *The Butterfly Storm* in 2004 to publishing *The Birdsong Promise* in 2018. I feel lucky to have so many fabulous friends who are supportive of my writing and who have helped and encouraged me over the past fifteen or so years. Thank you to all my ex-NHS Direct colleagues who have downloaded and read my books and have said such lovely things, not least of all Paula Worgan who has championed *The Butterfly Storm* in particular from the start (and in no small way helped make it such a success in 2013). Thank you to Sam Adie and Soula Grigoriadou for always reading my books and sharing social media posts and helping spread the word. Many thanks to my writer friends who have either critiqued, beta read, reviewed, encouraged and supported me – Judith van Duijhuizen, Elaine Jeremiah, AnnMarie Wyncoll, and everyone in the Bristol ALLi meet-up group including Debbie Young, Helen Blekensop, David Penny, Michael MacMahon, Jo Ullah. A big thank you to everyone who has read my novels, left a review and those of you that are a member of my Readers' Club – when I've doubted that I can actually do this writing and indie author life, your encouragement, emails and support is immense.

And finally, as always, without the support of my wonderful husband Nik and my lovely parents who have allowed me child-free time when they look after Leo, nothing would ever get written. Thank you all.

ABOUT THE AUTHOR

Kate Frost is the author of contemporary women's fiction and children's fiction. Her women's fiction, which includes *The Butterfly Storm*, *Beneath the Apple Blossom* and *The Baobab Beach Retreat*, often tackles serious subjects such as infertility, broken families and infidelity, often with a romantic element running through them. *The Birdsong Promise* is the long-awaited sequel to *The Butterfly Storm*, Kate's most popular book.

Kate Frost's children's books couldn't be more different – *Time Shifters* is a time travel adventure series for 9-12 year-olds. *Time Shifters: Into the Past* was published in autumn 2016. *Time Shifters: A Long Way From Home* and *Time Shifters: Out of Time* will complete the series.

Bristol, in the south west of England is home, which Kate shares with her husband, young son, and their Cavalier King Charles Spaniel. Bristol is a vibrant and creative city offering plenty of opportunities for writers. Kate's been involved in the Bristol Festival of Literature as well as the Hawkesbury Upton Literature Festival, which takes places in a village to the north of the city.

If you'd like to keep up to date with Kate Frost's book news please join her Readers' Club. To sign up simply go to www.kate-frost.co.uk/minetokeep and enter your email address. Subscribers not only receive a free ebook on sign up, but occasional news about Kate's writing, new books and special offers.

If you enjoyed *The Birdsong Promise* please consider leaving a review on Amazon and/or Goodreads, or recommending it to friends. It will be much appreciated! Reader reviews are essential for authors to gain visibility and entice new readers.

You can find out more about Kate Frost and her writing at www.kate-frost.co.uk, or follow her on Instagram @katefrostauthor, or search for Kate Frost - Author on Facebook.

11336458R00152

Printed in Great Britain
by Amazon